CATCH FIRE

TINA BROOKS MCKINNEY

Taboo Publishing

www.taboopublishing.com

TABOO PUBLISHING

Taboo Publishing

Catch Fire Copyright © 2013

Tina Brooks McKinney

ISBN: 0-9821089-2-3
ISBN-13: 978-0-9821089-2-5

DEDICATION

This is dedicated to my husband, William K. McKinney, my children, Shannan M. Young and Estrell S. Young, III and my parents, Ivor and Judy Brooks. God has graced me with an amazing family and I'm forever thankful for them.

Theresa Gonsalves, I can't tell you how much I love you! Your honest feedback on the initial edits meant the world to me. I thank you and my readers will too.

ACKNOWLEDGMENTS

As always, I have to give thanks to God for giving me this gift. This book almost didn't get finished. I had all but given up on writing. I was disillusioned with the business and a lot of the people in it. I don't do fake and I hate the crooks that prey on writers.

My Readers reminded me why I write. This book is dedicated to them. Special thanks go out to my real supporters. I'm gonna list some of them who really pushed me to NOT QUIT. Kim Floyd, Sharon Jordan, Joyce Dickerson, Patrice Harlson, Shelly Halima, Sabria Meadows, Marvin Meadows, Detris & Candice Hamm, Barbara Morgan, Muriel Murry Broomfield, Rhea Mayson, Sharaszad Cooke, Angie Byrd, Michelle McGriff, Franklin White, Octaviana Richardson, Mamie Abraham, Tammy Savage, Nane Quartay, Angela Simpson, Valerie Nixon, Antionette Gates. Theresa Gonsalves, you pushed me the hardest. You were always there to show me love and I can't ever repay you for this. You make me think I can do anything.

I could go on forever listing the wonderful people who have touched my life. If I didn't mention your name please understand, there is only but so many pages available in this book. Thanks for the love and support over the years. I hope I continue to make you proud.

Special shout outs to the publishers that pay their authors on time every time. It's a damn shame there are so many of them that are not doing it. Maybe that's why so many of us are turning to self-publishing. You do the math.

CHAPTER ONE

JORDAN BREE

"It's time to get busy living or die trying, Jordan." My doctor, Max, held open the door for me.

I heard his words but I wasn't really paying attention. The only thing I was focused on was the daylight. Regardless of the heat, I was ready to go outside.

Max snapped his fingers in front of my face, forcing me to pay attention. He allowed the door to shut and stepped in front of it. I was bothered by the delay. After four years of recycled air, I actually smelt real air! For a brief moment, I thought about shaking the shit out of Max to get him to open up the door. Realizing it wasn't going to work until he was ready to step aside, I sighed. I was not in the mood for any *Maxisms* today.

"Max, I can do this. Would you open the door, please?" I wasn't above begging if it would help.

"I feel like a parent about to send their child off to school on the first day."

I could care two shakes of a rat's ass about what he was feeling. This day wasn't about him; it was about me. However, I kept my thoughts to myself. I knew I had to indulge him if I wanted to get past him. This was another necessary evil in a series of many. "Max, you've prepared me well for this day." Even though I was smiling on the outside, I was raging on the inside. I knew Max liked to talk. My thing was if he was going to talk, the least he could do was have this conversation away from the door. I felt like he was tormenting me.

Max clapped his hands together excitedly. "This is a big step for both of us." He looked like a big-ass leprechaun jumping from foot to foot. Max wiped his hand over his forehead. How he figured himself in this equation was beyond me. He wasn't the one who was improperly imprisoned for four years. He had no idea what it had been like for me. Most of it I didn't remember even though I was there. Max only joined the party a few months prior to my release.

I attempted to placate Max. "It's going to be okay, Max, but first you've got to open the door." It was taking everything in me not to reach out and punch him in the throat. I knew he meant well but my patience was wearing thin.

Max paced before the door, clearly agitated. "Remember, I'm just a phone call away. I programed my number in the phone I gave you yesterday. If you need me just call. Don't forget to take your medicine, even when you're feeling good. Don't overdo it."

"I promise, Max." I lied, still trying to remain clam. I would've agreed to anything just to get him to move.

"Do you have the address of the home? Are you sure you don't want me to drive you?"

I sighed again. "Yes, it's in my purse next to the phone."

"What about the address?" He asked patting his pockets.

"I got it, Max. You have to let me do this by myself. It's bad enough y'all are making me go to a home, at least give me the dignity to get there on my own."

Max stopped pacing. "I didn't have anything to do with sending you to a home. The judge and your lawyer made that decision. If your mother had come forward to get you, then things might have been different …"

I winced. I didn't need reminders about the lack of parental support in my life. I never knew my dad. My mother lived in the same house I did while I was growing up but my siblings and I pretty much raised ourselves. Despite the pain this reminder caused, my face remained void of expression. I couldn't let Max see the rage I felt every time I thought about their betrayal. Short of death, I couldn't think of one acceptable excuse for their not visiting me. "I understand."

"The home is a temporary thing. It's only for a short time, just to get you acclimated to the outside world."

"If you say so." I clutched the seams of my pants to keep from choking him. My fingers dug deep into the excess jean material. A paper bag containing the rest of my clothes sat at my feet. My jeans hung low on my waist. My shirt practically swallowed me. The only good thing that came out of my confinement

3

was my weight loss. Always a chubby child, I couldn't wait to get some clothes that actually fit. My shoes were the only things I had that were suitable.

Max turned and looked out the door. With his back to me, I admired his physique. He wasn't a bad looking man albeit older. He was tall, slim but not skinny, wearing his hair close to his head. He placed his hand on the door causing my heart to race. This was it. My moment had come. Max turned around with a smile on his face. "Jordan, in order for you to move forward, you're going to have to remember for you to forget."

Another *ism*, it sounded confusing but I somewhat understood what it meant. I had either forgotten or blanked out many of the details from the last four years of my life. Max assured me those memories would eventually return. Until then, I had to get on with my life. "I'm ready."

Max exhaled; his conflicting emotions were written all over his face. "Just remember, I'm only a phone call away. You can call me if you ever need me as a friend or your doctor. My door, wherever it will be, will always be open to you." Max's eyes were moist. I could tell he was sincere in his words. However, my eyes were on the prize. Freedom had been a long time coming. The day was a picture perfect day for a new beginning. I may have come in as a child but I was leaving as a woman.

"Wait, where is your ride?"

I blinked as the door closed yet again. Shit. I lied when I told Max someone was picking me up. Had I known he would be standing guard at the door, I would have been better prepared. "I don't need a ride, Dr. Maxwell. I am perfectly capable of catching a bus or calling a cab for that matter." I used his full last name, letting him know I was irritated with him.

"Don't pay me no mind, Jordan. I'm just excited for you. It's been a long time since you've walked the streets of Georgia. Things have changed."

"Well, I know that. Haven't I watched enough television to see those changes?"

"The Real Housewives of Everywhere is not your reality."

"It might not have been my reality before I got here but it could be now. Once I get my settlement from the state, someone might ask me to be the next housewife."

"I sure hope you're kidding me. The last thing you need is a camera following you around twenty-four-seven."

"Why would you say something like that? That was just plain mean, Max." I pouted, folding my arms under my breasts, forcing them up.

Max's Adam's apple swelled. He coughed, somewhat nervously, with his eyes glued to my chest. "Sweet—" The rest of his words was bitten off.

I smiled. Max was into me. "I thought you said I was ready to go." My voice was seductively lower. Max looked away.

"You are; it's just me. Be careful. I care a lot about you. I don't want anything to happen to you."

"I'll bet," I mumbled as I reached for my bags.

"I'm sorry. What did you say?" Max sucked in air.

I fumbled. "Be careful of what? You keep saying that to me but you aren't telling me anything. First, you tell me to stick my neck out of the sand, and then, you warn me to put it back in. You can't have it both ways Max." I stomped my feet in irritation.

"When they shut this place down, it's going to be a lot of sick people roaming around the streets of Georgia. Add that to the hundreds of thousands already walking the streets, it could be dangerous for you."

"What? You think I'll be one of them?" I was pissed.

"No. Don't mind me." He appeared flustered.

He pulled his business card from the pocket of his white coat. I stared at the card for a second or two before I took it. "I put my home number and cell on the back," he seemed unsure of himself.

"Alright, Max, I gotta go." I pushed open the door half-expecting him to pull me back inside.

"Don't be a stranger!" he yelled to my fleeing back.

"Max, you betta not be looking at my ass." I fought the urge to turn around and catch him.

CHAPTER TWO

JORDAN BREE

My cockiness vanished almost as soon as the hospital was out of view. I didn't want to admit it to Dr. Max, but I was afraid. I walked for several blocks until I reached the bus stop. I sat down in the shelter and waited without making eye contact with anyone else. For some reason, the world appeared more colorful to my eyes. There was so much color, it hurt. The only time I looked up was when the bus approached my stop. Once I got on the bus, I panicked. I'd forgotten about money. I was so excited about leaving the hospital, I didn't plan my departure. I wanted to show my independence, so I didn't ask anyone for help. Now that I was free, I wanted to kick myself in my own ass.

"Are you alright, Miss?" The bus driver asked. I detected a hint of kindness in his voice.

"Uh, yes. Well, no. I don't have my Marta card."

"Do you have your fare?"

"No," I whispered. Flashbacks of my last bus trip flickered through my head. I had twenty dollars in my pocket and didn't want to squander all the money I had on a stupid bus ride. I backed down the stairs. Unfortunately, my retreat was stalled, as there were people behind me, blocking my way. I felt trapped.

I begged of the crowd, "Please, stop pushing. I need to get off." Although my voice rose slightly, it didn't reflect how I was feeling inside.

"You're holding everyone up." Someone shouted from the rear.

"I'm sorry, I didn't mean to." I wanted to get away but the people wouldn't let me.

"Hey, stop pushing. I got her fare. Just hold on a minute." An elderly lady in the front seat handed me three crumpled dollars. I didn't want to take it but I didn't have any other option.

"Thanks," I whispered as I received the money. For some reason, it burned my hands. My fingers were trembling as I jammed the money in the box. I knew these sensations were all in my head but I was unable to turn them off. This was not the way I wanted to start my first day of freedom. I knew I should have said something else to the lady to thank her for her kindness but I couldn't bring myself to look at her. I moved to the back of the bus and sat down. It felt like everyone was looking at me, even though I knew in my heart of hearts they were not. I rocked back and forth in my chair; my arms tightly wrapped around my duffle bag containing all my clothes.

"So stupid," I mumbled aloud. How was I going to take care of myself if I couldn't even remember something as simple as bus fare? What little self-confidence I had evaporated. This was a brand new world for me. Random thoughts were coursing through my head, making me feel like it were about to explode. I rocked faster, as if I could outrun my fears. I rang the bell and got off the bus.

I had too much going on in my head to sit still. I walked to the first gas station I saw and bought a pack of gum and some chips to make change. Seventeen dollars and fifty-four cents left. By the time I got back to the bus stop, another bus was arriving. This time, I quickly got on with the correct change. I smiled as I walked to the back of the bus. Even though it took over two hours for me to make it to the lawyer's office, I needed the time to get myself together. With my fake smile in place, I entered his office.

"I'm here to see Mr. Pressman."

"Do you have an appointment?" The receptionist asked.

"I told him I would come when I got out of the hospital. My name is Jordan Bree. He should be expecting me."

"Let me see if he's in."

I walked over to the sofa and sat down. I couldn't understand why the receptionist said she needed to see if he was in. Either he was or he wasn't. Unless he had another door out of his office, she had to know he was there. I was dying to ask her if she saw him today but I was afraid my question would come off sounding smart. I'd already fucked up once today, I didn't want to screw up again in such a short amount of time. I really needed to see him, especially since my funds were dwindling away.

"Miss Bree, Mr. Pressman will see you now."

"Thank you."

The receptionist led me down a hallway to his office. I had only seen Mr. Pressman once, when he came to the hospital with the settlement offer from the state. He was a pudgy little man, with short gray hair and faded blue eyes. Mr. Pressman looked up from his desk and smiled when I walked in.

"Jordan, so good to see you again, please have a seat."

I smiled back as I put my bag in the chair next to me and sat down. I was relieved to park that bag; it seemed to get heavier every time I lifted it.

"Thank you." My lips were already feeling the strain from having to smile so much. I didn't smile much in the hospital, so those muscles were a little weak.

Mr. Pressman opened his file and pulled out a series of papers. While he got himself organized, I looked around his fairly large office. From the look of the fine furnishings, I concluded he had to be doing very well in his practice.

"Can I get you something to drink? Coffee? Tea? Water?"

"I'd like some water please. I walked a good ways to get here and I haven't had anything to drink since I left the hospital." I neglected to mention the soda that I had snuck on the bus.

Mr. Pressman's head snapped back seemingly shocked. "You walked? The hospital is over twenty miles away."

"Well, I rode the bus some and walked some. It's okay. I'm so happy to be out of the hospital, I would have walked the entire way if I had to."

"That's absurd. You should have called me. I could have had one of my staff members come and get you or I would have come and gotten you myself."

"Really, it's okay. If you've been where I came from, you would understand. Dr. Maxwell offered to give me a ride but I wanted to get here on my own. I need to learn how to do things for myself."

Mr. Pressman frowned for several seconds. His disapproval was stamped on his face like a mask. He walked over to a portable refrigerator and got two bottles of water. After wiping the bottles for perspiration, he handed one to me.

"Do you need a glass?"

"No, the bottle is perfect." I unscrewed the cap and greedily gulped the water. I didn't realize I'd been this thirsty until I had finished the bottle. I wiped my mouth with the back of my hand. I had to keep in mind that my medication sometimes caused dry mouth.

"Wow, do you want another one?"

I was a little embarrassed. "Please." I held my head down, ashamed at how quickly I guzzled the first one. This time, I vowed to sip it. He handed me his bottle and went back to his desk. I wasn't exactly sure what was about to transpire. I hoped it involved money and a lot of it. After several more minutes, Mr. Pressman pushed some papers toward me with a pen.

"Jordan, we have a lot to talk about. First of all, I'm glad you're finally out of the hospital. What they did to you was deplorable."

"Thank you."

"There are actually two things going on right now that you need to be aware of. The state has settled on the unlawful confinement aspects of the case. However, we are still litigating the pain and suffering aspect. With the state's settlement alone, you are one wealthy young lady."

"That's good to know. How much am I getting?" I was afraid to get happy. Nothing good ever happened to me.

"Bear with me for a minute, it's a little complicated. In normal cases, I wouldn't accept a split decision such as this. I try to minimize the amount of time spent before the judge. This case is a little different because of a law that was passed back in 2007 regarding patients in mental institutions. This federal law requires the state to move patients from the hospitals into the community. The state, for whatever reason, did not act on this law. Your case bought their non-compliance to light."

"What does all that mean for me?" I was beyond confused.

"Your case closed the hospital for good. If it weren't for the law, I'd argue to have you moved to another hospital until the statement is finalized. Now, our only option to keep this aspect of the case open is to place you in a temporary group home."

I stood up so fast that I knocked over my chair. "Are you fucking kidding me?"

"Jordan, wait. It's not what you're thinking."

"You have no idea what I'm thinking. I should have known this shit was too good to be true." I was furious. Max had mentioned a home but I was under the impression that I'd be the only one in it.

"It's a strategic decision, Jordan. If you take this money and run right now, chances are it will be the only money you get out of this case. Alternatively, if you agree to the home for a short period of time, your settlement will likely increase immensely. In the end, it's your choice as to what you want to do."

My paranoia started to kick in. I really didn't know this man from the man in the moon. Who was he really? Was he working for me or the state? Why were they trying to keep me imprisoned, for what seemed like, the rest of my life? "My choice would be to take my money and get the fuck out of here. Can you make that happen?"

"So you want to forfeit your opportunity to get more money from your case?"

I didn't know what to do. "Why didn't you tell me any of this before I left the hospital? Why are you waiting until the eleventh hour and telling me all of this?"

"As I said, Jordan, there are two issues here. One is the closure of the hospital and the enforcement of the federal law. We didn't have the option of waiting for your case to be settled before you were moved."

"And I'm supposed to be okay with being locked up again?"

"The home we are talking about moving you to is not a prison. You will be free to come and go as you like. Except, maybe, at night. Other than that, you'll be technically free. I have to tell you, if your family had come forward, we wouldn't be having this conversation. I could have gone to the judge and told them you would be under adult supervision and that would be the end of it."

I felt like he had stabbed me with a knife. I didn't need to be reminded that my family had essentially disowned me. I was so overwhelmed with emotions, I started crying. None of this was making any sense to me. I wanted to know what I did that was so wrong that I was being punished like this. Mr. Pressman came around his desk to comfort me while I cried. At first, I pulled away. Then, it became too much for me to hold in.

"I know it seems bad right now, Jordan, but it really is the best case scenario. Can you just try it for a little while? If it doesn't work, we could meet again, and plot another course of action. Besides, we're not talking a lot of time either. It's only for six months and then you'll be legally free to do whatever you want."

I pulled away from Mr. Pressman. "What do you mean legally free? I'm already eighteen. I thought that was the legal age."

"Technically, it's sixteen. However, your circumstances were different. You've been hospitalized for a very long time, treated as a mental patient. The state requires some sort of supervision to make sure you're able to care for yourself. Given the fact that the state is paying you a lot of money, they want to make sure you can handle it responsibly."

"Sounds like some bullshit to me," I said sniffling.

Mr. Pressman walked back to his desk. "Like I said, Jordan, the choice is yours. I'm working for you."

"Are you?"

"Yes, I am."

"Then how come you haven't told me how much money we're talking about? I've asked you several times already."

"I'm sorry. I just wanted to make sure you understood everything before I told you. He pushed the paperwork back at me. The total amount of the settlement is two and a half million dollars. Taxes will take several hundred thousand of this money. You can take that amount and run but I feel it would be in your best interest to go for the remainder. Your case is huge, Jordan. What they did to you is reprehensible. You're entitled to get everything you have coming to you."

"And if I stay in the home six months, then what?"

"Hopefully, the remainder of the case will be settled. Even if it isn't, you will have fulfilled the state's requirements and it will keep your case active."

"Is the state trying to pull a fast one on me just because I'm young? If that's the case, I'm not signing a damn thing. I'll get my own lawyer and see them back in court." I stuffed the half-empty water bottle in my duffle bag, ready to leave the office. I didn't think far enough to know where I was going but I was getting the hell out of there.

"Jordan, please. I assure you the state is going to honor the terms of the settlement. But, uh, given the nature of the circumstances, the state wanted to be sure you were, uh, reasonably responsible enough to handle the situation."

"Oh, you mean they want to make sure my ass ain't nuts before they turn over that kind of money to a fruitcake."

Mr. Pressman's face turned red with embarrassment.

"And what happens if I don't agree. Then what?"

"Certainly that's your choice, but you have to understand, you can't have it both ways. If you don't sign these papers today, I don't have anything for you. We won't know how long it will take before the matter can be resolved."

"I saw commercials on television about long lawsuits and annuities. They said I could get my money now."

"Jordan, those commercials were made by lawyers trying to get paid. Your case is nothing like the ones on television. They are talking about cases where the settlement involves a lifetime payout. I'm trying to close your case, period, with a lump sum."

"So who pays your salary? Me?" I reached across the desk and picked up the agreement.

"No, my fees are paid by the state."

"Should I hire my own attorney to look over these documents?" I was bluffing. I didn't have the money to hire an attorney. Not to mention the fact that I needed money now. I couldn't afford to wait one more day, unless I wanted to sleep on the street.

"That is entirely up to you. If it would make you feel more comfortable, you are within your rights to do so."

"How much do you know about my case?"

"What do you mean?" Mr. Pressman ran his finger along his collar, as if his shirt was suddenly too tight.

"Do you know why I was detained?"

"I know that you were arrested but I can't recall why."

"There was a lady. I was real mean to her. I didn't mean it. I was sick and didn't know it. If I sign these documents, can you find this lady and give her a gift from me?"

"I'm sure that can be arranged, if the person's identity is listed in your records."

"I'm sure it is because she came to court to testify."

"What would you like for her to have?"

"I want to give her some money."

Mr. Pressman pulled out his legal pad and began taking notes. "How much money would you like her to have?" His pen was poised over the pad waiting for a response. I thought about it for several seconds before I answered.

"Fifty thousand dollars?" I wanted to give something, but I was unsure how much would be adequate enough to let the lady know I was sorry.

"That's very generous of you. What will you do if she refuses to accept it?"

I shrugged. "What can I do?"

"Alright, is there anything else?"

"How soon can I get the money? My pockets are a little empty." I hated to admit I needed anything. Especially to a stranger.

"As soon as you sign the paperwork, the money is yours. As trustee of the account, I'm authorized to draft the check."

"So you're going to just give me a check for the entire amount?"

"Less taxes, and your gift, of course. I just need to make a copy of two forms of identification for your file."

I couldn't move. I had so many thoughts going through my head. I didn't know which one of them to address first. I wanted so much to do everything by myself, but I couldn't. I began to cry again.

A startled Mr. Pressman said, "What's the matter, Jordan?"

I wailed, "I don't have two forms of identification. At least I don't have them on me. Everything I have is in that stinking duffle bag. I'm all over the place. If you give me a check, it's just a piece of paper and I won't be able to cash it. Then what? It's not just the money, it's everything. I've lost so much time that I can't get back; I don't know where to start."

"Oh, I see. Well there's no need for tears. Every problem has a solution." He reached over and patted my hand. He pushed the box of tissues at me. I grabbed several, dabbing at my eyes and nose. I also shoved a few in my bag. I hardly ever cried, even as a kid. Now, I was dealing with some heavy-duty, grown-up shit and I didn't know how to handle it.

"What can I do about it?"

"Do you have any family members that can sign on your behalf? We could grant them a temporary power of attorney?"

"Would that person have access to my money?"

"Yes, they would, so it would have to be someone that you trusted."

"Then I don't have anyone. You must have tried to reach my mother, and she ain't here. She never came to see me the entire time I was locked away. Would you trust your money to someone like that?"

"No, I don't believe I would. What about any other family member, sister, brother, aunt or uncle?"

I shook my head no. None of them had been there, when I needed them. I did have one cousin, who spoke to Brody, my reporter friend, on my behalf but I didn't know how to contact him.

"I see. This does make things more complicated. However, the problem is not insurmountable. I can open an account with you as the signatory. You will be able to access it just like you'd access any other account. We could set that up today, order you an ATM card and it's done. Would you like for me to do this?"

"What does that mean? Will you be working for me?"

Mr. Pressman laughed. "No, dear, this is just a temporary solution so you can have access to your money while you get yourself established."

I liked the sound of that. I would contact Dr. Maxwell and Brody. Between the two of them, I was sure they could help me gather the information that I needed. "I'm going to need some money right now. None of my clothes fit and I swear I'm sick of walking around with my pockets on empty."

"That's not a problem, how much do you want?"

"Ten thousand dollars," I said smiling.

"Jordan, that's an awfully large sum of money to carry around with you. I don't think that's such a good idea."

I felt stupid. Of course that was a lot of money. What was I thinking, especially since I was going into a home. "Can I get half that? I promise I'll be careful. I swear, I need so much. I won't have it with me for long."

"Jordan, it's your money. I'm only offering some advice. Give me a moment to get my secretary to set this up. I'll be right back."

"Okay." I finished the rest of my water while I waited. I was feeling a little bit better about my situation now that I knew I would have some money. I looked up when Mr. Pressman came back into the office.

"I'm going to drive you to the home personally. We'll sit down and talk with the woman, Mrs. Gates, who runs the place. If you have any questions whatsoever, this will be the time to ask them. I want you to be comfortable there, Jordan. I don't want you to view this as a form of punishment. All I ask is that you give it a try."

"Okay, I'll do my best. What's six months when I've already done four years, right?"

"Exactly."

CHAPTER THREE

LAWRENCE MAXWELL

My face burned with shame when Jordan straight up busted me for looking at her ass. Feelings of regret and uncertainty filled my heart. I realized that Jordan probably thought I was old enough to be her father. To her, twelve years might seem like an eternity. Despite our age difference, I still wanted to tell her how I felt. Yet, I let her leave knowing there wasn't anyone else in the world that cared for her as I did. Fear of rejection kept me silent.

I was still staring out the door when I noticed a car pulling up to the curb. My heart lurched even though I knew it couldn't possibly be Jordan coming back, especially since she was walking. The hospital occupied the entire block and was officially closed. Therefore, there was no reason for anyone to stop, unless they had business at the hospital. A feeling of dread came over me as I squinted to see inside the tinted windows of the Honda CRV. The windows of the truck were so dark; it should have been illegal to drive. Curiosity kept me glued to the door as I impatiently waited for someone to emerge from the vehicle. I was already on edge from saying goodbye to Jordan. I didn't need anything else to happen. Just for the hell of it, I wanted to snatch the driver out of the truck and beat the living shit out of them. The desire to hurt someone was so strong, it scared me.

"What the hell are they waiting on?" I shouted as I glared at the car. Something tells me to walk away; however, my feet aren't cooperating. "Get out of the fucking car already." I thumped my fingers impatiently against my legs. Something important was about to happen. Something game changing, I could feel it. My stomach felt like I had tiny moths flying around inside as I rigidly eyeballed the vehicle. I felt myself smiling expectedly, as if I were about to win the Publishers Clearing House Sweepstakes. My smile immediately disappeared when I recognized my arch nemeses, Brody Mason, a freelance reporter, as the vehicle's occupant. If that wasn't bad enough, the mofo had the nerve to be carrying flowers. I scowled as he approached me.

"Dr. Maxwell." Brody tipped his head in greeting. His smile was as wide as the bouquet he was holding. His eagerness offended me.

I nodded my head without bothering to open the door. As far as I was concerned, Brody had no business with the hospital. His eyes dipped to the door handle as if he were waiting for me to open it. He attempted a smile, which didn't reach his eyes. I chuckled. I didn't believe in smiling in a person's face and stabbing them in the back the moment they weren't looking unless it was business. My beef with Brody Mason was personal.

"Mr. Mason," I said through gritted teeth.

Brody tested the door, finding it locked. His smile turned into a frown as our eyes locked. He removed his hand. "I came to pick up Jordan; has she finished checking out yet?"

Anger surged through my body. I could not believe his unmitigated gall trying to pick Jordan up right under my nose. When I first met Brody, I was fooled into believing he was a reporter interested in lobbying the state for more funding for research on mental illness. Since this was a subject near and dear to my heart, I opened my doors and shared classified information, which resulted in the closure of our hospital. Needless to say, I had a score to settle with Brody Mason.

I unlocked the door and stepped outside. Suddenly, I was happy that Jordan had already left. I put on my biggest smile. "Why, yes. She's finished. In fact, she's already gone." I was gloating as I turned to go back inside. Brody grabbed my arm stopping me. I was outraged by his balls to touch me. He didn't know me well enough to put his hands on me. I snatched my arm back.

Brody fired questions at me as if he were entitled to an answer. "Gone? What do you mean gone? Gone where?"

"Exactly what part of gone did you not understand?" I replied.

"What's your problem, dude?"

"Dude? You must have me confused with someone else." I turned around again ready to put some distance between Brody and his offensive flowers. I had no doubt in my mind who the flowers were intended for and I was happy Jordan was not there to accept them. It didn't help my self-esteem any that Brody was at least ten years younger than I was and possibly more appealing to Jordan. I needed to get away from Brody before I did something foolish like punch him in his arrogant face.

"Hold up, I'm not finished talking to you."

I was fuming. "I don't have anything else to say to you. You asked me where she went and I told you she left. End of discussion."

"Dude, if you're upset about the article I wrote for the paper, it wasn't anything personal," Brody said.

"I don't give a pig's nuts about your stupid little article. What I do care about is getting back inside to finish closing down this hospital." I wasn't being one hundred percent honest when I said I didn't care about Brody's article. That 'little' article flipped my life and those of my colleagues', upside down. Many of them were facing unemployment for the first time since graduating from college. Unlike some of my colleagues, I cared more for the welfare of my patients. Therefore, I actually agreed one hundred percent with what young Brody wrote. Of course, I wasn't about to tell him that.

"Come on, man..." Brody was clearly frustrated.

My contempt for Brody went beyond the article. His pompous attitude and cocky stance infuriated me. I felt like he used me for a flash of fame, without any regards to the consequences. No story, in my opinion, was worth all that. At the very least, he could have acknowledged my work and showed me some more respect. I wasn't like my counterparts and he did little to let the world know it.

"Excuse me; I have more work to do." Brody did not try to physically stop me this time.

"Where could she go?" Brody's voice was almost like a wail and it cut through me like a knife. It made me realize we both cared about Jordan far more than we should. How could I get mad at him for that? Essentially, we were in the same boat.

"I asked Jordan if she was getting a ride and she said she didn't need one." I shrugged my shoulders.

"Well, I don't understand how you could just let her leave like that." Brody's indignant tone pissed me off.

"What was I supposed to do? Throw her to the ground and sit on her? She was ready to go and I understood why she felt that way."

"But Doc, she wasn't ready. She shouldn't be wandering the streets alone. What if something happens to her?"

My mouth dropped, appalled by his insinuation. "You should have thought about that shit when you started writing letters and filing lawsuits. At least when she was here, I could keep an eye on her."

"You kept her drugged." Brody shouted in retaliation. His anger showed for the first time.

My fist shot out and punched him in his jaw. Brody stumbled back and landed on his ass. I stood over him shouting, while silently begging him to get up so I could hit him again. "You're a damn liar. Obviously, you didn't read your own research. I'm the one who took her off the drugs. When I came on staff, she was so doped up she could hardly move without assistance. How dare you include me in what went on at this hospital before I started working here."

Clearly, Brody was not expecting my aggressive response. I felt immediate shame for my reaction, as

I extended my hand to help him up. He stared at my outstretched hand for several seconds before he took it. My body was tense. If he punched me back, I was determined to take it like a man. I shouldn't have sucker punched him. Real men didn't do that. "I'm sorry. I was out of line." I didn't know if he would accept my sincere apology.

Brody massaged his jaw. "What will she do?"

"Jordan is socially retarded, not mentally. She has a brain and she can think. As long as she continues her medication, she should be fine. Of course, I would have preferred to have her continue with her therapy a little longer but thanks to your crusade, that option was not available. If you had consulted with me prior to your printing that article, we could have planned this better. Now there is nothing either of us can do. Even though you probably thought you were doing some good, in actuality, for her, you made things worse."

"Now you wait just one minute. I take offense to that." Brody had balled up his fist like he was about to take a swing at me. I braced for his attack, even if it meant we were going to do battle in the middle of the sidewalk.

"Whether you take offense or not, the truth is the truth. Your little article may have gotten five people released from the hospital because they didn't need to be here, but what about the other two hundred people that were rightfully being treated here? Did you ever stop to think about what would happen to them? Right, you didn't because it's written all over your face. Thanks to you, those people will more than likely wind up in jail or dying in the streets. Those patients suffering from dementia, without their medication, will be wandering the streets, too confused to even tell somebody they need help. So don't you dare try to judge me."

Brody looked uncertain and confused. "I assumed those patients would get shipped to another hospital?"

"That's why you should never assume. It makes you look like an ass. In fact, you should probably stop talking now before I lose what little respect I had for you." I was mentally exhausted, as I tried to leave again.

"How can I fix this?" Brody said, practically pleading for my help.

"I don't know that you can. The state can barely afford to keep places like this open. Most of the people who were being treated are without medical insurance. With minimal staff, lower wages and deplorable working conditions, we were hanging on by a thread. Now with the lawsuits that are popping up like stinky farts, you may have bankrupted the entire state."

I could tell Brody was finally getting the bigger picture. I almost felt sorry for him because he would have to carry around this burden for the rest of his life. Heaven forbid someone died, I seriously doubted if Brody could handle it.

"I get it. I fucked up man. You don't have to keep beating me over the head with it. Tell me what I could do to fix it. How about doing that Einstein?" He sarcastically responded.

I felt my nostrils flare as my temper heated up once again. This little snot was getting on my nerves. *Why should I be the one trying to fix something I had nothing to do with breaking?* As much as I wanted to throw my hands up in the air and walk away, there were still innocent lives hanging in the balance. I sighed. "Son..." Brody's shoulders stiffened. He obviously didn't like being called son, any more than I liked being called dude. I rephrased my response. "I don't have all the answers. I suggest you use the same amount of vigor you used to get Jordan out of the hospital to get help for the others you managed to displace. For the record, I didn't agree with Jordan's earlier treatment but in a lot of ways, she was better off here than at home." I couldn't resist throwing that last bit of shade at him.

Brody gave me the side eye. "Why do I get the feeling there is something else I need to know from you?"

"I have no idea what goes on in that head of yours. I'm under no requirement to say anything to you." I replied nonchalantly. Just looking at him made my blood pressure rise. Every time he opened his mouth, it rubbed me the wrong way. Perhaps it was because of the way he spoke. He talked way too fast for my comfort. I remember my dad telling me that if a person talked real fast like Brody, I could pretty much assume they were lying.

Brody stuttered, "I, I didn't mean it like that. I'm just trying to wrap my arms around what's going on here. You're the only person left in this place who actually acts like they care. So what else am I supposed to do?"

I ignored his question. "Where you from, Brody? You obviously aren't from around these parts."

He looked confused. "I'm from Baltimore. Why?"

"Nothing, I uh…" I was sure my face had turned red. He was from the north which confirmed my dad's convictions about fast talkers.

"You uh what?" Brody flexed his arms like he was trying to get an attitude. His cheeks were all puffed up like he'd stuffed some cookies in them.

I flexed my own muscles in return. Lest he forgets, I wasn't about to let him clown me.

Brody paced back and forth, clearly disturbed. As much as I disliked the young man, I couldn't allow him to walk away when it was evident he needed someone to talk to.

"Listen, I'm about done here. Would you like to go somewhere and have a drink?" When Brody hesitated, I bristled. I felt like I was extending the olive branch to a bomb waving terrorist instead of a confused man.

"I guess!" Brody fished his keys from his pocket and turned to his car.

"Hey, man, don't feel like you're doing me any favors."

"Shit, are you this difficult with your patients?" Brody's smile was so bright I had to smile back.

"Only when I'm dealing with knuckleheads like you. Are we drinking?" I thought I needed a drink just as much as he did.

"Yeah, we're doing it. I'll follow you."

I rushed back inside the hospital to lock up. As I walked, I hoped this wasn't one of those decisions I'd regret in the morning. Brody and I shared a common bond, Jordan. He knew things about her that I didn't, so I was going to use this time to find out what that was.

CHAPTER FOUR

JORDAN BREE

"Aaugh." My head was pounding as if someone was actually beating a drum inside of it. The sound was so loud it felt like my ears were pulsating.

"Make it stop," I moaned aloud. My words sounded muffled even to my own ears. Everything hurt. I felt like my head was encased in a football helmet filled with some sticky, gooey substance clogging my ears. My lips were weighted like mini cinderblocks. Even with all this going on, I didn't panic. I was used to waking up dazed and in pain. This was the reality of my life. The only difference of today from yesterday was the voices. For a brief moment, I felt abandoned by the only friends I had.

Without opening my eyes, I reached over to my nightstand for the glass of water that always graced my bedside. I gingerly groped around until my fingers touched the plastic tumbler. The glass, wrapped in plastic keeps the creepy crawlers from swimming in it while I slumbered. It was a nuisance but a necessary annoyance.

My lips were so cracked. I expected my fingers to be wet with blood when I touched them. I ripped off the plastic and emptied the glass in two long gulps. The water was warm but did little to satisfy my thirst. I needed more. Forcing my legs over the side of the bed, I attempted to stand. The bathroom sink was exactly twenty-two steps from my bed. Ice would sooth my parched lips, however, I ruled out taking the extra forty-eight steps to the community kitchen of my half-way house to get it. When I got out of the home, the first thing I was going to do was buy a small refrigerator to place beside my bed, especially if I had to continue to take the medicines that robbed my body of fluids.

Although it was only twenty-two steps, it felt like I'd walked the length of a football field, as each step echoed in my head. I gasped from the pain, caused by movement, bringing tears to my eyes. Seventeen steps left to go. Once I satisfied my thirst, I would pop three Tylenol and a few Benadryl for my stuffy nose.

I started my days trying to figure out which medication I would need to deal with the cards I'd been dealt for the day. I shared my miserable existence with five other females, who were in my opinion, as fucked up in the head as I was. We were all financially dependent on the state. Most of the ladies were under the age of eighteen and had grown up in the system. The only exception to the bunch was Lacy. Lacy had aged out and was awaiting placement in income subsidized housing.

My case was different. The home was a way station for me. This was a chance for me to get acclimated to other people before stepping out into the world on my own. Fortunately for me, the home was temporary and I only had a few months to go. As long as I continued to be on my best behavior, things would be good. The only problem was, being good wasn't easy while the voices in my head implored me to do bad things.

By the time I reached the bathroom, I was mentally drained. Fragments of my reoccurring dream still lingered in my head. I knocked twice on the door, which sent currents of pain to my head. My tongue was hanging out my mouth, as if it was searching for moisture from the air. My fingers clutched the plastic tumbler close to my chest.

"Go away," Lacy yelled through the door.

"I just need water," I pleaded. I didn't feel like fighting with Lacy today. She was another bitter bitch and I wasn't in the mood.

"Fuck off."

I have an arsenal of tools to deal with anger. Things I should do before I react, however, I couldn't think past the raging fire I felt coursing through my veins. Normally, Lacy didn't fuck with me. She knew I came to them by way of a mental institution. Her victims were often more passive than I was.

I rapped on the door again, as I leaned heavily against its frame. I should have started counting myself down. Or better yet, took those painful extra steps to the kitchen to get my water. I knocked again.

"Are you hard of hearing, bitch?"

The only person who was allowed to call me a bitch was my mother. For anybody else, it was going to be a problem. Without giving it a second thought,

I rammed my foot against the thin door. The force of the blow shattered the thin plywood. I furiously tried to jerk my leg from the door as tiny wood splinters scraped against my skin. "I got your bitch right here! As soon as I get my foot out this door, I'mma show you," I bellowed. In my head, Lacy was as good as dead. She just didn't know it yet.

"Oh shit," Lacy was caught with her drawers down and nowhere to run.

"Your ass is mine," I hissed through clinched teeth. This bitch was about to pay, just as soon as I freed my foot. For the moment, my thirst was forgotten. The only thing that mattered to me was getting my hands on the scrawny heifer who had the nerve to call me out my name.

"I'm sorry, Jordan. I didn't know it was you knocking on the door." Lacy's eyes were wide with fear.

In my haste to get at her, I was pushing my foot in instead of pulling it out. My entire thigh was now encased in the door.

"You'll be sorry alright, when I get my hands on you." My heart thumped purposely inside my chest.

Lacy started crying. "Damn, I said I was sorry."

My arms were seized from behind. "I need some help up here," the RA shouted.

"Get your hands off of me." This added a new dynamic to my struggles. I hated restraints of any kind. I bucked back like a wild bull trying to free both my arms and my leg. The sound of running footsteps broke my trance. Seconds later the familiar sting of a hypodermic needle pinched my arm. The effects of the drug were instant. I slumped against the RA knocking her off balance, my foot still affixed in the door.

"Get her off of me!" Rough hands yanked my leg clear of the door and hoisted me to my feet. "That's going to cost you, Jordan," another RA declared as I was led back to my room. My head lolled to the side as I observed Lacy sashaying from the bathroom. Our eyes locked. It wasn't over and we both knew it. The plastic tumbler rolled from my pliable fingers as the drugs took effect.

CHAPTER FIVE

LACY BATES

I knew from the moment I saw Jordan, she would be a problem for me. Based on the way the RA's treated her when she first arrived to the home, I could tell she was different. Things around the home started to change almost immediately.

Jordan got assigned a coveted room on the first floor. That in itself was enough to make me hate her. There were two bedrooms on the first floor. Those bedrooms were larger than the rest of the bedrooms. Since there were only two bedrooms on the floor, they only had to share the bathroom with each other. Upstairs, where I stayed, I had to share the bathroom with four other girls. The other stark difference between Jordan and the rest of us was she didn't have to keep the same schedule we did. She was allowed to sleep later, stay up longer and wasn't compelled to participate in group therapy. She also had the ability to leave the home, during the day without supervision. This was something we all coveted.

Group therapy was a means for us girls to get to know each other better. Through this knowledge, we learned tolerance for each other. We didn't know shit about Jordan other than the fact she was a little nutsy. I resented the hell out of that fact. I didn't understand how she could opt out of therapy and I couldn't. I didn't think it was fair that she was given special privileges right off the bat, when we had to work for them.

The decision to use the downstairs bathroom for a change wasn't premeditated. I thought I'd be able to get in and out without being detected. I was so careful as I tiptoed down the stairs. The rest of the house was sleeping. I eased into the bathroom, locked the door and kept the lights out while I took a leisurely shit. I'd just start shitting when I heard the knock. Once I got started, it was difficult for me to stop. I assumed she'd go away if I stayed quiet long enough. Apparently, I was wrong.

"Girl, why in the world did you want to rattle Jordan's cage today?" Keisha, our RN, demanded.

I was not in the mood for some of Keisha's inane chatter today. Keisha always asked a lot of questions. For right now, I didn't feel like giving any answers. "Ain't nobody thinking about Jordan. She walks around here like she's God's gift to the world. She ain't no better than anyone in here and she'd better recognize it."

"Why do you let her get under your skin so much? She's not treated any differently than the rest of the girls."

"Who said she gets under my skin? I ain't thinking about that bitch."

"You could have fooled me. She's the only person you gripe about in group, and I see the way you roll your eyes at her. Does she remind you of someone from your past?"

"Why am I even talking to you?"

"Because I asked you why she bothered you. And because I'm trying to decide what to do with you."

"What to do with me? I didn't kick in the fucking door. You act like you're scared of Jordan too. Walking around here on your tiptoes like you're afraid to make any noise."

"I'm not scared of anybody. I get paid to keep the peace around here and you just disturbed the peace." Keisha walked off.

I got nervous. Although Keisha was the RA, she was different from the other RA's that had worked in the house. She came from the system and empathized with the girls. This was the first time she'd taken a side and it pissed me off. Anne, another resident, crept into my room. "Anne, why the hell are you sneaking around all the time?" I couldn't really cuss Keisha out but Anne was fair game in my opinion.

"Because I don't see the point of making noise everywhere I go. My momma used to say, children are meant to be seen, not heard."

"Your momma? Is that the same momma who used your pussy to pay the rent?" I needed to shut Anne down quickly and this low-blow was the fastest way to do it. Anne was very sensitive to conversations dealing with her mother. She should have never mentioned her in group. Personally, I didn't understand why she continued to defend her mother after all she'd been through.

"Hey, leave my momma out your mouth." Anne was trembling as she spoke.

"If you didn't want me talking about your momma, you should have never brought her up in the first place. And in the second place, you ain't no child. In the state of Georgia, you are deemed an adult after the age of sixteen. As far as I'm concerned, if you can lay on your back and fuck like a woman, then you're a woman."

"I'm done talking to you, Lacy. You're not my friend."

"Where are we, high school? You better grow the fuck up and get a set of balls."

Anne's lower lip quivered as a fire smoldered in her eyes. What I said was a clear violation of the code of conduct in the house. I had used some sensitive information she shared against her. Anyone else would have slapped the shit out of me but Anne was different and I knew it.

"You are going to get yours."

"From who? You?" I started laughing at the very idea of Anne doing anything to anyone.

"It doesn't have to be me. I only hope I'm around to see it."

"Humph, spoken like a true coward. If you want to be a bad bitch, you got to be that bitch. Don't get caught sleeping. You might not wake the fuck up." Even though I started out trying to shut Anne down, I was also offering words of advice. She did need to toughen up and stop letting people, places and situations get the best of her. If I didn't teach her this lesson, I didn't know who would. I was the closest thing to a friend she had in this house.

"Lacy, I know I didn't just hear you threatening Anne." RA Kim walked up beside Anne and placed a hand on her trembling shoulders. She patted her back a couple of times causing Anne to rest her head on her shoulders. I wanted to puke.

"Uh, no. I wasn't threatening her; I was err…, um… We were just joking around. Ain't that right, Anne?"

"Save it, Lacy. Anne, go back to your room. I need to speak with the comedian for a minute."

Anne's smile mocked me as she left the room. Her words about my big payback cast a shadow in my mind. I turned my attention to Kim, the newest addition to the RA staff. RA was an acronym for residential assistant but I considered them to be regulating assholes. Of all the RA's, Kim was the worse in my opinion. She was young, hungry, and trying to make a name for herself. Since she was closer to the ages of the other girls in the house, she tried to be our friend. She burned a couple of girls who made the mistake of trusting her. Therefore, I avoided her like the plague.

"What do you want?" Kim knew I didn't like her so I saw no reason to pretend that I did. I turned my back hoping she would go away.

"For starters, I want to know what the world happened in the bathroom?"

I started making up my bed and cleaning up my room. "Why you asking me? Jordan started it."

Kim laughed. "Because Jordan is taking a nap."

If this was a joke, I didn't think it was funny. "The bitch needs to be put to sleep permanently."

"Whoa, that sounds like a threat too. Should I be preparing a little cocktail for you as well?" Kim toyed with her whistle from the chain swinging around her neck. One blast from it and it would mean lights out for me as well. It was an intimidation tactic and it was working.

I kicked the first thing my foot came in contact with, a sneaker under my bed. "I said I didn't do anything to that bitch. I was in the bathroom, minding my own business, when she busted through the door like a wildebeest. If anything, she was trying to attack me." My bowels were still giving me a fit.

"You've got such a smart mouth. I believe you said something to set her off." Kim tapped her whistle against her open palm.

"Were you there? Did you hear me say anything to her?"

"I didn't have to be there. I'm saying, based on what I know about you, you did something to provoke Jordan. I only need to prove it."

"How the fuck could I provoke her when I was in the damn bathroom with the door closed. I swear to God, I don't know how the fuck they hire some of you retards." Once again, my mouth was writing a check that my bank didn't want to cash.

"Who the hell are you calling a retard?" Kim had lost her own cool as she stepped up close behind me and twisted my arm behind my back and pushed me forward. Leaning over my bed, with my face mashed against the wall, I felt a twinge of fear. I wasn't afraid of physical retaliation. Kim was too smart to actually hit me; however, she could punish me in other ways.

Unlike my earlier confrontation with Jordan, which was loud and boisterous, this scuffle was whispered and more menacing. "I think it's time you and I come to an understanding. I'm only in this shit hole for a short period of time. You are not going to make my time miserable. I already have to do some extra paperwork explaining what happened to the bathroom door. That's the last report I'm going to have to write because of you. Do we understand each other?"

Apparently, I had underestimated Kim. Despite her small stature, she was no punk. I couldn't move my head from the pressure she'd applied on my arm. "Fine."

"The way I see it, we did your stupid butt a favor by breaking up that altercation when we did. If Jordan would have gotten ahold of you, you'd be cleaning up more than your shitty drawers."

Measuring my words, I said, "Can you let go of my arm now?"

"What? No please?"

This bitch was really feeling herself now. All it took was a little bit of power and the shit went right to her head. I remained silent. Stubborn was my middle name and she was about to find out.

Kim stepped up on my bed without loosening her grip. She leaned close to my ear, her lips dangerously close to touching me. "You really don't want to get on my bad side."

"Everything alright in here Kim?" The senior RA asked.

I'd never been so glad to hear that old biddy in my life. As the pressure was lifted from my wrist, Kim stepped off my bed. I angrily shook out my arm.

"Everything is just fine. Me and Lacy were having a come to Jesus meeting."

"Jesus? Is that what you call it?" I was relieved not having to say please to Kim.

"Lacy was just telling me why she was even in the bathroom on the first floor when she knows she is prohibited from using it. We were also discussing how she planned on fixing the door so we don't have to. Ain't that right, Lacy?"

I was stunned at her suggestion that I be made to fix the door. "Why should I be the one to have to do it? I didn't kick it in." Stunned or not, I was still going to stand up for myself.

"Because you provoked Jordan, plain and simple. And you broke the rules." RA Gates intoned, taking sides with Kim.

They were ganging up on me and there was nothing I could do about it.

Mrs. Gates said, "Good, I'll run to Home Depot and get the door and some paint. Kim, make sure you get your report on my desk as soon as you get a chance with your recommendation for punishments. I'll be back soon."

"Punishment? What punishment? Isn't fixing the door enough?" At that moment, my griping stomach exposed my inner turmoil with a vaporously loud fart. The fart was as loud as it was putrid.

"Jesus, Lacy, did you just fart or crap your pants?" Kim used her hand to cover her nose, as she backed out of the room fanning her face.

I was beyond humiliated. Just when I thought the day couldn't get any worse, I farted. It couldn't have been a sneaky fart either. It was an odorously, noisy fart that I couldn't even pretend didn't emanate from me. I wanted to get back in bed and start my day again but I had to make sure I hadn't shit my panties first. Grabbing a towel, I went to the bathroom for a quick shit and shower.

CHAPTER SIX

JORDAN BREE

I was feeling more or less normal by the time the drugs wore off and I'd taken a shower in the bathroom. While I was sleeping, someone had repaired the door and the housemates were relatively quiet for a change. Unfortunately, I couldn't enjoy the peace and quiet because I was summoned to the RA's office. Rather than make matters worse and bitch about it, I decided to see what the old battle-axe wanted and be done with it.

I knocked on Mrs. Gates' door and waited for permission to enter. She made me wait for several seconds before she answered me.

In my most contrite voice I said, "You wanted to see me?"

"Come in and shut the door." Mrs. Gates had her head buried in some files on her desk. Since this wasn't a social call, the somberness of her voice didn't unduly upset me. I took a seat and waited while Mrs. Gates reviewed the folder which I assumed was mine.

"Kim has given me a report of this morning's incident and before I determine punishment, I'd like to hear what you have to say."

Punishment? I was taken aback and nervous at the same time. I had never received a punishment since I'd been at the home. "I woke up this morning feeling sick. I really needed to get into the bathroom but the door was locked. I thought it was Tamika and I begged her to open the door. I was wrong about that. It was Lacy and she told me to go fuck myself. I kept knocking on the door but she wouldn't open it. When she called me a bitch, I guess I lost it." I probably should have censored my response but she asked me what happened so I told her, especially if she was going to dole out some sort of punishment.

"I think I understand what happened without your colorful language."

"Actually, that wasn't my language, it was Lacy's. I just repeated it."

Mrs. Gates waved her hands in the air as if dismissing whatever else I had to say. "Be that as it may, I have made a decision. Regardless of the circumstances, we can't have this type of physical aggression happening around here. Someone could really have gotten hurt, not to mention the damage done to my home."

"But —"

"Excuse me, I'm not finished."

"I know but Lacy shouldn't even have been in my, I mean, that bathroom. She should be the one in this room, not me." I was getting upset.

"Will you wait a minute?"

I swallowed any further objection.

"As I was about to say, Lacy has already repaired the door. However, going forward, I am going to need you and Lacy to learn how to work together."

"Fu—" I stopped myself short. I was going to make Lacy pay for all of this shit. I also didn't forget that she called me a bitch either.

Mrs. Gates continued, "Starting tonight at dinner, you and Lacy are on kitchen duty. You will be responsible for clean up after meals. During your punishments, you are not allowed to use the dishwasher. You will either wash or dry the dishes at every meal. Whichever chore you don't do, Lacy will have to do the other. In addition, I expect the floors to be mopped and swept at the end of each meal. Once again, you will either mop or sweep with Lacy doing the other chore. In the event one of you fails, both of you fail, so I suggest you two communicate or it's going to be a very long punishment."

"That's not fair." I shouted as I jumped to my feet. I was so upset I was ready to tear some things up. I looked around her cramped office to determine what I could toss first.

"Sit down, Jordan, unless you want me to sedate you again."

I paused. As mad as I was, the threat of another medical knock out stopped my tantrum before it began. Defeated, I slumped back into my chair. This was all Lacy's fault and one way or another she was going to pay for it.

"If you both do a good job, the punishment will be over in a week. If not, it will be a permanent assignment until you leave the home. I'd make it work in the first week if I were you." Mrs. Gates closed my file and folded her hands on top of it.

"If you're going to punish me, I'd rather do my punishment all alone. I work better by myself," I said hopefully.

"Then you would be missing the point of the punishment. In life, sometimes it's necessary to work with others, despite your differences," Mrs. Gates smiled. I wanted to bash her teeth in.

"I guess there isn't anything else that I can say?" My lips were pressed firmly together. My arms folded under my breasts to keep from choking the older woman.

"No, not really. You're free to go."

Lacy had an ass whipping coming with her name on it. I just had to figure out a time when she'd receive it. Sulking, I went back to my room. I shut the door because I didn't feel like being around the other girls, especially since I was in such a foul mood. I could not believe I allowed Lacy to get me in trouble. I had purposely kept my distance from every person in the home until today. A lot of good it all did me now.

***

All chatter in the dining room ceased when I entered the room. I assumed everyone knew about my punishment and they were watching me to find out what I was going to do about it. I decided not to be the entertainment for the evening. As far as I was concerned, these witches could catch fire. I'd wash the damn dishes, and even mop the floors, but it would be the last time I would suffer at someone else's hands. I learned, a long time ago, that folks don't have to see you being angry for you to be mad. Actions spoke a lot louder than words.

Lacy walked into the kitchen fire cracker hot, as I was fixing my plate of baked chicken and rice. I looked in the last pot and turned my nose up at the sweet peas. Ever since I was a kid, I hated peas. If I had my way, I'd throw out every single can we had in the house.

"I'm not washing any dishes," Lacy announced as she began fixing her plate. "And I'm not mopping the floor either."

Lacy was like a little gnat flying around, annoying as hell. She craved attention from everyone around her. She was baiting me to swat at her, but I wasn't biting. I had no problem washing dishes or mopping the floor, so she really needed to sit her silly ass down somewhere.

The food was cold so I popped it in the microwave for a minute. I hated cold food. I liked to see steam coming off my plate before I put it in my mouth. When I was in the mental hospital, all my meals were cold. I attributed most of my weight loss to cold food and the medication they had me on. Lacy pulled out a chair and sat at the end of the table mimicking me each time I raised my fork to my lips.

"Would you hurry the fuck up? I've got better things to do than watch you stuff your face." Lacy slid her empty glass along the table and it careened off the side, falling to the floor. Fortunately, the glass was plastic. I could tell Lacy had never had a beat down before in her life. She was used to letting her mouth do the talking for her and had never been put to the test. I so wanted to be the one that schooled her on what a real ass whipping was about. If she pressed on, I was going to throw caution to the wind no matter what the consequences.

"Little girl, you'd better stop taunting me."

"Who the hell you calling little girl?" Lacy jumped up knocking her chair over in the process.

"Would you rather I call you a ratchet whore?" The dining room had cleared out of other people. I mentally calculated how long it would take me to reach across the table and ram my fork in her neck. Seconds, if she didn't move. It was tempting. Every single day I had to ask myself was it worth it. At this particular moment, she was not worth a return to the mental hospital or jail. I had to think of another way to squash this worrisome pest.

I stepped over her glass when I put my dishes in the sink. I rolled up my sleeves and got to work washing the dishes.

CHAPTER SEVEN

LACY BATES

I was two seconds away from winging the glass pepper shaker at the back of Jordan's head. I probably would have, if I thought it would actually hit her. I sucked at sports when I was in school. I couldn't hit the side of a barn with a two-by-four, let alone a fat head with a two-inch pepper shaker. I had to think of something else to bring that bitch down a peg or two. I angrily stomped out of the kitchen so I could think.

The group home was locked down every night at six o'clock. Smokers were allowed on the enclosed porch with permission from the attending RA. I wasn't much of a smoker but I kept a pack for emergencies such as this. Taking the stairs two at a time, I ran to my bedroom to grab a cigarette.

I stood outside of Keisha's office with a cigarette in my hand. "I need to take a smoke."

"Since when did you start smoking?" Keisha asked while peering at me over her black rimmed glasses.

I bit back a smart remark since outside privileges was at the discretion of the RA on duty. "I know. I'm trying to quit. It's hard in here with nothing else to do." I feigned a smile.

"You should. They are bad for your health." Keisha got up from her desk and looked around its top for her keys. She had the messiest desk of all the RA's and I hated her for it. Chaos led to confusion.

"Like I said, I'm trying." I held up the cigarette again, trying to keep my irritation out of my voice.

"Give me a minute. I can't seem to find my keys. I quit smoking a couple of years back. It wasn't easy so I feel for you."

"Bitch, please," I mumbled. Ain't nobody asked for her sympathy.

"Excuse me?"

I panicked for a second. I didn't realize that I had spoken loud enough for her to have heard me but I wasn't sure.

"I said, quitting is a bitch. Got my nerves all frazzled."

"Oh, okay. How long have you been smoking?"

I threw my hands up in the air in frustration. I didn't want to have a discussion. I wanted to fucking go outside. "Do you need some help finding the keys?" By this time, I was ready to push everything off the desk and stick my foot up her ass.

"No, I got it. Give me a minute. They have to be around here somewhere." She opened up the drawers of her desk and rummaged around inside.

This type of disorganization would have driven me nuts. I was an orderly person who liked everything in its designated place. I had a serious case of OCD. This was another reason why I hated living with other people. *How difficult could it be to keep up with a fucking set of keys?*

Vigorously shaking her jacket, which was discarded over the back of her chair, Keisha exclaimed, "Found them."

Stepping aside, I followed Keisha to the door. She wasn't in any hurry, which further irritated me. I was beginning to believe she was doing it on purpose. She tried several keys before she got the right one. "One of these days, I'm going to label these keys."

"Yeah, heaven forbid we ever had to get out of this place in a hurry." Being locked inside had to be against some kind of rules for residential housing. It wasn't something that I thought about looking into before, but it definitely deserved further consideration.

"If you're serious about quitting, you should take up a hobby or something."

"I tried drugs and alcohol. Look where that got me."

"To a place where you learn to make better choices? I sure hope so."

My sarcasm seemed lost on Keisha. She finally opened the door and followed me to the porch. I didn't bother trying to hide the horrified expression on my face as I watched Keisha sit down. This was not part of my plan. I had no intention of actually smoking the cigarette. It was supposed to be a prop but she was leaving me with no choice. I stood on the opposite side of the porch turning my back to her.

"You don't have to sit out here with me."

"It's no biggie. Even though I don't smoke anymore, I still like the smell of it."

I couldn't tell if she was testing me or really telling the truth. This was a problem with all the RA's, they had an opinion about everything and we were supposed to listen to them. I'd like to switch places with any one of those heifers to see how they liked being locked up twenty-four hours of the day, three hundred and sixty-five days a year.

I quickly lit the cigarette, pretending I couldn't wait to inhale the nicotine. The stench irritated my nose as I fought back the desire to cough. I could feel Keisha's eyes watching me. I raised the cigarette to my lips and inhaled deeply exhaling the smoke into the air. It was torturous, but I did it. The lengths I was willing to go for a moment of privacy scared me sometimes. This time my plan backfired.

"So what's the deal with you and Jordan? You seem to hate her."

"I don't hate anybody. I just don't like the girl." I lied.

Keisha snorted, "Why? She hasn't done anything to you. She keeps to herself and minds her own business."

"How do you know what goes on around here? You're only here eight hours a day." I felt myself getting mad.

"I've seen the way you look at her. Does she remind you of someone?"

Was I that obvious? "Look, I came out here to smoke, not to be analyzed."

"I'm not trying to analyze you. I'm just trying to understand. From the first day Jordan came here, you've been different. We've never had any problems with you and now you're like a ticking time bomb."

"Did it ever occur to you that I might be sick of this place and these people?" I expelled the remaining smoke in my lungs as I sat down on the chaise lounge. Surprisingly, I was beginning to enjoy the smoke.

"My sister used to do me like that. Poor kid. I didn't give her the time of day."

Fuck my life. This bitch was about to tell me her life story. I didn't want to hear her shit. I inhaled again.

"She used to try to go everywhere I went. Always snitching on me too. She was four years younger than me. No friends of her own, trying to be like her big sister."

In spite of myself, I became interested. Her story was starting to sound similar to mine, except, I was the little sister. My sister ignored me too and I hated it. "So how come you ignored her? Would it have been so hard to spend a little time with her?"

"I just didn't want to be bothered. She was such a brat. Since we were siblings, she knew exactly how to get to me."

I knew what she meant; I always went for the jugular when I was dealing with my own sister. The only weapon I had, which could effectively shut her down, was my mouth. "You probably knew how to get to her too."

Keisha nodded her head appearing to be lost in thought. I turned away from the pained expression on her face. I didn't want to see her like this. Her vulnerability was endearing and caring for her was the last thing I wanted to do.

I had finished smoking my cigarette. Keisha didn't appear to be in any hurry to go back inside and neither was I. I wasn't in any rush to get to the chores in the kitchen either. Jordan couldn't mop the floor until I swept them. I liked keeping her waiting. The thought gave me a wicked feeling of glee. I eased back onto the chaise.

"She got to me alright. I'll carry her with me for the rest of my life."

A feeling akin to fear settled in my heart. "What happened?" I knew it wasn't going to be good.

"She killed herself."

Keisha openly cried as I helplessly watched. Her admission didn't surprise me, as I understood the despair her sister must have felt. "Sorry." I didn't know what else to say. I couldn't imagine living with that kind of pain. Nosey me wanted to know how she killed herself and why. Even at my lowest, I never once considered taking myself out. Taking my sister out would have been more my speed.

"You're done with your smoke. I hear those dishes calling your name." Keisha was all business again. She'd dropped her guard for a minute but the bitch was back.

Any sympathy or compassion I may have felt for Keisha evaporated the second she mentioned the dishes. It was just as well, I didn't have to feel sorry for anyone else. "Whatever." I brushed pass Keisha leaving her alone with her misery.

CHAPTER EIGHT

BRODY MASON

I was beginning to second guess my decision to have drinks with Jordan's doctor. When I first met him, I was on the fence trying to figure out the role he played in her life. He made his intensions clear when he punched me in the jaw. Dr. Maxwell wanted more from Jordan, and, thus far, he hadn't got it. I had to admit, he had every reason to hate me. The story I wrote caused the closure of the hospital, effectively putting him out of work. If I were in his shoes, I'd hate me too. Despite my misgivings, he was my only connection to Jordan. If I wanted more information, I really had no choice but to grit my teeth and bare it.

We arrived at Marietta Fish Market. I wasn't sure exactly what Maxwell had in mind. "Are we eating or drinking?"

"Can't we do both? I haven't had a thing all day."

"That's fine. I just wanted to know if we were sitting at the bar or a booth."

"We can do a booth. It's more private."

Luckily, the restaurant wasn't crowded and we were immediately shown to a booth in the corner of the restaurant.

Maxwell chuckled, "Aren't you the lady's man?"

"Huh?"

"Don't tell me you didn't notice the way she was swinging her hips. I know she wasn't doing it on my behalf."

"Oh, she's like that every time I come in here. I don't pay her no mind."

"Judging by the scowl on her face, she must've noticed that too."

The scowl on the hostess' face surprised me. I had been there many times before and had never given her any indication that I was interested in her. I shrugged. "She probably thinks we're gay."

"Well, then it's a good thing she won't be serving our food. Home girl is looking at you like she wants to stab you. You sure you didn't hit that?"

I found Maxwell's comment to be offensive. He didn't know me like that. "Trust me, ain't nobody got time for all that." The waitress came over to the table.

"Hi, welcome to the Fish Market. Are you ready to order or do you need a few minutes?"

"Hi Crystal. I'll take my usual," I said smiling.

Maxwell asked, "What's the usual? I've never been here before."

"I'm gonna have the crab cakes. They are the best I've had since I moved to Georgia."

"Really? I'll get some as well. They better be good."

"Trust me, they're good. You are talking to a brother from Baltimore, the home of the crab cake.

Let us have a couple of Heineken's to wash them down, okay, Crystal?"

"Got it. I'll bring your beers after I place your orders." Crystal took our menus and left us alone.

"How often do you come here?" Maxwell inquired.

"I'm telling you man, the crab cakes are good. Whenever I'm feeling homesick, this is my spot." I was really trying to be nice to this guy even though he rubbed me the wrong way. I couldn't get over the feeling that he was hiding something.

"I hear you."

I waited until Crystal had given us our drinks before I started talking. "I'm glad you asked me for drinks. I think we got off to a bad start and I owe you an apology." I could tell by the expression on his face that Maxwell wasn't expecting me to say this.

"I guess I also owe you an apology. I shouldn't have hit you." Maxwell leaned back in his chair and stretched his legs out under the table appearing to relax. I, on the other hand, wasn't ready to trust him.

Maxwell leaned towards me. "Let me ask you something. How did you get involved with Jordan's case in the first place?"

"It started with the video of her on television—"

"Can you believe I never knew about the video until your little story hit the papers?" Maxwell said interrupting me.

I was annoyed. I hated when people interrupted me when I was talking. "Anyway, turns out she's a distant cousin of one of my frat brothers. He told me she was getting the shaft and asked me to look into it."

Maxwell sneered. "What you did went well beyond mere curiosity."

"Hey, what can I say? I'm a reporter; digging deep is what we do."

Maxwell didn't look convinced. "So you smelled a story, saw an opportunity to get your name in the press and you took it."

I didn't like his tone. "Yeah, I saw a story but once I started digging into it, it wasn't about my getting recognition. I happen to care about people who couldn't speak for themselves."

"So what made you move to Atlanta?" Maxwell had switched subjects.

"Are you kidding me? I was sick of those brutal winters. A brother can only shovel so much snow before he has to say fuck it and move. I was at that point."

"I feel you. I used to live in Boston and that snow ain't no joke."

"Boston? Damn man, I feel like a punk complaining about the little bit of snow we get compared to y'all."

We both started laughing and I could feel some of the tension wash away from both of us.

"So why Atlanta and not Florida or California?"

"Seventy-five percent of the time those states might be alright but the other twenty-five is a beast. I'm not down with no fires or hurricanes. They can have that nonsense."

"You ain't lying. I'm not trying to board up my house every year in case a rogue storm wants to hit. You see those cats living in those million dollar homes but they got to monitor the winds for brush fires. That is crazy to me too."

The waitress brought our food. "Can I get you anything else?"

Brody said, "Yeah, can you get me another brew. You can't eat crab cakes without a beer."

"I'll take another one too." Maxwell bowed his head and said grace.

"Amen." I said as he made the sign of the cross on his forehead.

Maxwell picked up his fork and tested the golden brown cake "Mmm. This is good."

"I told you, and for the money it's a good size too."

"With this beer, my mouth is in heaven right now." Maxwell said, as he held up his bottle.

"It's almost like having a nut in my mouth." I embarrassed myself.

Maxwell laughed. "You are telling the truth. Too funny."

I was glad I didn't offend him. "So how long have you been at the hospital?"

"A little less than six months."

"Ouch, and now you got to find another job, thanks to me."

"Fortunately for me, finding a job won't be that difficult. If push comes to shove, I could open up my own practice to pay my bills."

"If you don't mind my asking, why wouldn't you want to do that anyway instead of working in the hospital?"

"Because, it's not all about the money for me. I didn't get into this field to make a boat load of money. I did it because there was a legitimate need for my services."

"Commendable, but is it smart? You spent all that money for school yet you're working for peanuts." I was trying to figure Maxwell out.

Maxwell shrugged. "I was fortunate enough to get scholarships. Money has never been an issue for me. As long as I have food in my mouth and a roof over my head, I'm good. If I open a practice then I'd have to worry about paying for office space and all those other headaches that come with it."

"But you'd be making a decent salary, so it wouldn't make a difference. Hell, you could hire someone to handle all that other stuff for you."

"You're missing the point, son. The people I'm trying to reach can't afford those types of trappings." He pushed his empty plate away and drained the rest of his beer.

"Oh, I get it. You didn't become a doctor just to get a fancy car and a trophy wife."

Maxwell sighed. "Something like that."

"Actually, I like that. Sounds pretty damn noble if you ask me." As much as I wanted to hate Maxwell, I was beginning to like him.

"What about you? What's your story? What made you decide to write?"

"I don't know really. It wasn't like a conscious decision or anything like that. It kind of happened and I just rolled with it." We fell into silence as the waitress cleared the table of dishes.

"I didn't think I was going to like you but you're growing on me," Maxwell confessed.

I shook my head because I was thinking the same thing. "You took the words right out my mouth! I thought you were going to be a grade A dick, but you're not so bad after all."

"I'm glad we took the time to get to know each other."

"Let me ask you something completely off the record, scouts honor."

Maxwell looked leery. "What is it?"

"Now that the hospital is closed, would you please share with me what was really going on inside? I mean, I have my suspicions but I really don't know."

"If we're going to get all deep, I'm gonna need something stronger than this beer."

I signaled the waitress and ordered two double Patrons. He drank half before he started talking. I ordered another round.

"Georgia Regional isn't much different than any other hospital struggling to stay afloat in these hard economic times. Every time Congress cuts the budget or the taxpayers get tired of footing the bill, hospitals have to adjust. Especially, state funded mental institutions. They did what they felt they had to do under their financial constraints."

"Come on Maxwell, people were dying and no one seemed to care. What about *Sarah Crider*? She was only fourteen when she died."

"That was way before I came to the hospital."

"I realize that but didn't it concern you?"

"Of course it did, but I didn't know about it until you brought it to my attention."

"Then how did the administrators explain what happened to Jordan and the others? Twelve people locked in the hospital for years for no reason. How do you justify that?"

"I don't have to justify it; I wasn't there. Just because I was wearing a white coat when you came in, doesn't mean you can attribute all their atrocities on me. In 1999, the U.S. Supreme Court ruled that under the Americans with Disabilities Act, all states must move individuals with mental illness out of ailing state-run institutions and into settings integrated with their communities. Georgia, among other states, ignored this ruling and continued to build larger facilities. Those facilities became under funded by the government."

"Yeah, yeah, yeah. I know all that. It was part of my research for my article. I'm trying to find out why these people were seemingly lost in the system. Jordan, in particular, was held for over four years. That shit ain't right."

"Who you telling? I might have been as shocked as you were to find out she wasn't even supposed to be there. Jordan's records did not contain any notes as to why she was in the hospital. Believe me, I checked."

"Man, I kept thinking if I didn't do the article, she might never have gotten released."

"Before you go patting yourself on the back, I think you should think about the other side of the coin."

"What's that supposed to mean?"

"Like I said before, you may have helped a few but what about the rest of them?"

"I didn't make the rules, Doc."

"You can call me Maxwell or Max. Don't call me Doc. I hate that shit."

"Sorry, no disrespect intended." He nodded his head and continued speaking.

"People don't like to talk about the mentally ill. Everybody has that crazy cousin or loopy aunt or uncle. Most times, families pull together and take care of them so you don't hear about them. But what about those people who don't have families? What about those people that were sent to hospitals instead of jail to reduce overcrowding? They ain't crazy. They may play crazy to get out of jail and those cases make it harder to manage the patients that really need help."

"So what are you saying? Did you condone what went on at Georgia Regional?" Maybe it was the alcohol but I was starting to feel like Max was talking in circles from a contrived speech.

Max frowned. "I didn't say that. I'm just trying to get you to understand that there were other factors which needed to be considered. When I first got to the hospital I was surprised by the amount of patients and the levels of medications given to them. I immediately started trying to change things and I quickly learned my lesson."

"What happened?"

"Before I say anything else, is this conversation still off the record?"

"Come on Doc, I mean Max. I thought we were beyond that."

"Is it or isn't it? The hospital may be closed but I still need to work."

"Completely off the record."

"I'm not playing with you."

His words were beginning to slur. "Okay, I said it was off the record so chill out."

"I got my ass in a knot because about eighty-eight percent of the patients were, in my opinion, receiving entirely too much medication. Most of them, including Jordan, were doped to keep them docile. I objected and systematically started reducing their medications."

"Good for you."

"Don't applaud me yet. One of those patients had killed both his parents and his baby sister. He pled insanity and won. He was sent to our hospital and kept heavily medicated. I didn't know his history because it was sealed by the courts due to his age."

"Damn, did he hurt anybody at the hospital?"

Max kept talking like he didn't even hear the question. "He was just a kid and smart too, when he didn't have all those drugs in his system. I got to admit, he fooled me. Had me thinking he was a victim and feeling sorry for him. After about a week without the drugs, we used to talk. I mean really talk. He spent all day watching television and when I came in at night, he'd be ready for me. Used to follow me around all night long, asking me questions." Max shook his head and fell silent, apparently lost in his thoughts.

"Dag, man, you gonna leave me hanging? What happened?"

"He attacked one of the nurses. Damn near broke her neck because she changed the channel."

"Oh wow." I was shocked.

"Yeah, it was deep. The hospital hushed it up and the patient got transferred back to prison where he belonged."

"What about the nurse? Is she okay?"

"She's alright. She was appointed as hospital administrator."

"Shut the front door."

"Exactly, and she became a royal pain in my ass."

"So, technically, I did you a favor too by exposing the whole thing."

"You helped me but you fucked hundreds in the process. I'm a grown man. I can take care of myself. What about the rest of those people that can't?"

He was either getting drunk or agitated. Either one wasn't good. "How many times am I going to have to apologize for that? Just like you didn't know what was going to happen when you changed those medications, I didn't know what was going to happen when I published that article. My only concern was Jordan. Who knew it would start a federal probe? I certainly didn't."

"Fine, let's move on. What's done is done and we can't change it." Max nodded his head in agreement.

I thought about it for a few seconds and then I asked the main question that had been on my mind. "Do you know where she went?"

"Uh, I do but I'm not sure if I should tell you. I feel like if she wanted you to know, she would have told you herself."

I never knew it was possible to see red, but I really did. By this time, I was a little drunk too. "What are you implying Doctor Maxwell. You think me and Jordan ain't friends or that she might not trust me or something? Because if you are, you need to squash that nonsense. Jordan and I are close. Really close. She's a lot closer to my age. I bet she don't tell you half the stuff she tells me." I wagged my finger in his face. I probably shouldn't have mentioned the age difference because when I did, it seemed like something in Max snapped.

"What does age have to do with anything?" He reached for his wallet and started peeling bills off a roll, throwing them on the table.

"Hey, don't get upset. I was just saying; that's all."

"Like I said, if she wanted you to know, she would have told you. I think that should be enough to cover the check. If not, make up the rest. I'm out." Max pushed back his chair and gruffly pushed the table. My only source for information about the woman I had grown to love walked out the door.

CHAPTER NINE

JORDAN BREE

I left the house as soon as the breakfast dishes were done. I had a lot of ground to cover and not a lot of time. Jogging the two blocks to the bus stop, I kept looking at my watch. I arrived just as the bus was turning the corner. I separated three one dollar bills from the crumpled ball of cash I had in my pocket to pay my fare. Stepping onto the bus, I took a seat next to the rear door. I liked sitting next to the door just in case some shit popped off and I had to get off in a hurry.

I settled back in my seat and tried not to think about what I was about to do. I had some unfinished business in my old neighborhood.

The bus was relatively empty at that time of the morning. I slid over to the window seat, rested my face against the cool glass and closed my eyes. I didn't need to see to know where I was going. I knew the route by heart. Every stinking bump in the road read like braille in my head.

Last night, I didn't take the sleeping pill that normally put me under each night. While the pills quieted the voices and allowed me to sleep, the aftereffects sometimes left me feeling muted for most of the day. I couldn't afford to be muddled in the brain today. In my neighborhood, muddled could get you killed.

I opened my eyes a short time later. There were more passengers on the bus but none of them seemed to notice me. Everyone seemed connected to some type of device to entertain them. I welcomed the distraction of people watching because going back to what used to be home was never easy. It was supposed to be a revitalized neighborhood, however, it reminded me of a dressed up skunk or a wolf in sheep's clothing. It was like they moved the cemetery but forgot to take the dead bodies with them. The stench reached my nose before the bus came to a stop outside the housing complex. I took a deep breath and got off the bus.

I was immediately transported back to a time before the face lift. On the surface the potted plants in the windows and the children playing on the plastic jungle gym, suggested a gentle lifestyle, void of the seedier elements of life. The picture perfect location, minutes from downtown Atlanta, was a façade. We used to call the place Little Vietnam. It was named one of the most dangerous places to live in eastern DeKalb County. Little Vietnam was a community of thieves. You could get anything you wanted in the courtyard of the apartments: drugs, shoes, guns, handbags, dresses and murder. Many of the killings were done right there, on the playground, amongst the kiddies. All the deals went down before the kiddies.

"I got that stuff." A small boy, old enough to be in school, sided up to me.

"I need ATM."

The boy paused. A frown marred his otherwise handsome face. His eyes narrowed in suspicion. He didn't recognize me from a can of paint, so I understood his concern. Many of the faces I knew were no longer around. I raised my fingers in salute. He nodded and I followed him to building seventy. Outdoor deals were obviously a thing of the past. He walked to the door and rapped three times in rapid succession. Someone behind the door opened it a crack. The only thing I could see through the door was an eye, pressed in the seam.

"What you want?" The eye asked the boy.

"It ain't me; it's her." He pointed at me. I swallowed a knot of fear that developed in my throat.

"I need ATM." ATM was the king of East Meadows. Nothing went on in the complex without his knowledge.

"Who you be?"

"It's me, Theresa's sister, Jordan."

The door opened wider and ATM stepped forward. I forced myself not to run away. I was a little nervous because I'd never addressed ATM before. One word from him and I could end up dead or missing.

"What do you want?"

The little boy was still standing beside me with his hand underneath his shirt. I envisioned him gripping the butt of a gun, with a bullet that had my name on it. I glanced at the boy and then back at ATM. He nodded to the boy who then turned and left.

"I need some half and half."

"How much?"

"Double deuce." I hoped it was enough. I had no idea how much drugs I actually needed. I just hoped I had enough money to cover it.

"Wait." He slammed the door in my face.

I felt stupid hanging out in the corridor of the apartment building but I didn't know what else to do. If I turned and ran, I was so sure I'd be shot in the back in broad daylight. I looked around trying to appear nonchalant. I noticed a man sitting on the steps. He was watching me intensely. This only served to confirm my fears of being shot. I nodded my head in greeting to the watchman. He didn't acknowledge my greeting. I kept my hands at my side, just in case I made him as nervous as I felt.

"Oh, please hurry up," I whispered without moving my lips. I wanted to get what I came for and get the hell away from this place. It was no longer my home. I was completely out of my element. Even though I had lived amongst these people all my life, I never dealt with them. I didn't realize they scared me until now. The door was snatched open as abruptly as it was closed.

"Give it to me."

I took the wad of cash from my pocket and pressed it into ATM's hand. I waited while he counted it. Satisfied with the amount, he passed me a folded paper bag. As much as I wanted to look into it and confirm my purchase, I didn't dare. I didn't even ask him if I was owed any change. "Thanks."

ATM shut the door without saying a word. He banged my sister on the regular until she let the drugs take over her life. The very least he could have done was ask about her. The guy on the steps went back inside the upstairs apartment. I exhaled the breath I'd been holding. Finally, I felt it was safe to go. I pushed the bag into the cup of my bra and walked as quickly as I could to the bus stop. I was terrified that someone was watching me, ready to either knock me over the head or worse, arrest me. My heart rate didn't return to normal until I was safely back on the bus headed home.

***

I was feeling rather proud of myself as I rounded the corner to the house. I'd checked off another thing on my list of things I wanted to do before I moved on with the rest of my life. My enthusiasm died a little bit when I spied Lacy sitting on the porch. She had her head down and appeared to be reading something. She looked up as I opened the front gate but quickly lowered her head when she saw me. I wasn't offended when she didn't speak. In fact, I was elated. I didn't want to speak to her ass either. Lacy smirked as I mounted the stairs; then she pulled the brim of her black baseball cap down lower over her eyes. For a second, I thought about complimenting her on her look. With my luck, she'd take that as a sign I wanted to be friends. "Fucker," I mumbled and went to my room to find a suitable hiding spot for my stash.

Finding the right spot was very important. Not only did I spend a lot of money, I needed to keep it a secret at all cost. If the drugs got into the wrong hands, there was no telling the type of trouble I'd get into. Therefore, I took my time looking for the perfect hiding place. Coming from a family of crack heads, I had to learn the hard way how to hide things in plain sight. It seemed like the more complicated the spot, the easier it was for them to find it. Go figure.

Pulling out the third drawer in my dresser, I got one of my old push-up bras. Sitting down on the bed, I removed the padding from each of the cups. I removed the baggies containing the drugs and shaped them to fit inside my bra. After several attempts, I was satisfied with my handiwork. I threw away the padding and put the bra back in the bottom of my drawer. As I was closing the drawer, I noticed one of my t-shirts peeking out of the last drawer. The hairs on the back of my neck stood up. I was meticulous with my things, so I knew I didn't leave it that way. Someone had been in my room. Hastily I pulled open the drawer looking for anything else out of place. Suddenly hiding the drugs in my bra wasn't such a good idea. I realized what was missing almost immediately. "Arrugh! I am not believing this shit." The timing of this invasion of my space could not have been worse. I needed to fix this quick, fast and in a hurry. I was livid when I marched down to the RA's office. I knocked once and barged in. I was pissed. Keisha was in her office, reading a book.

"I am about two seconds away from stomping a mud hole in that heifer."

"Which heifer?" Keisha lowered her glasses on her nose, peering at me over the top of the lens.

"Lacy!"

"If this is about the dish detail, you will have to take that up with Mrs. Gates."

"This ain't about no damn dishes!"

"Hold up now. I'm not the one. My shift just started and I'd rather be at the house chilling. So, I think you better take it down a few decibels." Her finger was poised over the panic button. One click of the button and I'd be face down on the floor with another sleepy time cocktail.

My blood felt like molten lava. I felt like I was going to erupt if I didn't hit something. I cracked my neck from side to side, attempting to calm myself down. Lacy was trying to push me over the edge in order to get me in trouble. Even though I was conscious of her plan, I still reacted the same way.

"Whew. Help me Jesus. You just don't know how upset I am."

"Well, you called the right one if you have a problem. He can take care of it. Oh, yes He can!"

I wasn't looking for an amen. I wasn't even expecting Jesus to intervene. In fact, Keisha could catch fire too as far as I was concerned. I was so peeved I was trembling.

"What happened now?" Keisha moved her hand away from the button, which would have brought the rest of the staff running.

"Lacy has been in my room fucking, I mean, messing with my stuff."

"Did you see her?"

"No. If I saw her, I'd be whipping her ass right now."

Keisha's brow went up in disapproval. "Then how do you know she's been in your room if you didn't see her?"

"Because she's wearing my hat." I said between pinched lips.

"Well, did you leave your hat in the common area?"

I spoke real slow, enunciating my words. "No. I don't leave my stuff lying around like those other girls. It was in my room, in my dresser drawer. The trick took it."

"Are you sure it's your hat? Maybe we should go talk to her and get to the bottom of this."

I was dangerously close to nutting up. If it weren't for that button on the desk, it would've been on like popcorn. Talking was the last thing I had on my mind. I couldn't believe that silly skank had the nerve to steal my shit and wear it in my face.

"While we are standing here flapping our gums, that bitch is wearing my hat."

"Do you have any proof that it's yours?"

"Are you kidding me? You mean like a receipt or something?"

"That will work," Keisha said smiling.

"Well, I don't have no damn receipt. That hat belonged to my sister and I want it back. She got her name on the brim."

"Okay, that will be sufficient. What's your sister's name?"

"Theresa. Now can you go get my hat?"

"I'm going to go get Lacy. I don't want this situation to escalate, so can you please not call her a bitch, trick or a skank?"

I was not about to make any promises. How I reacted depended on the situation. "I'll try." Keisha gave me a stern look and left the room as I continued to seethe. It did not take long for them to return. It didn't help my attitude none to see she was still wearing my hat.

"Have a seat, Lacy." Lacy sat down while Keisha was walking back to her desk. She didn't look at me but I felt like she was wagging her tongue. The urge to punch her was so strong; I had to sit on my hands.

"Lacy is that your hat you're wearing?"

She reached up and touched the hat as if she'd forgotten she was wearing one. "Yep, sure is."

"She's telling a damn lie." I exclaimed.

Keisha shot me a warning look but addressed Lacy. "What's the name inscribed on the brim?"

"Huh?" Lacy looked dumbfounded.

"Stupid cow probably doesn't know what inscribed means."

Lacy spoke around a big wad of gum she had in her mouth. "I don't know. Let me look."

Before she could take it off, I reached over and snatched it trying my best to get some of her natural hair in the process.

"Ouch," Lacy yelled grabbing her head.

"See, I told you it was mine; here's my sister's name." I pointed at the name penned inside the ban. I sat back in my chair with my hat safely back in my possession.

"Where did you get the hat, Lacy?"

Lacy ignored the question. "She didn't have to snatch it like that. I think she got some of my new growth."

I rolled my eyes. "She's lucky all I did was snatch it. Tell this girl to stay out of my room and keep her hands off my stuff."

"Ain't nobody been in her room. I found the hat in the living room. Had I known it was hers, I wouldn't have put the nasty thing on my head. She probably has lice or something."

Furious, I jumped up from my chair. Lacy jumped up as well and took a defensive stance.

Keisha shut us both down. "Don't make me push this button. We will not be doing this today. Y'all are not about to ruin my day. Both of you sit down now!"

Reluctantly we sat.

"Snitch," Lacy whispered loud enough for me to hear.

I got so angry. I was ready to take a needle if it meant I could beat the shit out of Lacy before they gave it to me. Where I was from, being called a snitch was worse than being called a bitch.

"And you're a lyin' thief who needs to stay the fuck out of my room."

Keisha rolled her eyes. "This isn't getting us anywhere. I have half a mind to turn you both over to Mrs. Gates since you don't want to act like the young ladies you're supposed to be. Of course, you know, if I do that, she'll have y'all cleaning bathrooms too."

"That's not fair. She stole from me. I didn't do anything to her."

"And she kicked down the bathroom door while I was taking a dump and I got punished."

"That's my bathroom. I had every right to get in there. I asked your stank ass nicely to open the door and you told me to fuck off."

"Enough! What is it with you two? Are you sure you two aren't related?" Keisha allowed her anger to show for the first time since we'd entered her office. If she was waiting for a response from me, she wasn't going to get it. I didn't know what Lacy's deal with me was. Frankly, I didn't give a shit. Making friends in this house wasn't part of my deal. My freedom was a few short months away. I didn't want to do anything to jeopardize it.

"Fine, I borrowed her stupid hat. Big fucking deal."

Keisha folded her arms across her body. "If you took it from her without her permission, you stole it. We do not tolerate theft around here."

"For crying out loud, it's a cheap-ass hat. I can get a better one at the Dollar Store. It wasn't worth nothing to begin with." Lacy said, while plucking threads from the hem of her cut off shorts.

I saw the door of opportunity open and I was going to take full advantage of it. "I don't feel safe. I feel threatened. I want the key to the lock on my door." Unknowingly, Lacy did me a favor by stealing my hat.

Keisha let out a nervous laugh. "Jordan, don't you think that's a little extreme? I'm sure Lacy won't be giving you anymore problems. Ain't that right, Lacy?" The pinched expression on her face exposed her only tell.

I folded my arms across my chest. "What you think doesn't matter. It's how I feel. I think I need to call my lawyer. This isn't working for me." I smiled. If this were a chess match, I was about to claim the queen and challenge the king.

Lacy jumped to her feet again as her mouth dropped open. "She's gonna sue me for a stupid hat? What kinda shit is that?"

"Go to your room Lacy. I'll deal with you later."

"Go to my room? What am I, twelve?"

"Go!"

Lacy stood for several seconds with this incredulous expression on her face before she stormed out of the room and slammed the door. "Bitch."

"That chick has anger management issues," I stated.

"She just wants some attention."

"Whatever. I don't fuck with her 'cause of her mouth. She calls everyone a bitch and I don't get down like that."

"About that key …"

"Yeah, I'm gonna need that." I could tell Keisha was nervous and she should be. I wasn't going to let this golden opportunity pass me by.

"I don't think that's gonna fly. There are rules and safety measures to think about."

"I hear you, but I still want a key. Lacy is not going to leave me alone just because you say so. If she's so brazen that she steals from me and flaunts it in my face, then a warning from you is not going to change anything."

"I can see your point. However, there are still safety concerns that need to be addressed. What if we need to get in your room for an emergency?"

"I want to talk to my lawyer. He might want to shut this place down like he did my other one…" I enjoyed testing Keisha. She wasn't such a hard-ass when I pinched her nipples.

"I will talk to Mrs. Gates about giving you a key. Don't get your hopes up."

"I'll be back to use the phone once I check my room to see if anything else is missing." I didn't wait for a response. I just walked out the door.

CHAPTER TEN

LACY BATES

I couldn't wait for Jordan to come out of the office. I was dying to know what was going on behind those doors. I paced back and forth in the hallway waiting for her. In my head, I played through all kinds of scenarios. All of them ended with Jordan getting kicked the fuck out of the home. My hopes were dashed when she finally emerged with this big-ass smile on her face. This shit wasn't making sense to me. Jordan had all but threatened Keisha, yet she came out smiling. What was I doing wrong? I didn't want to stampede into the office right away but the suspense was killing me. I reached the door and gave three short raps.

"Come in?" Keisha barked. I almost chickened out about going in.

I peeked around the door. "What was that all about?" Curiosity was oozing from my pores.

"That was about you taking something that didn't belong to you."

"Not that, I mean the lawyer thing. Can I call my lawyer too?"

Keisha was playing busy with some paperwork on her desk in an attempt not to meet my eyes. She stopped the second I mentioned a lawyer.

"You don't have a lawyer."

"Hell, if it could get me a lock on my door, I'll get me one. Where do I sign up at?"

"That's not going to work for you. Jordan has special circumstances."

"I knew something was different about her! Uh, what special circumstances?"

"That's really none of your business. Besides, I can't discuss it with you." Keisha appeared to be extremely agitated, which only added to my determination to get some answers.

"Okay, if you don't want to talk about it with me, then maybe you'd like to discuss it with the whole house. I think we should have a group session and talk about it. How about that?" I turned to leave the room hoping she would take the bait.

"What do you mean?" The look in her eyes told me that she knew exactly what I meant.

"I mean, that I'm going to talk to every single girl in this house and tell them that your precious Jordan is getting her own key. Do you think that they are so blind that they can't see what's going on around here for themselves? Do you think we don't talk about it? They may not be as vocal as I am, but you can bet your sweet ass, they see it."

"I've got to speak with Mrs. Gates. It's not my call; it's hers."

Crap. I knew Mrs. Gates would not be bullied. I had to contain this conversation to this room if I wanted to prevail.

"She's going to think you can't handle a bunch of adolescent girls. How's that going to look on your resume?"

"This one won't be on me, and unless you want to earn yourself a ticket out of here, I suggest you let it go."

"Fine. We'll see what the other girls have to say." If she wasn't going to provide answers to me, I'd incite the other girls to get the answers for me. I had almost opened the door before she stopped me.

"Wait, let me think."

She couldn't see the smile on my face because my back was turned. I wasn't sure what I was about to hear but I was certain either way it went, I won. I only needed to find out what the prize would be.

"Sit down. You have to promise me this conversation does not leave this room. I could lose my job for even thinking about discussing another person with you."

"I understand." It was a struggle to keep my facial expressions blank. Keisha's entire demeanor changed. She was not the imposing authoritative figure I was used to. I almost felt guilty for forcing her hand. Almost.

"Jordan's story is sad. She was lost in the system and misdiagnosed. She's only here until her records can be expunged and her court case settled."

I'm not sure what I was expecting to hear but this wasn't it. So what she became lost in the system. To a certain extent, we were all lost in the system. Another number or tick marks representing impoverished children whose parents didn't give a damn. Why should she be any different from me? All of the girls had their own horror stories. I didn't see anyone knocking on the door trying to help them. It was so unfair. "Big fucking deal. Name one of the other girls out there that haven't gotten a raw deal. This is bullshit."

"It is different. She was picked up by the police for an altercation in the street. They sent her to a hospital for evaluation. Somehow or other they forgot about her. It's really tragic when you think about it. She was in the mental hospital for several years before they found her."

"Well maybe the bitch is crazy. Did you think about that?"

Keisha shook her head. "When Gates hears about this, she's going to flip. Fuck my life. This is not good."

I'd never seen Keisha so distraught and I couldn't understand why. "So what, she gets a key. We should all have keys. We're not supposed to be in jail. Mrs. Gates be trying to run this bitch like it's a prison."

Keisha shook her head again. "You think its easy trying to manage a bunch of unruly girls? She has to be hard on you girls or you'll take over."

"You know what, I never thought about it that way. To a certain extent, you're right. Give me an inch, I'd definitely take a mile. It's the only way that I know to get ahead. But on the flip side, I want to be treated with respect. Giving me a key to my own room is a small way of doing it."

Keisha stopped toying with the papers on her desk and let out a long sigh. "I guess I can't put this off any longer." She stood up from her desk, forcing me to stand as well.

"I hope you tell her whatever she does for Jordan, she's going to have to do it for us too. It's only fair."

"Whoever told you that life was fair lied."

***

I wasn't sure what I was going to say to Jordan but I knew I had to do something to end the feud I started. Since both Keisha and Mrs. Gates were tied up, I decided to take advantage of the opportunity just in case things went left. I was nervous when I knocked on her door.

"Who is it?" Jordan called through the door. She still sounded angry, which was not the best way to start a conversation with her.

"It's me, Lacy." There was no other sound coming from her room. I waited patiently for her to open the door or tell me to fuck off. She snatched open the door after several seconds.

"What do you want?" She demanded with her hands on her hips.

"I came to say I'm sorry."

"Yeah, right. And I'm supposed to believe you?"

I suppressed the urge to get angry. It's what I would have said if the situation had been reversed. "I'm actually being sincere. I mean it."

Jordan looked leery. "Did Gates put you up to this? Because if she did, you can go back and tell her it didn't work."

"Ain't nobody put me up to nothing. Why can't you just accept my apology?"

"Why should I? You've been fucking with me from day one."

I smiled. As much as I hated to admit it, she had a point. "So, I'm a dick head, sue me."

"You got to have a dick to be a dick head. Unless you've got something else to tell me." She smiled for the first time. She really needed to do it more often.

"So we're good?"

"You think a lousy apology is going to make me like your ass?"

"You ain't got to like me, Bitch. I just owed you an apology." I was done trying to hide my annoyance.

"I done told you about calling me a bitch!" Jordan took two quick steps getting in my face, breathing the same air as me. Her eyes were like smoldering embers.

"If you didn't act like one, I wouldn't call you one." She was not intimidating me by being in my space. What did concern me was the trouble I'd get into if we were to start fighting in her room. At the very least, I needed to drag her ass into the hallway so I could say she attacked me. I stepped back, keeping my hands to my side. Even though we were both angry, neither of us raised our voices. It was as if she wanted to keep this confrontation as quiet as I did.

"I'm not going to ask you again to leave me alone. I don't want any friends. I'm not interested in getting to know you. To be blunt, I don't need you. So fuck off." She slammed the door in my face.

Oh no she didn't. I was too stunned to move. I had heard some pretty fucked up things in my day but it never made me feel like I did at that moment. "Well fuck you too…Bitch!" I hightailed it away from her door feeling slightly vindicated for some odd reason.

CHAPTER ELEVEN

JORDAN BREE

Lacy was speeding up my timetable. Originally, I'd planned on dealing with her on the eve of my departure from the home. However, her actions made it clear she wasn't going to go away. Whipping her ass in front of witnesses was not an option. Ignoring her wasn't working. She wasn't leaving me much of a choice. I was interrupted in my musings by another urgent sounding rap on the door.

"What?" I couldn't believe that girl's tenacity. I yanked open the door ready to bury my fist in Lacy's face. "Oh, it's you. I thought it was Lacy again."

"Can I come in?" Keisha's face was like a mask and unreadable. I stood back from the door, allowing her to enter. If I were in real trouble, I would have been summoned to Mrs. Gates' office, so I took this as a good sign that Keisha came to me.

"I would offer you a chair if I had one." I crossed the room and sat on my bed, leaving Keisha standing near the door.

"Gates has agreed to provisionally give you a key."

"Provisionally? What does that mean?" I was cautious.

"It means under certain conditions."

"Okay, I'm not sure I like it, but what are the conditions?"

"One of them is that you don't tell the other girls. The other is that your door remains unlocked anytime you are in your room."

"That's some bullshit right there. It totally defeats my purpose for getting a key."

"I'm sorry. I thought you wanted a key to protect your things when you weren't around to do it yourself. Isn't that what you told me?"

"You don't have to worry about me telling those other girls shit. I don't speak to half of them anyway. What makes you think that Lacy won't tell them? These girls rattle my door knob every day trying to piss me off. First time it happens and it's locked, Gates is gonna come at me all sideways. I'm not having it."

"I actually agree with you but I'm not in charge."

"How's she going to know if I lock my door at night? She gonna come by every few hours and check?"

"Your guess is as good as mine. I just work here."

Keisha sounded defeated and for a split second, I almost felt sorry for her. "Can I talk to Mrs. Gates?" It was evident to me, Keisha wasn't going to be able to help me.

"I don't know. She was pretty upset."

"She's upset? Are you kidding me? Was her stuff stolen?" I walked over to the door. "I'm done with this. Can I use your phone?"

If it were possible for a black woman to turn white, Keisha did it. "I can't give you my phone. I'd get fired."

"Well, I'm not doing a back and forth with you. I want to see my lawyer today. I don't care who calls him. I want to see him." This meeting was over and my opening the door signaled the end of it. In my head, I was already working on what I would say.

***

I was a little nervous when I walked into Mrs. Gates' office. However, I wasn't the only one feeling the strain. Mrs. Gates looked as if she'd swallowed a lemon with her lips tightly pressed together in a grimace. She sat behind her desk but I could hear her feet rapidly tapping on the floor. Mr. Pressman was seated in one of the chairs facing her desk and I walked over to the other. I nodded to Mr. Pressman and he returned my greeting with a smile.

"It's good to see you, Jordan. How have you been?" Mr. Pressman asked.

"This meeting ain't private?" I sat down and waited for Gates to leave.

"Um, I'd really like to stay if this discussion relates to things going on in this house." Mrs. Gates stated.

I was agitated. I didn't want to show my hand in front of Mrs. Gates until I knew if I had a leg to stand on. Right now it was all a bluff. If Mr. Pressman told me to sit down and shut up, I'd look foolish.

"Jordan are you comfortable with this?" Mr. Pressman asked, as he placed his brief case on his lap. I waited while he reached inside and retrieved a pen and pad, presumably to take notes.

"Do I have a choice?"

"Of course you have a choice. We just need to find somewhere we can speak in private or you can come to my office in the morning." Mr. Pressman looked at Mrs. Gates.

Mrs. Gates cleared her throat. "I thought you said you didn't want to do the back and forth, Jordan."

"Fine, we can do this here. Mr. Pressman, this isn't working for me. I feel like I'm in jail or back at the hospital."

"That's ridiculous. There are no bars on these windows or locks on these doors with the exception of the front and back doors." Mrs. Gates responded.

"I'm sick of this place. We don't have any privacy. People come and go in my room, taking things and I'm not okay with it." I turned in my chair and faced my lawyer. "If I'm not being punished, why am I here?"

"Jordan, this is only a temporary place for you until your settlement is approved. As you know, the state will probably appeal but we should have the first payment soon."

"So, why do I feel like I'm being punished? You told me this place was a halfway house. My question to you is: halfway to what? What about the rest of these girls? Why are they here? Are they criminals? Did you know they can't even go outside? What kind of foolishness is this?"

"The other girls are not your concern, Jordan."

Mrs. Gates sounded very angry. She ignored everything else I'd said except the part about the other girls. What was she trying to hide? Well she wasn't the only one angry. Mrs. Gates had been virtually inaccessible to me. The only time I ever knew she was in the building was when she was chewing someone out. "I told you Lacy was messing with me and what did you do? You made us work kitchen detail together."

"I was trying to teach both of you a lesson about working together."

"So you're my teacher now? I didn't know I was in school."

Mrs. Gates waved her hands in front of her face. "Mr. Pressman, my role with these girls has never been questioned."

"Well maybe it should be. If we're not in trouble with the law, why can't we have locks on our doors? Why can't they go out unsupervised too? I don't want to make this about anyone else but fair is fair. No wonder the other girls hate me. You made it that way." My tears surprised everyone, including myself.

"The girls don't hate you."

"Mr. Pressman, I don't know what I'm supposed to learn here. I'm no more prepared to go out into the world than the first day I came here. So what's the point? " What started out as my quest to get a lock on my door turned into something much bigger.

"These girls are my responsibility. I can't have them running around the street. It's bad enough you do it."

"We are not girls. We are young women. It's about time you recognized it. Most of these women have been through more in their young lives than you. If you're supposed to help us, damn it, teach us about life outside these walls."

Mrs. Gates stood up from her desk. "You will not speak to me like that."

"What you gonna do? Drug me again?"

Mr. Pressman's jaw dropped as his head switched between me and Mrs. Gates. He stood up, his face as red as if he'd been on the beach all morning. "Ladies, please. Jordan, I'm not sure what you want me to do here. I can't tell Mrs. Gates how to run her house."

Mrs. Gates smiled for the first time since I'd entered the room. Her look said she won but I was about to bust her bubble. "Mr. Pressman, perhaps I made a mistake in calling you."

"That's right, dear, you wasted this man's time." Mrs. Gates' smile stretched.

"I think I should have called my reporter friend, Brody, instead. He won't need permission from the court to print a story. And we all know what happened the last time he took pen to paper. I'm pretty sure I have his number in my room. I'll be right back." I stood up as well and walked to the door.

Mrs. Gates hands flew up to her face trying to cover her surprise. Mr. Pressman sat back down so fast his briefcase fell to the floor with a small thud. The unexpected noise in the otherwise quiet office startled Mrs. Gates.

"This is ridiculous. How am I expected to run this home if there are no rules? Mr. Pressman, I've tried but I can't do it. She's threatening me."

"Mrs. Gates, she is not threatening you. She's just upset. Can we all just sit down and talk about this like adults."

Mr. Pressman didn't want me to call on my reporter friend either. Aside from the negative publicity, he had a fiduciary duty to the court to check on me, file reports and he didn't. Calling in Brody would not only be bad news for Mrs. Gates, it might also screw up my own plans in the process. I returned to my seat. Once everyone was seated Mr. Pressman took control of the meeting.

"Good, now, Jordan, can you please tell me what it is that you want?"

"Why are you talking to me like I'm trying to launch a prison take over? All I wanted was a key to my room."

"Then why are you asking about the other 'ladies' ability to leave?" Mrs. Gates inquired.

"Don't you see why this is creating problems for me?"

"So what do you suggest, Jordan?" Mr. Pressman continued.

"How about affording them, I mean, us dignity and respect? It wouldn't hurt your program if the ladies were allowed to do things outside of the house to help them, like going to school or getting jobs."

"If I open those doors, then I have to deal with boys, drugs, pregnancy and a whole host of other problems, which I don't have the time or staff to deal with."

"I beg to differ. You could start out by allowing them a couple of hours of freedom once a week and see what happens. If they fuck it up, then it's on them. But punish them individually, not the entire house."

"Well, that sounds reasonable to me." Mr. Pressman commented, clearly uncomfortable with the back and forth.

"Mr. Pressman, I appreciate what you're trying to do. However, I'm afraid I can't implement those types of changes without consulting with the Board of Directors." Mrs. Gates was sitting staunchly in her chair, her face firmly foreboding.

"Perhaps you can meet with them and get back to us." Mr. Pressman suggested.

"We only meet quarterly. I will make a note to add this as an agenda item for our next meeting."

"We? Are you on the board, Mrs. Gates?" I asked sarcastically. I had come to the conclusion that Mrs. Gates was an idiot in a skirt.

"Why yes, I am." I was waiting for her to pop her collar. If she had, I would've gone over the desk and punched her in the throat.

"Let me guess…president?" Her smile confirmed my suspicions. "Then I'm sure you won't have a problem getting them together sooner should this story hit the papers." Check and mate.

The look of surprise on Mrs. Gates' face was priceless. I had thrown down the gauntlet. She produced a key from her center desk drawer. She placed it on the corner of her desk. "I'll work on a new schedule for the girls and post it tomorrow. Satisfied?" I could tell Mrs. Gates wasn't used to conceding. It wasn't a look she wore well.

"What about keys for the other ladies?" I couldn't care less whether the other women got keys. I was not trying to make friends. I only wanted them to stay out of my business and leave me alone.

"There are safety issues involved; I can't make that decision on my own."

"Very well." I picked my key up from her desk. I wasn't going to press that issue as long as I could lock my own door. By anyone's standards, I'd won. The girls would be so consumed with their own freedom, they'd forget about me.

"That's great. I'm glad we were able to work this out in-house." Mr. Pressman was pretty much ineffective, giving me cause to wonder how he would handle the state's appeal. I made a note to look for alternative counsel.

CHAPTER TWELVE

JORDAN BREE

I had taken a few weeks off to allow things around the house to settle down. When the ladies found out that the outdoor restrictions had been modified, they went wild. The house was a hornet's nest of activity with people coming and going. Now that the novelty had worn off, there were more people around to take the focus off my not being there. I needed for there to be some uncertainty as to my whereabouts. Since I spent the majority of my time in my room with the door closed, it would be easy to assume I was in there. Unless someone came specifically looking for me, no one knew what I was up to.

I dressed with care and slipped out of the house before my fellow housemates had begun to stir. Spring was definitely in the air. However, I had the feeling winter wasn't finished with us. It was already May and we'd yet to see a day that reached above seventy-three degrees. This was highly unusual for

Georgia. We tended to skip spring all together and go directly to summer. I sorely regretted not grabbing a jacket when I left the house. I was too afraid of anyone seeing me to go back and get one. I practically ran the entire way to the bus stop and hid in the shelter until the bus arrived. I was so cold, I was shivering. To make matters worse, the bus was freezing too. It was so cold; the windows were covered with condensation. I resisted a childlike urge to scribble my name on the window.

I got off the bus in my old neighborhood again and it felt as if I'd never left. It wasn't a good feeling. Every insecurity and negative feeling I'd ever felt came rushing at me with a tidal wave of emotions. I stumbled back from the pain, each memory like a physical assault. Coming back so soon may have been a mistake. This trip was different from the one I'd made a few weeks prior. The last time I tried to sneak in unnoticed. This time, I was coming home. "What was I thinking?" I wondered aloud. Many of my memories were vague and unpleasant. I wanted so desperately to forget but I dreamed about it so much. I had to see it just one more time. I needed to experience it, smell it, touch it and get over it. Doctor Max said I needed closure.

Trash littered the side walk, the streets reeked of urine. Children didn't play in this neighborhood; it was too dangerous. The streets belonged to the junkies and their suppliers. In this neighborhood, everything came with a price. The only way I survived as a child was because of my siblings. They might not have been good for anything else but they knew these streets. The corners protected them and therefore, me. My brother, Rick, died on these corners. He paid the way for me to go to school but his protection lasted only as far as the neighborhood. After that, I was on my own.

Though these were the streets I dreamed of, in the light of day, they didn't look the same. The streets I dreamed of were much nicer. I had forgotten about the filth and despair that plagued these crossroads I called a neighborhood. I had forgotten all about the desolate faces I needed to pass to get where I was going. *How could I have not seen it before?*

This time, I expected to feel welcomed by the familiarity. Instead, I felt more alone than I'd ever felt in my life. The people I passed didn't see my pain. Caught up in their own misery, their frowns were etched deep in their faces, much like badly crafted tattoos. It's hard to believe I escaped even though my road out wasn't an easy one.

I tried not to think as my feet carried me to my old housing complex. Our building had yet to be renovated. As much as I wanted to believe I didn't care about the family that abandoned me while I was in the hospital, I did. My heart started beating faster as I approached the courtyard.

The voices in my head begged me to stop. What little love left in my heart, drove my feet forward. I pushed the automatic door opener. Nothing happened. I didn't have the needed keycard to get in. It was somewhere in the boxes of personal effects I took from the hospital. I stepped away from the doorway waiting for someone to come out. It was a busy building, so I didn't have to wait long. A small gaggle of children burst through the door, shrieking with glee, oblivious to the dangers that lurked in the courtyard. They weren't as careful as the adult residents in the building. They didn't notice me slipping through the opening. Once inside, I exhaled the air I'd forgotten to swallow. "So far, so good," I murmured.

I had no intention of knocking on our old apartment door. I just needed to know if my people still lived there. Broken glass and cigarette butts littered the hallway. I gingerly stepped over the shards of glass, checking the names on the mailboxes. We lived on the fourth floor. Back then, it might have had a glorious view of downtown Atlanta, if the other housing projects weren't so close to each other. Now, ours was the last one standing. The windows were so dirty, I couldn't see out of them.

My eyes were slow to adjust to the dimly lit corridor. The faded names on the mailboxes were difficult to read. Or maybe my eyes didn't want to see. Whatever the reason, it took me several minutes to locate the name I was looking for. My heart sank when I realized they were still here. Had the name been blank or unrecognizable, I could walk away believing that they'd moved. A strong surge of resentment and anger boiled in the pit of my stomach. They were there the whole time. My shoulders slumped. I wanted to believe they'd gone and didn't know where to find me. I turned away from those damning mailboxes, anxious to get as far away from that damn building as my feet would carry me.

The front door banged against the concrete wall; someone was coming. Without giving it much thought, I ran for the elevator, stabbing the button repeatedly. "Urgh," I moaned in frustration. My heart was racing. It might have been the children coming back. They had such short attention spans. Nonetheless, I didn't want to wait and find out. With my luck, it would probably be a security guard or worse, someone who knew me. I gave up on the elevator after a few more jabs at the button. Taking the stairs as fast as my heeled sandals allowed. My tiny feet sounded like a herd of cattle as they pounded the stairs. I couldn't tell what was making the most noise, the click-clack of my heels or the symphonic beating of my heart. Within seconds, I was winded and pissed off. Why was I running? I didn't do anything wrong and had every right to be in the building. My people lived there.

I stopped running on the third floor landing. I realized it wasn't the children I heard coming through the door. They would have found me by now. Whoever it was, they were taking their sweet-ass time coming up the stairs. While I tried to catch my breath, I peeked over the railing. I couldn't see a damn thing. I willed myself to relax. If I got caught, there was only so much they could do to me. I'd be escorted out or beat the hell up, depending on who caught me. I'd been thrown out of much better places, and had my share of beatings. So what was the big deal? "Fuck it."

Out the corner of my eye, I saw an empty syringe on the floor in between the railings. It looked as if someone had stashed it there with hopes of coming back for it later. Nine times out of ten, its owner was scared away much like I was. I bent and picked it up without thinking about the inherent dangers of touching a used needle. I put it in a zippered compartment of my purse. I wasn't sure what I was going to do with it but I was fairly certain I needed it. I leaned over the railing again. Nothing. Relieved to have dodged the bullet, I started walking back down the stairs deep in thought.

Even though I was curious about my family's lack of concern about me, I now knew I wasn't ready to face them. I would have to do it one day. However, today wasn't the day. When I saw them, I wanted to have all my ducks in a row. I was already more financially sound than my entire family put together but there were still some areas in my life I needed to improve. First and foremost, my living conditions. Tucking a wayward hair behind my ear, I began negotiating the stairs. It was taking a lot longer to get down than it was to go up. I was concentrating on my heels and didn't notice the woman doing the two step shuffle coming up.

"Shit," the woman hissed as she tripped, nearly falling.

I fought the urge to reach down and catch the woman. I was in the wrong neck of the woods for that shit. In this neighborhood, if you reach out and touch someone, you're liable to get touched back with a quickness. Kindness and compassion weren't common place around here.

The woman was so frail. Her arms looked like tiny twigs. Her legs looked like her arms should have looked, with feet attached to them. Her dusty brown skin looked unnatural. She was wearing a brown mangy wig which she may have put on backwards. The bangs were hanging down her neck and what was left of her nappy hair poked out the front. She used the railing too pull herself up, one step at a time. Shuffling her feet, with her head down, I couldn't guess her age.

I crossed to the other side of the stairwell, so as not to run into the woman, hoping to avoid any down-draft aromas. This woman was a stark reminder of where I came from. One of the roughest tenements in Atlanta, the last one standing. My sudden movement startled the woman. As our eyes locked, I recognized her. She was no ordinary woman. She was my older sister, Theresa. For a brief moment, I felt giddy. I finally saw someone who truly knew me, down to my stinking drawers. All of my previous apprehension and fear disappeared. With renewed energy, I was ready to give my sister a wet kiss and a big hug. I rushed forward. My sister held up her skinny arm.

"Oh, no you don't."

Her eyes were ablaze with hatred, luminous pool, so intense I had to step back. Didn't my sister recognize me? "Theresa, girl, don't you know who I am?" I felt like I'd walked into an episode of the Twilight Zone where reality was altered.

"I know who the hell you are." My sister spat at my feet, as if some dirty bug had flown into her mouth. "What I want to know is what are you doing here?"

My sister appeared angry with me, as if I'd done something wrong. If anyone had a right to be angry, it was me. Righting my shoulders, I pulled myself up and threw back my head. I was not about to give my sister the satisfaction of knowing that my feelings were hurt. Coming there was a bad idea. I didn't realize how bad until now. Of all my siblings, I felt closer to Theresa than anyone. If she wasn't happy to see me, no one else would be either. It was a bitter pill to swallow.

"What did momma say?" Theresa had reached the second landing. Her eyes were on the floor, as if she were searching for something and vigorously scratching her arm. With a growing certainty, I realized what she was looking for. For a split second, I considered giving the needle back to her. For some reason, I decided against it. Regardless of how she treated me, I still loved her.

"Momma? I haven't seen her." My pride wouldn't let me admit I was afraid to. If Theresa was this strung out on drugs, ain't no telling what my mother looked like. Drugs or not, it didn't excuse why I hadn't heard from them.

Theresa smiled, "still chicken shit ain't you?" For a few seconds she sounded like the sister I once loved.

"I'm not scared."

"Then why are you sneaking around in the hallway then?" Theresa's eyes narrowed to tiny slits. She stepped closer to me and the aroma nearly knocked me down.

I covered my nose. "When's the last time you washed that ass?" Not caring whether I hurt her feelings, I blurted it out. If someone hadn't already told her she stunk, she should have smelled it herself. The stench was horrible.

Theresa opened her mouth to say something and immediately closed it. She was covered in so many layers of dirt, it was hard to determine where the dirt ended and her complexion began. "Ain't none of your damn business." The fire was gone momentarily from my sister's eyes. She had to know how bad she smelled. I felt bad for her. She'd been the last one of my family members who said no to drugs. I wondered what changed.

Theresa eyed me up and down, making me uncomfortable under her scrutiny. "You didn't see no shit on the floor did you?" Her voice sounded pitifully hopeful.

"What type of shit you looking for?" I wasn't sure what I would've done if my sister actually told me the truth.

"Never mind." We stood in awkward silence for a few seconds.

"I guess I should go."

Theresa's head snapped up; her red rimmed eyes appeared to glow. "Go where? Ain't no room for you here now."

Something inside of my head popped. "Who said anything about staying in this roach infested hotel? Bitch, please." I was hurt, angry and confused. Why did it have to be this way? Why did my sister hate me so much?

"Bitch? I changed your shitty diapers and you're going to talk to me this way?"

I was ashamed of my outburst for about a hot neo-second. I had nothing to feel guilty about. I wasn't the one who started this argument. Theresa was having a difficult time standing still. She kept lifting her arms and looking at them as if they belonged to someone else. She attempted to scratch her hair but the wig was so matted, I doubted her slender fingers did anything to relieve the itch.

"Where you going to go?" Theresa's voice was so low it sounded almost childlike.

"Back to my apartment." I lied. I might not have my own place yet but where I was, was a hundred times better than where she was.

"You have an apartment? Where at?"

"It's in Lenox." I prayed she didn't ask me where Lenox was because I didn't have a clue. I had seen it on television and it looked like a nice place to live.

"Lenox? Get the fuck out of here. You wish." Theresa laughed.

I shrugged my shoulders, neither confirming nor denying her statement. She was going to believe what she wanted to believe anyway. "Alright, I got to go. Take care of yourself." I tried to step around my sister but she had other ideas.

"How many people live with you? You in a group home or something?" She coughed up some phlegm and spit it on the floor.

"No, it's just me." I lied again.

"Right, I might be a little loopy now but I ain't crazy. How you going to afford a place by yourself? Fuck you talking about." She was angry again.

"I don't know what you want me to say. I told you the truth."

'You got some money?" Theresa's timid voice was gone. She had put a little bass in it.

I wasn't intimated any more. Theresa used to kick my ass but now, she might have weighed seventy-eight pounds; give or take a few. If she wanted to act crazy, all I had to do was blow and she'd fall down the stairs. "I got enough."

"Let me see." Her eyes appeared to twinkle like she was about to receive a Christmas present.

I almost started laughing. She must have thought I had boo-boo the fool written on my head. I only had about twenty-five dollars on me but there was no way in hell I was about to pull it out. "For what?" Even though my tone was even and calm, I was getting upset. It was clear what was really important to my sister and I wasn't it.

"I just wanna see it." Theresa started scratching her arm in earnest. I knew what this meant. It was time for my sister to feed her addiction.

"This ain't no show and tell."

"I knew you were lying. I don't know why I let you waste my time like this. Get the hell out of here."

'Fine." I tried to step around my sister again but she blocked me once more. She tried another tactic.

"How 'bout you lend me twenty dollars?"

"How you gonna pay me back? You got a job?" I replied sarcastically.

"Do I look like I have a mother fucking job?" A large vein in her neck pulsated.

"Do you really want me to tell you how you look?"

Theresa winced. "I've been sick. Yeah, yeah, I'm sick. I need to go to the store and get me some medicine." She coughed clutching her chest as if she were in pain. It was a pitiful act, transparent as glass.

I pretended to play along. "What's wrong with you?"

Theresa looked confused. She obviously hadn't sorted her lie out completely in her head before she opened her mouth.

"I, uh..."

I was overwhelmed with sadness. I came here wanting answers but this was not what I wanted to see. I knew my mother had started dabbling in drugs before I left. If Theresa was this bad, my mother had to be worse. "Mom strung out too?"

Theresa looked surprised, as if it were some kind of secret. Her face turned crimson red. I didn't know whether it was anger or shame that caused it.

"Ain't nobody doing no drugs. If you ain't going to give me no money, just say so. You don't have to make up no shit about us to keep your stinkin' money."

"Fine. I won't give you money. I'll feed you if you want me to, but that's all I can do for any of you."

"Snotty nose bitch. We got food at the house. Fuck I need food for?"

We were back to square one. Coming there was a huge mistake. I had the closure I needed. I only had one more question that I needed to know the answer to. "How come none of you ever visited me in the hospital?" I couldn't keep the pain from seeping into my voice as I fought back tears. Visiting someone was such a small thing to do. So small, it was inexcusable that they didn't do it.

"Momma said that your crazy ass wouldn't know the difference. We saw you acting a fool on television." Theresa laughed at me. I hated when people laughed at me.

"I'm not crazy! I wasn't then and I'm not now." I didn't know why it was so important to me that she knew it. If she heard me, she didn't let on.

"Momma has a new baby now." This conversation took a sharp right turn, and, for a minute, I thought I misunderstood what she'd said.

"Say what?" I was floored. This was the last thing I wanted or needed to hear. My mother was in her late forties and, in my opinion, way too old to have another baby. Not to mention the fact that she was a horrible parent. If this was true, I felt sorry for the kid. Growing up in the projects was hard enough under the best circumstances.

"Yeah, you got another baby sister. She's three."

I had heard enough. I didn't want to know about another baby. As far as I was concerned, my mother didn't take care of the children she already had. This new one meant nothing to me. I needed to get out of that building before some of its filth rubbed off on me. "I got to go, Theresa."

"Ain't you gonna come upstairs and say hi?"

"For what? You already told me there wasn't any room for me there. Besides, if your mother wanted to see me she would have made an effort before now. You take care of yourself. Despite how both of you treated me; I did love you at one point in time." I gently pushed my sister to the side, going down the stairs as quickly as I could.

"Wait, how are we supposed to get in contact with you?"

"You can't." I never looked back, I couldn't. It was heart breaking to know that if I ever saw my sister again, it would probably be in a pine box. Life was so unfair. I wanted to cry so badly but I couldn't. This was not the time or place for tears. In this neighborhood, tears were a sign of weakness. In this place, you took the shit life gave you and kept it moving.

My feet sounded like hoofs on the pavement as I stomped angrily down the street. I needed to do something to clear my head. This was a dangerous place for me to be, both physically and mentally. As I walked to the bus stop, I fished through my purse for my phone. When Max gave it to me, I never imagined myself using it. Instinct told me to keep it charged and I'm glad I listened. The phone only had three numbers in it. I prayed that one of them would answer my plea for help.

"Max, its Jordan. I really need to talk to you." I could not describe how happy I was to hear his voice.

"Jordan, it's so good to hear from you. Are you okay?"

"No, I'm not," I cried.

"Where are you? I'm coming to get you."

CHAPTER THIRTEEN

LAWRENCE MAXWELL

I did not recognize Jordan when I met her at the Applebee's. She looked amazing. "Wow, Jordan, you look good. If you hadn't called out to me, I wouldn't have recognized you." She wore a purple sundress with some high heeled sandals. I wasn't into fashion but she looked like she could have been on the cover of some magazine. Her dress coated her hips like a second skin. Her heels emphasized her shapely legs and thighs. I had to remind myself she was once my patient and not some woman off the street. She was definitely the type of woman I was attracted too. Even while I treated her, I found her attractive, now she was stunning. Her oversized sunglasses hid her beautiful brown eyes from me.

Jordan allowed a hint of a smile to touch her lips. "Thanks." She appeared to be a little nervous. I couldn't blame her; I was nervous too. Despite my nervousness, it was good to see her and I was pleased she called me. I pulled up my chair close to the table.

"You said over the phone that you weren't doing okay. I have to tell you, you had me worried."

"I'm sorry. I didn't mean to trouble you. I needed to talk to someone. I don't have a lot of people in my life right now. I hope you don't mind my calling on you."

My heart practically skipped a beat. If she only knew how much I had thought about her. In my dreams, she was the one I envisioned lying next to me. When I didn't hear from her after she had left the hospital, I had all but given up believing I would ever see her again. Her call came as a very pleasant surprise. "Just the opposite. Didn't I tell you I would always be there for you?"

"You did, but people always say things that they don't really mean."

"I rarely say things I don't mean. You know you asked me for some information before you left and I've been holding on to it for you. I wasn't sure if I was supposed to call you."

"Oh, wow. I completely forgot about asking you for help in getting my birth certificate and social security card. You must think I'm still crazy."

"Jordan, you were never crazy. Confused, maybe, but never crazy," I said smiling. Even if she was crazy, I wouldn't have cared. She was very special to me; I felt a certain responsibility toward her.

"I can't believe you remembered. I want to get my driver's license and won't be able to get it without it."

"Yeah, I got them. I just didn't know what to do with them." I had so many other questions to ask her. I didn't know where to begin. I didn't want to scare her away by interrogating her. She said she wanted to talk, so I decided to do what I did best...listen.

"Did you want to get something to eat while we talk?"

"Actually, I could use another drink."

I raised a brow as warning bells went off in my head. Drinking didn't necessarily agree with the medicines I'd prescribed for her and I knew she was under age. "Are you sure that's wise?" I was on a slippery slope wanting to please her, while still being concerned for her wellbeing. Technically, I was no longer her doctor. However, it wasn't easy to turn off that switch once it had been turned on.

"Relax, Max. I don't plan on getting shit-faced. I just need something to help me unwind. I left my pills at home, so I'm good."

"Are you still taking them?"

"Yea, Max, I'm taking them. Maybe not as regularly as when I was in your care but I still take them."

"Jordan, in order for the medicine to be effective, you have to take them as prescribed."

"Can you take off the doctor's hat for fifty fucking seconds and just be my friend?" Her irritation was evident in her voice.

"Of course I can. Cut me a little slack, Jordan, this is new to me."

"Good. You need to chill. You work too hard anyway."

She gave me a sexy smile that damn near made me nut in my pants. I couldn't believe how incredibly stimulating she was without even trying.

"Point well taken. Actually, I have been *chilling* as you say. I haven't started working yet. I've been taking it easy. I think I'm going to take off the rest of the month. Then, maybe open up my own practice. I don't think I want to go back into another hospital. Too many politics for me."

"Good for you. You've got a good heart, Max. I want to see you happy."

My heart soared. "Oh, I'm happy. Especially now that I've gotten to see you again. I think of you often." This was as big of an admission as I was willing to make right now.

Jordan's smile slid off her face. She removed her glasses revealing very somber eyes. "Remember when you told me I had to remember in order to forget?"

"Yeah."

"Well I went by the old neighborhood today." She put her head down while playing with her fingers.

I wanted to reach across the table and give her a reassuring hug. "Let me go get you a drink. What would you like?"

"I'm drinking Zinfandel." She continued playing with her fingers, a silly game about the church and all its people that I used in therapy with her to get her to open up to me and other people.

"I'll be right back." I could have waited for the waitress to come back to her table but I needed a stiff shot myself. "Give me a Jameson on the rocks and a White Zinfandel for my lady." Calling Jordan my lady, was a complete slip of the tongue, but I liked the sound of it. I paid for our drinks and carried them back to the table. Jordan still had her head down and I wondered what was going through her mind. It bothered me that she was hurting and that there was nothing I could do about it.

"Thanks." Jordan's fingers gently brushed my hand causing a surge of electric lust to rush to my dick. I felt my face flush with embarrassment. It was a good thing I was sitting down or she would have seen my erection. She picked up the glass and took a generous swig.

"Just what the doctor ordered." I smiled and raised my glass in a mock toast.

Her gaze was thoughtful, as she took another healthy swig from her glass. "It tastes good too."

"Why'd you put your glasses back on? I can't see your eyes." I felt like she was hiding behind those dark frames. She took them off and placed them on the table. They became something else to play with.

"I saw my sister. She looked bad, smelled even worse."

"Is she sick?"

"You could say that. It's self-induced. I'm pretty sure she's on that shit."

"That's too bad. How did that make you feel?"

Jordan raised her brow. "This ain't no session, Max. I just wanted to talk to someone."

"I can ask you how you feel without trying to analyze you. Obviously, it made you feel some kind of way or you wouldn't have called me."

"Touché. I'm a little fucked up by it. She was experimenting with it when I left. I never thought she'd go over the ledge. She saw what it did to other people in my family. I don't get it."

"That had to be tough. Did she know who you were?"

"Fuck you mean? Of course she knew who I was. It was my sister for Christ's sake. She changed my shitty drawers and was quick to remind me of it." Jordan snapped. She emptied her glass and slammed it on the table.

"I didn't mean it like that. Jordan, calm down." The last thing I wanted was for Jordan to start a scene in the restaurant. Especially since she admitted she was not on her pills and had been drinking.

"How did you mean it then?" She was still pissed.

I held my hands up and drew a womanly shape in the air. "The hair, clothes, make up... you don't look anything like the little kid she might remember. You're a beautiful woman now."

Jordan's head jerked up. She smiled fully showing all of her teeth. "You think I'm beautiful?" She seemed genuinely surprised.

"Are you kidding me? You're gorgeous." I wanted to say more.

"That's the nicest thing anyone has ever said to me."

All vestiges of her anger had disappeared. Her smile was brilliant and lit up the room for me. I felt like we were the only two people in the restaurant. "Do you want another drink?" Suggesting this went against my better judgment. She hadn't begun to talk about what was bothering her. I had a feeling she was going to need another drink to continue.

"Yes, please. I promise to drink this one slower." She graced me with another sexy smile. I quickly turned away before she could see the affect she had on me.

"Hold that thought, I'll be right back." I practically skipped to the bar.

She pinched her fingers together as if holding an imaginary thought. I liked it when she was acting silly. It didn't happen often. She was still smiling when I returned to the table with the drinks. We were off to a good start. If it were in my power, I'd make sure she had something to smile about every day.

"Okay, where were we?"

Her smile slipped several notches. I frowned as I realized things were about to get serious again. She was so young; how was I ever going to explain to her that into every life some rain was going to fall? And that it was okay because those things never lasted for long.

"My sister told me my mother had another kid, a girl and she's about three years old."

"Really?" I wanted to ask her how that made her feel. Yet, I didn't want her to accuse me of analyzing her again.

"Do you have a family, Max?"

Her question took me by surprise since she'd never asked me anything of a personal nature before. "I have an older brother, no sisters."

"Do you get along?"

"Yeah, sure. I mean, he beat my ass when we were little, but we're good now."

"That's nice. I was beginning to think all families hurt each other." She played with her glasses again. She picked them up, and for a moment, I thought she was going to put them back on.

"Unfortunately, we can't pick our families. Sometimes it turns out good. Sometimes it's an epic fail."

"Mine is a big ass failure. I used to ask God for a do over. I wanted to pick the cards up and throw them in the air. I'd give anything to be able to pick them all over again."

"Jordan, don't you see, you already have a do over. You never have to see your family again if you don't want to. The choice is yours."

"I guess that's true. I wanted them to tell me what I ever did to be treated like I was treated. It still doesn't make any sense to me. I was a good kid you know?" Tears leaked from her eyes.

"I believe you. You can't beat yourself up about this. The way I see it, it's their loss, not yours."

"I asked my sister why they never came to see me. She said my crazy-ass wouldn't have known if they did or not. Was I that far gone, Max, that I wouldn't know my own family?"

"I don't know what you were like in the beginning. When I got to the hospital, they had you on some heavy duty drugs. I'm not saying you needed them. I think they were able to handle more patients if they kept them doped up. I really believe you spent your days in a medically induced stupor. You were unresponsive for the first couple of weeks after I weaned you off those drugs. I don't know how much of that you remember. On a brighter side, you're better now."

"I want to see my file. Do you think they will have that kind of stuff in there? For all I know, I could've been raped."

"Whoa, slow down a minute. I'll admit members of the staff were, in my opinion, negligent, but I don't believe they were physically abusive. At least I didn't see any evidence of it."

Jordan's eyes grew. "Did you examine me down there?"

"No, of course not." It was a good thing she wasn't able to read my mind. I might not have looked while she was my patient but given the chance, I would've loved to check her out now. The thought made me feel like a lecherous old man.

"I'm sorry, Max. I just don't want to wake up one day, five years from now, with some horrible memories that I had blocked. You don't know what it's like to have so many gaps in your memory. The last thing I really remember was going to court. Everything after that is a blur."

"I can understand how that would make you feel. This has to be especially difficult since you are a woman. But, from what I understand, most of the staff at that time was women."

"Is that supposed to make me feel any better? Women abuse women too."

"Damn, I guess you're right."

"Can you get me the records?"

"Sure. I don't know how much good they will be. Don't worry, I'll get them." I took a big gulp from my drink.

"Thank you, Max. I really owe you one for this. I don't know what I would have done if you couldn't have met me today. I was so upset."

"Are you feeling better now?" Max inquired.

"Yes, I'm fine. Thank you."

"Did you get the answers you were seeking?"

"Yes and no. I don't know why they hate me so much. Other than that, I'm willing to spend the rest of my life not knowing. As you said before, it's their loss."

Jordan smiled and it looked like a beam of sunshine to me. I could only hope that she actually meant what she said. Instead of saying what she knew I wanted to hear. We sat in silence for a few seconds, each of us lost in our own private musings. I was feeling so relieved at seeing Jordan again. For me, it was a feeling of satisfaction. I couldn't help but wonder how it was for her. It had to be more bitter sweet. She probably needed to see a familiar face in a sea of unfamiliar ones. I was all about Jordan regaining her memory if it would make her a whole person again. What concerned me were those unpleasant memories she had yet to remember. Those were the thoughts and fears I assumed woke her up in the middle of the night.

"I can't begin to tell you how happy I am to see you. I thought you were going to just disappear off the face of the earth. I ..."

Jordan put her fingers to my lips. It was the first time she'd touched me. I fought against the urge to lick my lips so that I could taste her touch. Without realizing it, my eyes closed. For a brief moment, I got lost in my own fantasy. Her touch was much softer than I'd ever imagined. I pursed my lips ready to claim the softness of her lips.

"Max! What are you doing?"

Talk about a reality check. My head jerked forward. Something wasn't right. I heard the righteous indignation in Jordan's voice as my head swiveled around to see what could have offended her. It took me a few moments to realize it was me. "Oh, God! I'm so sorry. I thought..."

"You thought what?" She was shaking. Her eyes were wide and wild giving her a caged in look.

"I, uh, don't know. I'm so sorry." I couldn't lie and I damn sure couldn't tell her the truth based on her reaction.

"I knew this was a mistake. I should have followed my instincts." Jordan stood up, her disdain for me written all over her face.

"Jordan, wait. I said I'm sorry." I was humiliated. I'd had my fair share of rejections in the past, yet it was never because I'd misread the signals. Even when I was young, I hadn't made those kind of mistakes. Except, maybe the one time I tried to kiss the teacher's aide who was twelve years older than me.

"Don't worry about it Max; it won't happen again."

My heart sank. I could deal with this public embarrassment. I could not deal with the thought of never seeing her again, even if it were on a friendly basis.

"Jordan, please. I'm a jerk. I wasn't trying to be disrespectful. I promise you it won't happen again." I felt like a lecherous old man. Her expression told me everything I needed to know. Jordan would never see me as anything other than her doctor. I might gain good friend status but that was as far as it would go with us. It was a difficult pill for me to swallow after all the fantasies I had about us and a painful reality I had to accept.

Jordan managed to pull herself together. She still looked like she'd eaten a spoon full of shit but at least she was civil. "It's okay, Max. Look, I really need to get going. Can you send me the files I asked for? Or do I need to arrange to have them picked up?"

I flinched. "I have the files boxed up in my apartment. We could swing by and get them if you want."

"Max, I—"

"Don't worry; I ain't gonna bite that dog no more."

After several moments, she finally agreed to go with me. "Fine, but don't make me have to beat the shit out of you. I also need to run by the store before I go home. I feel the need to binge on chocolate chip cookies."

"You won't have any problems out of me." If being her friend was the only way I could be close to her, I would have to content with that.

CHAPTER FOURTEEN

JORDAN BREE

It was just a dream, yet every bone and miniscule muscle in my body hurt. A tear slid down my face as I remembered. Its track felt like it was burning my skin. I was in agony. The loud pounding inside my head reminded me of a calypso band I'd once seen on television. I wanted someone to turn if off so I could rest. I didn't know how to convey my wishes without moving my tender lips. "Argh." My mouth was dry, like I'd been sucking on cotton balls or sand. I needed some water but the stupid faucet, in my dream, wouldn't work. "Help." My mouth didn't move as I rolled over.

In the distance, I heard a woman, with a nasal sounding voice call out, "Hey Doc, that patient you've been drooling over in bed five is waking up."

My body seized with fear when I realized the patient they were referring to was me. I was being afforded a birds-eye-view of my time in the hospital through my dreams. For once, I didn't want to wake up. I had to see. In my mind, I opened my eyes. It seemed as if I were watching myself on television. I listened for other sounds with a keen ear. Something was definitely wrong. I viewed myself thrashing on the bed, as a watchful observer. It was easier to handle this way. It was clear that whatever was about to happen to me was painfully important.

Sensing movement near me, I turned my head to the right. A sharp pain raced through my body causing me to cry out in pain again. "Argh."

"Jordan, can you hear me?" A male voice asked.

The voice in the dream did not sound familiar to me. "Mum."

"Raise her head up and put a cuff on her. Get me some ice chips too," the male voice ordered, taking control of the situation. His tone was stern yet conciliatory.

Hands groped me, catching me off guard. I could feel what was happening to 'her', as if it were actually happening to me now.

"Stop," I whispered as they lifted my head. Pain radiated from the top of my head, shooting down my back and through my legs. I was so dehydrated. I was scared. I'd never heard of anyone ever being able to experience pain in a dream. It was like viewing a train wreck about to happen. I couldn't stop watching.

"Can you open your eyes?" the voice cautiously asked. I wanted to see who was talking but the face was hidden from me. Instead of answering, I gently moved my head from side to side. I tried to raise my arms but they would not move.

"Here, these ice chips should soothe your throat. Does it hurt you?"

I could almost feel the cool chucks of ice on my parched lips. I greedily licked them, causing shooting pain to radiate through my toes. My discomfort must have been imprinted on my face.

"Are you in pain?"

"Head," I weakly replied. I wanted the pain to go away and for all the noise to stop.

"My name is Lawrence Maxwell. I'm a doctor. I'm going to give you something for the pain. Not enough to knock you out. Just enough to dull the pain. Do you understand?"

"Yes."

"I can't give you anything to drink but I can give you some more ice chips. Do you want them?"

"Oh yes." I heard the clickety-clack sound of running feet and heavy breathing, before I felt something cold against my lips. This time, I opened my mouth and sucked on the plastic spoon. The cold nuggets felt great inside my mouth even though they dissolved quickly. "More," I whispered as I rolled my tongue across my lips.

"No problem."

The doctor pressed the spoon against my lips. I tried to lift my hands to grab the cup but couldn't. My hands were strapped to the bed. This was important. I wanted to press pause on the memories so I could digest what I'd learned. Unfortunately, the mechanics of the dream didn't work that way. I teetered on the edge of wakefulness as my mind whirled through the possibilities of why my body was being restrained. I saw no physical evidence of an accident. The last thing I remembered was riding the bus coming home from school. I inhaled quickly, swallowing several pieces of ice causing me to choke. "Awk, awk," I sputtered as I felt the chips lodged in my throat.

I couldn't breathe and started to panic. This wasn't part of the dream. I felt the oxygen leave my lungs. I was suffocating for real.

I bolted from the bed, my heart racing. Frantic, I paced the room. When my heart rate settled, I sat back on the bed. My face was wet with tears. I was finally remembering.

"Oh, God." I muttered aloud. I glanced at the clock on my nightstand. It was still early, too early to be wandering around the house. I felt like I'd received some of the answers but there were still a lot of gaps. I knew I had to go back to sleep if I wanted to remember the rest. I eased back on the bed gripping my sheets. I needed to go back this time more like a spectator. I wasn't sure if it were possible, as I drifted effortlessly back into my memories.

***

The young doctor reacted quickly, untying my hands and lifting me to a sitting position. He raised my arms over my head. This caused shooting pain in my limbs. Even in my dreams, I had a potty mouth. "Shit," I exclaimed. I was relieved to know that my arms worked. I needed to know why they felt the need to tie me down in the first place. I continued to watch.

"Are you okay?" Max asked as he tried to shine a light in my eyes.

"I'll be fine if you'd get that bright-ass light out my eyes." The fear of choking gave way to anger and outrage. "Where am I, and why the hell were my hands tied?"

"Hold on now. I know you have questions. I need to make sure you're okay." Max checked my pulse, blood pressure and temperature.

From my vantage point on the outside looking in, I could see angry welts on my arms. The welts appeared old, indicating that I'd been restrained for a long time.

The only problem was I couldn't remember why I was being held prisoner.

Max stepped back from the bed, his brow furrowed as if in deep thought. "Now, as I said before, you're in a hospital. We had to restrain your arms to keep you from hurting yourself."

"Hurt myself? Why on earth would I hurt myself?"

"That is the million dollar question we've been asking ourselves. You've got some serious scratches on your face that, according to our records, were there when you arrived. Which leads us to believe you would hurt yourself if we didn't stop you."

"Scratches? That is ridiculous. I'd never hurt myself." I lifted my hands to touch my checks. I was confused, I didn't feel any marks. "I don't understand."

"How much do you remember about coming here, Jordan?"

I wanted to press the pause button again. I wanted to stop the imaginary tape to give myself a chance to take in all that I'd witnessed. Unfortunately, dreams don't work like that.

"I don't remember this place at all."

"Well, what is your last memory?" Max wrote something on a pad that even from my spectral vantage point, I couldn't see.

"I, uh. What are you writing?"

"Does it bother you?"

"Yes, uh, I mean no. I don't know what I mean."

"That's completely understandable as well. You've been heavily sedated and things may be a little foggy to you right now."

"A little foggy? Are you kidding me? You can't begin to comprehend how I'm feeling right about now."

Max sighed. "You're right. I don't know which is why I'm asking you questions."

"Well I have a couple of questions for you. Why am I here? How long have I been here?"

"Initially, you were sent for evaluation. However, for reasons I have yet to figure out, you've been here for over four years."

"Four years? Did you just say four fucking years?" This would explain the absence of marks on my face.

"Now I know this must come as a shock to you…"

There had to be a plausible reason. "Was I in a coma?"

"Well," Max started. A blind man could tell he didn't want to answer the question, which only fueled my anxiety and anger. A nurse, who had been hovering behind Max, stepped forward handing him a needle. My eyes widened in surprise, daring him to use it. Max looked down at the needle and twirled it in his fingers. "I don't want to have to use this, Jordan. That's not the way I operate. Don't think I won't use it, if necessary. Do you understand?"

"I understand a threat when I hear one. Is that the way you operate?" I was pissed.

Max slid the needle in his pocket. "I just needed you to know, I have to protect myself, my staff and you. Your file says you have a mean right hook. I'd rather not test it out, if you know what I mean."

"I hear what you're saying, but put yourself in my shoes for a second. You wake up, in pain, in a strange place, and someone, whom you don't know, tells you that you've been there for four years. How would you react because this is baffling the shit out of me?"

Max's face softened. "I feel you. To tell you the truth, I don't know how I would react in similar circumstances. If it makes you feel any better, I'm actually here for you. I'm new to the hospital and my sole reason for being here is to take care of you and the other patients like you, who appear to have been forgotten by the system.

***

I always dreamed in color but rarely remembered any specific details of my dreams. This dream was different because I remembered every detail which led me to believe it was more of a memory than a dream. My meeting with Max probably inspired these recollections but what freaked me out was my ability to feel the pain.

I woke up, drenched in sweat and extremely sore. My room was dark, which only added to my fears. I reached over to my nightstand trying to turn on my bedside light. I winced as my wrist rested on the table. Terrified, I examined my wrists, looking for welts. As crazy as it was, I fully expected to see some marks. Thankfully, I didn't. There wasn't any doubt in my mind seeing Max triggered these memories. The only thing I needed to figure out was what to do with them.

I was too distraught to go back to sleep. The bathroom was down the hall so I donned a robe and my slippers. I carefully opened the door, trying not to wake the other members of the house. Even though my room was the only occupied bedroom on the first floor, I didn't feel like dealing with anyone after my horrific dreams. Our RA, Keisha, reminded me of my mother, with her multiple personalities. Some days she could be so nice and others she was like a hornet guarding her hive, stinging everyone in her wake.

Thinking about my mother only made my head hurt worse. I made it to the bathroom without stepping on any noisy floorboards. I quietly shut the door and turned on the light. Dried tears streaked my face and my nightgown clung to my damp body. I turned on the tap and waited for the water to cool. Fragments of my dream were still fresh in my mind. After spending four years in a hospital, the only thing I could remember was being restrained. Odd. I was now more determined than ever to remember my past and seek retribution in the present.

CHAPTER FIFTEEN

JORDAN BREE

Karma is the influence of an individual's past actions on his/her future lives or reincarnations. The only problem is, karma takes its sweet-ass time, and the results were often unpredictable. Since I did not have the time or the inclination to wait on karmic results, I decided to tip the hand in my favor.

Chips Ahoy! Chewy Gooey Chocofudge Cookies were my weakness. There wasn't a chocoholic alive that I knew who could resist the temptation. Thanks to Max, I was able to get some on my way home. However, I didn't plan on eating them. In a house full of females, those cookies didn't stand a chance. I carefully opened the bag and removed the cookies, lining them on my desk. The chocolate aroma was enticing. Using the dirty needle I'd taken from my old apartment building, I infused a tiny bit of peanut oil into each chocolate chip. It was a tediously time consuming process. Using too much oil would make the cookies greasy. Using too little would simply be a waste of a good cookie. I saved the last two cookies for myself. I carefully loaded the remaining cookies back in their tray and closed the bag.

Satisfied with the results of my hard work, I once again snuck down the hallway and placed the bag of cookies on the kitchen counter. "It ain't karma. It's a bitch."

CHAPTER SIXTEEN

LACY BATES

Sweet Auburn Festival is a free musical festival held near downtown Atlanta and a few of the girls and I were planning on making a day of it. Since I didn't have much money, I decided to raid the coffers of the house and pack myself a lunch.

"Dem bitches gonna starve." I chuckled to myself. Nine times out of ten, the other girls would scramble to pack their own lunches if they saw mine. I wasn't about to let that happen. I packed up the rest of the chicken from the night before, placing them in a baggie, followed by chips, two apples and an orange, completing my lunch. I was about to close the bag, when I spotted the premium cookies on the counter.

"Oh wee, chocolate chips are the shit." The house didn't splurge on expensive cookies. These had to be someone's personal stash. Too bad for them, they fucked up leaving them in a common area. Grabbing an extra baggie, I stuffed as many cookies as I could into it. With no regrets, I placed the near empty bag of cookies on the bottom shelf of the pantry. Someone's loss was my gain. Armed for whatever, I was ready for the day.

Taking the stairs two at a time, I raced into the bathroom and grabbed two towels. "I'm heading out. I'll meet y'all at the spot." I ran back down the stairs without waiting for an answer. I wanted to get out the house before someone noticed I'd stolen their cookies.

**

One of the benefits of travelling solo was not having to compete for attention. Wearing my daisy duke shorts and white cutoff shirt, I was garnering a lot of cat calls from both males and females. The girls were like bitch bye, but the boys, they were off the chain. The positive feedback bolstered my wilting self-esteem.

"You wearing them shorts shorty," a cute Hispanic guy said.

"Thank you, boo." He was cute but he didn't look like he had two nickels to rub together. I was broke as a joke and I was looking for a sponsor.

"How about letting me holla at chu?"

"And get my man all mad?" I commented over my shoulder never breaking my stride. I was lying through my teeth. I never had a boyfriend, much less a man. Besides, the dude couldn't even speak right.

"Lucky man," he shouted back.

I was trying to get over to center stage where the main attractions were performing. It was slow going. Mention the words free and good weather, folks came out by the bus loads. After months of looking at the same people, day in and day out, at the house, I felt like I'd died and gone to heaven.

After standing in place for several minutes, I realized I was approaching this situation all wrong. Rather than try to walk through the crowd to get center stage, I'd walk around the masses to get closer. It might equate to more overall steps but I thought it would take less time. My initial attempts to turn around were stone walled. Wall to wall people were pressed up against each other. I started to get anxious, which isn't a good feeling in a crowd. My gut instinct was to push against the throngs. I resisted the temptation. Guys were using our close proximity as an excuse to grope my ass. It was pissing me off.

"Watch your hands, buddy!" I shouted. I turned around ready to punch the shit out of the closest person to me.

"Sorry Ma, I didn't mean it."

Dude was drop fucking dead gorgeous. He had the deepest dimples and the whitest teeth I'd ever seen. His chestnut face sat atop broad shoulders and sinewy arms. He was a little taller than me with my heels on. Perfect. He could touch my ass anytime he wanted.

"It's so many people." If that wasn't the dumbest thing I'd ever said in my life, I didn't know what was.

"I know. I'm about to break free. Wanna come?" He held out his hand and I gladly took it. If he was going to lead the way, who was I not to follow? He rushed through the crowds like a quarterback, with me closely on his heels. If he ruffled any feathers, I couldn't tell. We didn't stop until we were on the outer fringes of the crowd.

"Now we can breathe," cutie said smiling.

"I know. It got thick so fast. Where did all these folks come from?"

He threw his head back and laughed. "You know how we do. Don't lie. If this shit wasn't free, you probably wouldn't be here either."

He spoke the truth. I didn't mind coming out to hear the music or enjoy the weather. But I wouldn't have paid for it, even if I had money. "You got that right. The only way I'd ever pay to see someone perform was if they were in an air conditioned building with assigned seats."

"See, you ain't right. If you hadn't come down here today, I wouldn't have gotten the chance to save you."

I blushed at the backhanded compliment. "How you gonna be my savior and I don't even know your name?"

"How rude of me? I go by Seven." He blessed me with another beautiful smile.

"Is that your government name? The one you put on your license?" I was making an assumption that he drove. At least I hoped he did. I couldn't imagine myself spending time with nobody riding the bus.

"No, it's the only one I'll answer too. You got a problem with my name?" He was still smiling so I assumed he was kidding.

"I think it's interesting." I actually thought it was stupid but I wasn't about to tell him that.

"So what's your name?"

"Eight." I tried my best to keep a straight face.

"Ah, a woman with a sense of humor. I like it."

I was beside myself with happiness. He looked to be in his early twenties, yet he called me a woman. This would have never happened if I'd come with the other girls. They would have busted me out at the first opportunity. "It's Lacy. Thanks again for your help." I turned to leave. I didn't want to ruin his illusions about my maturity. I doubted if I had enough clever retorts to continue to dupe him.

"Yo, you gonna leave me just like that. What I do? I was about to blaze a doobie."

Warning bells should have been ringing in my head. We'd been warned about the use of drugs. Failure to obey this rule would result in severe punishments which included the loss of any personal freedom. *So why wasn't I running?* "Where? Right here?" I could not deny the feeling of excitement I felt.

"No, silly. The police would be on us quicker than Grant took Richmond."

I had no idea what he was talking about. Who the hell was Grant or Richmond for that matter? "Where you gonna do it then?" I looked over at the portable toilets lining the street and shook my head. "I ain't going in those nasty toilets."

"Me neither. My truck is over on the next block. We can do it there."

"Oh, okay."

We started across the street where the crowd was denser. The walk gave me time to think. What the hell was wrong with me? I wasn't anybody's dummy, yet I'd agreed to get in a vehicle with a complete stranger. I had to be out of my damn mind.

"You come here by yourself?"

I stopped walking. "I don't know about this. You're beginning to freak me out."

Seven stopped walking as well. I expected a negative reaction from him. However, he seemed to be hurt. He held up his hands. "What did I do?" He appeared sincerely upset. It was hard to be uneasy while he was looking at me with his chocolate brown eyes.

"You didn't do anything. I shouldn't be going anywhere with someone I don't know." I waited for him to tell me to fuck off, but he didn't. He pulled out his wallet and handed me his driver's license.

"Now you know my government name. Feel better?"

His response was so unexpected, there was no way I could turn him down. Especially since I knew his real name. I handed his license back to him.

"Yeah, I'm good, Hector."

"See, that's why I didn't want to tell you my real name. Folks always wanna clown me about it."

I grabbed his arm playfully. "I'm sorry. I couldn't resist. I think Hector is a nice name … for a white boy." I started laughing. Seven merely watched without smiling. "Dag, what happened to your sense of humor?"

"I love jokes as much as the next person. This one is played. I've been hearing it all my life; it's old."

He took the fun right out of it. "I'm done. You won't hear me say it again. I promise."

"Good."

My good sense told me to turn around and go back to the festival. The village idiot in me continued to follow Seven in silence. I wanted us to get back to the carefree banter we had shared earlier. "Are you going to be mad at me for the rest of the day? 'Cause if you are, I can leave right now."

"I'm not mad. I'm just ready for a smoke. My car is right here." We stopped at a grey Jeep Cherokee. He used the key fob to unlock the doors and climbed in the driver's seat. I would have liked for him to have opened the door for me. Cute or not, he needed some manners. I got into the car. It was hot; the leather seats burned the back of my legs. I jumped back out of the car. "Ouch, that's hot."

Seven gave me a hearty laugh, displaying his dimples, once again endearing himself to me. I unrolled one of the towels I'd taken from the house, draped it over the seat and got back in the car. "It's hot as hades in here. Can a sista get some air?"

"Yeah, give me a second." He reached across the seat and pulled a blind down over the windows, making the inside of the car dark. He started the car, "The air won't get cold unless we start driving. At least we can take some of the heat out of the car. I probably should have left the window cracked."

"I'm sure it will be okay." Sweat was pouring off me like I was standing in the rain. Seven had my undivided attention as I watched him roll the blunt. I never once considered it sexy, until I saw his lips around the end of the blunt. I imagined those same lips on mine. He lit the joint, inhaling deeply. He held the acrid smoke inside for a very long time, before blowing out the smoke in the air. "This is some good shit here."

He passed me the joint. I held it for a few seconds trying to get up the nerve to leave. I wanted to place my lips where his had once been. I decided one or two totes wouldn't kill me. If I doused myself in perfume, and stayed to myself, the scent would wear off before I got home. That's what I told myself.

Unfortunately, the drug went straight to my head, relaxing all of my inhibitions. I took another long tote before passing it back.

"Ain't it good?"

"It sure is." I waited patiently for him to take his turn and pass it back. We passed it back and forth until it became too small for me to hold. The last thing I wanted to do was go home with tell-tale burns on my fingertips.

"Want me to roll another?" Seven asked as he turned on the radio.

"Not unless you plan on smoking it all by yourself. I'm good." I was more than good. I was high as hell.

"Naw, I'm straight. The only thing I need now is something to eat. Damn joint got me hungry as hell."

I could relate. I hadn't had anything to eat all day. I was practically starving my own self. Suddenly, I remembered the lunch I'd packed before leaving home. "Hey, I got some chicken in my bag. You want to share it?"

"Hell yeah! Pull that shit out."

He handed me some paper towels from the back seat and I split up the chicken. "Hope you like cold chicken or at least it was when I first packed it."

"Are you kidding me, cold chicken is the best chicken in the world. Did you cook this?"

I was about to lie but since he didn't say whether he liked it or not, I decided to tell the truth. "No, a friend made it."

"Well, when you see that friend, tell them they're are the best damn cook I know."

For the next several minutes, the only other sound in the car, besides the radio, was the smacking of lips. We tore through all five pieces of chickens, like greedy rats devouring trash.

"I swear for God, this chicken did not taste this good last night."

"I guess we've got the munchies bad. What else you got in that bag?" I thought about giving him an orange or apple. I didn't want him thinking I was lame. The only other thing that I had was my cookies, and quite frankly, I didn't want to share them. "I'm thirsty. Maybe we should go back to one of those vendors to get something there."

"Girl, I done ate. I'm high. I ain't feeling that walk right now. I've got some beer in the cooler in the back." He reached over the seat and pulled out two beers, handing me one of them.

Another series of bells went off in my head. These bells were louder. I could probably hide the smell of the joint with some perfume but I thought the beer would linger on my breath for hours. I remembered my mother waking up the next day, still smelling like beer. "No thanks, I'm not a beer drinker."

"Not a problem; more for me. Hold on, I think I got a pop in here too." After several seconds, Seven shook his head. "I guess I must have drunk it." He opened his beer and took a long gulp followed by a loud belch. The sound was so unexpected, I started to giggle.

"How rude," I snickered reaching for the beer. I was having too much fun to worry about any potential consequences.

"That's my girl." Seven upended his beer can again.

I wasn't sure if I liked beer or not. I'd never had one. However, I was betting the beer would be amazing, just like the chicken. After struggling to pop the top, Seven opened the can for me.

"Thanks. I did not want to break a nail."

"Heaven forbid that would happen," Seven said sarcastically.

"Have you ever broken a nail down to the quick? Hurts like a son of a bitch for weeks."

"Naw can't say I have. I keep mine kinda close." He held up his fingers for my inspection. He had long fingers and well-manicured nails.

I tentatively sipped the beer. Although I was skeptical about drinking the beer, I wasn't worried about the consequences of getting caught. The way I figured it, as long as I got back to the house before Keisha came on duty, I'd be good. Keisha was like the hall monitor. Whereas, Mrs. Gates rarely came out of her office, unless there was a problem and Kim was working nights this week. I finished my beer while Seven rolled another blunt. The paranoia didn't start until after we'd finished the second joint. Seven turned the radio down. "Be quiet, did you hear that?"

I was giddy. "What?" I whispered in between fits of giggles.

"Sounded like something was outside the car."

"Of course it's something outside the car. We're at a fucking festival. There's a whole lot of something outside the car."

"No, I mean right outside the car. They might be listening."

I wanted to be serious but everything was so fucking funny. Even the somber expression on Seven's face. "Hey, want a cookie?" My munchies had kicked up into high gear.

"You got cookies? What kind?" Seven blessed me with his dimples again.

"Chocolate chip." Seven provided the smokes and the beer; the least I could do was share my cookies. I stingily pulled four cookies from my bag and gave him two.

"You've been holding out." He practically shoved the entire cookie in his mouth.

"No I wasn't. I was saving them for the perfect time." Cookies went great with milk. Beer was a close second. I ate my cookies almost as fast as Seven did.

"Aw man, talk about good." He said smacking his lips. He had cookie crumbs in his goatee. I was about to tell him when my stomach started cramping. The pain was unexpectedly intense.

"Ouch, I guess cookies don't go with beer; my stomach is pitching a bitch."

"Don't you dare fart in my car. These leather seats hold smells."

He laughed. I couldn't tell if he was actually serious or making a joke. "I don't fart."

"Bullshit, everybody farts. I know you women like to sneak a fart. All I'm saying is aim that shit out the window and not on my seats."

"Well you've got crumbs and shit in your beard. Makes you look like a pig with no home training." I was getting angry and scared. My stomach was hurting real badly. To make matters worse, my arms felt like they were on fire.

"What's the matter with your face? You've got all these ... and your arms. What the fuck is wrong with you?"

Stunned, I looked down at my arms. There were long red welt marks on them. "What the fuck?" I was really scared now. Something was terribly wrong. I clawed at my throat. It felt like it was on fire. I was convinced something in the car was eating at my skin. I groped for the door, trying to get away.

"Wait, what are you doing?"

"I can't breathe; I think I'm going to throw up."

"Shit, girl, the bathroom is right over there." He raced out of the car and opened the door for me. Pulling me out, I pushed him aside stumbling toward the portable bathroom. I didn't know if it was fear or the drugs that had my heart racing. It was getting more and more difficult to breathe.

"I'm out of here," Seven shouted jogging back to his car. I heard the screech of his tires as he abruptly pulled away from the curb.

"Fucker," I rasped as I fell to my knees. My bladder erupted spilling piss, and possibly shit down my legs. I was certain I was gonna die.

"Miss, are you okay?" A male voice yelled at me.

I felt like I'd fallen down in a hole and couldn't get up. As much as I wanted to answer, I couldn't.

"Somebody flag down those EMT's. I think this lady is having an allergic reaction!"

Peanuts, I'm allergic to peanuts. I was yelling but my lips didn't move. I clutched my necklace imploring the man with my eyes to read it. My medical history was inscribed on it. I yanked furiously at the chain hoping it would say what I couldn't. After several attempts, he took the medallion from my fingers.

"Where is your pen?" the stranger shouted.

There was no way I could tell him Seven took off with my purse still in his car. I closed my eyes for what I was sure would be the last time.

CHAPTER SEVENTEEN

BRODY MASON

A trip to Grady Memorial Hospital on a Saturday night was like visiting a zoo. A vast cornucopia of people, jammed into the tiny waiting rooms, anxiously waiting to be seen. Varying degrees of injuries, ranging from gunshot wounds, traffic related injuries and general sickness, plagued the visitors. An occasional outburst of obscenities was not uncommon.

Everyone there needed help. Whether they were waiting on news of a loved one, or seeking assistance, it was clear to me that Grady had a shortage of both space and personnel. Part of me wanted to give up my seat and go home. The other part of me was curious to know if the girl I had assisted earlier that afternoon would live. As I waited, I felt the familiar tug of another story brewing in my head.

I was an independent journalist selling my stories to the highest bidder. My last story of medical abuse in psychiatric hospitals resulted in the closure of several Atlanta mental facilities. However, I was accused of reckless reporting, which could have done more harm than good. To top it off, I lost touch with the very person I was trying to help. Consequently, I was looking for a way to redeem myself.

The cops grilled me seven ways to Sunday on what happened to the girl. I kept telling them I didn't know who she was. They seemed convinced I wasn't telling the truth. Were it not for the other witnesses, my night might have ended in a jail cell instead of a hospital waiting room. I didn't even know where the girl came from. One minute I was walking along minding my business, and the next, she was standing there in apparent distress. I caught her as she was falling.

I waited patiently for another hour for information. I was about to give up when I was approached by a female dressed in green scrubs. "Are you Mr. Mason?"

Standing up, I nodded my head. I was hoping for the best but bracing myself for the worse. "I'm Doctor Broomfield. I was told you were waiting for information on the young lady brought in this afternoon from the festival."

"Yes, I found her."

"She's fine now. We're going to keep her overnight for observation."

"That's good to know. I wasn't sure she was going to make it."

"She gave us a scare too. If it wasn't for her medical alert, we might not have been able to bring her back. People don't realize how important those identifications are, especially when you can't communicate yourself. They could very well save your life."

"I can vouch for that. I didn't know what was wrong with her when I first saw her. Thanks for letting me know. I didn't want to leave without knowing, especially since I don't even know her name."

"You're welcome. Actually, she's asking for you. Normally, I wouldn't allow this but under the circumstances, I'll make an exception. You have to agree to keep your visit short. She really needs her rest now."

"Really? I'll only stay a few minutes, I promise."

"Good. I'll show you where she is." The doctor turned and started walking away. I felt a little weird following behind her. Everyone else in the waiting room was either waiting for medical attention or information. However, the doctor didn't appear to notice their stares. We went through a series of corridors until we stopped in front of a closed door. "She's in here for now. We'll move her into a room as soon as space becomes available. Remember, she needs all her rest."

"I will." I was nervous as I pushed open the door. Her eyes were closed and I almost backed out of the room, not wanting to disturb her. She looked so much different now that she wasn't in distress. I was pleasantly surprised by the difference, not that it mattered. I would have helped her even if she looked like a dog.

"I can smell your cologne."

"Oh, is it bothering you?"

"I can tell who you are by smell. My eyes are still swollen."

"I'm glad you're okay."

"Thanks to you. Do you have my purse?"

"Uh, no. I don't think you were carrying anything when I saw you."

"That bastard must still have it."

I was confused. "What bastard?"

"The guy I was with when it happened. He told me to get out of his car. He didn't want me to mess up his seats."

"Nice guy."

"I thought so. Guess I was wrong."

"My name is Brody by the way."

"Thank you, Brody. My name is Lacy."

Her voice was raspy, almost sexy. I couldn't tell if this was her natural voice or one caused by her sickness. "Glad that I was able to help. I promised the doctor I wouldn't stay too long, so I'd better go."

"Can I ask one more favor before you go?"

"Uh, sure." Normally I didn't agree to do things before I learned what they were but under the circumstances, I made an exception.

"They had to cut off my clothes. I don't have anything to wear when I leave here."

"Don't you have any family or friends you can call to bring you some?" Stupid me, I didn't even think to ask her if she wanted me to notify anyone about what had happened to her.

She started crying. "No, I live in a home and they are probably going to kick me out since I missed curfew."

"They can't kick you out if you got sick. Do you want me to call them? I can explain."

"I don't even know the number. Would it be too much to ask if I told you the address, to go over there and pick up something for me to wear?"

My gut told me to just say no. Unfortunately, my bleeding heart said otherwise. "No, it's no problem. Where is it at?" What was I thinking? Without a doubt, I would have to listen to a barrage of questions that I didn't know the answers to. Then, I would have to come back to the hospital to give her the stuff. Why didn't I leave when I had the chance?

"I wrote it down." She pointed in the direction of the table next to her bed. A small pad and a pen rested on it. I walked over and retrieved it. I was such a sucker for a woman's tears.

"I'll go by first thing in the morning."

"No, I need you to go tonight. If you wait until the morning, those bitches might steal my stuff." She was trying to get up but I gently pushed her back.

"Will they even answer the door at this time of the night?"

"Yeah, if I know Keisha, she'll be on the front porch smoking. She thinks we don't know she smokes. She lied and told me she quit but I've seen her. Wish I could see her face when you bust her."

"Alright, I guess I can go, if you're sure it's okay."

"It will be. Just don't tell her about the drinking and the weed. I'm in enough trouble already."

"Hey, I don't know anything about that."

"Good. I'm really tired now." She turned over, dismissing me.

"I'll see you in the morning." I waited for a few seconds for a response. When it didn't happen, I quietly left the room.

***

It was after midnight when I pulled up in front of the house. The front porch was screened in and the light was on. I assumed they left the light on for Lacy. For me, going to the door was risky. I didn't know what was waiting for me and it had me nervous. I sat in the car with the engine running, trying to get my nerve up. I was almost ready to pull off when I noticed movement on the porch. Without giving it any more thought, I got out of the car and approached the walkway. "Excuse me, are you Keisha?"

"Who wants to know?"

"Lacy asked me to come."

"Is she hiding in the car?" I detected major attitude.

"No, she's in the hospital."

"What?" The screen door opened and the lady stepped out into the light.

"She had an allergic reaction to something and had to be rushed to the hospital."

"Who are you?"

"My name is Brody Mason. I was with her until the EMT's arrived."

"With her? What were y'all doing?"

"No, not 'with her', with her, as if we were together. I was passing by and she looked to be in distress."

Keisha looked dubiously at me. "You still didn't tell me where you were."

"Oh, my bad. At the Sweet Auburn Music Festival."

"A couple of the other girls went there too. They came back hours ago."

"I don't know about all that. She was alone when I saw her. We've been at the hospital for hours. I waited around because I didn't know if she was going to make it. I didn't even know her name. I just got in to see her and she asked me to come by, tell you what happened and bring her something to wear for when she's released tomorrow."

"Where are her clothes?"

"She said the doctors had to cut them off." I was beginning to feel like a pervert even though I had done nothing wrong.

"Um hum. What hospital is she in?"

"Grady. I don't know what her room number will be. The doctor said they'd move her once they had a bed for her. I'm sure they will tell you when you call."

"I'm not calling anywhere. That is not in my job description. My job is to watch these girls in this house. She ain't here. She ain't my responsibility."

Damn. I expected at least a little compassion. I was standing out there, being bomb dived by mosquitos, and I'd never confirmed who I was speaking with. "Are you Keisha? Lacy told me you were cool." I got the classic black woman head jerk.

"I am cool. But Lacy should know I'm not about to wake up this entire house getting clothes for her. Now you can come back in the morning and I might be able to accommodate you. This had better not be some trick either. I'm gonna need paperwork from the hospital before she can come back in here. Goodnight." She stepped back on the porch, allowing the door to slam and turned off the light. So much for southern hospitality. I had just committed myself to yet another unplanned trip.

I actually felt sorry for Lacy. She cried when I mentioned family. It only made me want to know more about her and the circumstances that brought her here. Had she been in foster care? Was she abused, abandoned? Would she be the source for another story for me? Tomorrow, I'll find out.

CHAPTER EIGHTEEN

JORDAN BREE

Lacy didn't come back last night after being gone all day. The entire house was a twitter with excitement as we gathered in the kitchen. She was fixin' to be in big trouble. Just about every woman in the house had felt Lacy's wrath, at one time or another. I couldn't be happier but I tried not to show it. I made a point of not saying anything while they were discussing her.

"What do you think happened?" one of the girls asked.

"Bitch ditched us at the festival. Probably somewhere shit faced," another suggested.

"Well, I hope it was worth it. Keisha's mad as hell. I walked passed her and she was in Lacy's room going through her things."

"They might get rid of the bitch."

"If they do, I want her room."

Keisha searching Lacy's room was news to me. I backed out of the kitchen to see for myself what was going on.

"Are you packing her shit?" I didn't have to pretend with Keisha that I liked Lacy. She already knew the deal.

"Not yet. Seems Lacy is in the hospital. I'm getting some things together for her."

"Pity."

Keisha stopped rummaging through the drawers. "You feeling sorry for her?"

"Are you kidding me? I believe in keeping it one hundred. She don't give a fuck about me and the feeling is mutual. She can't come for me, unless I send for her."

"I just think you two got off on the wrong foot. She ain't so bad, once you get to know her."

"Whatever. Ain't nobody got time for that." I was a little surprised to hear Keisha defend Lacy. Seeing as how she had something smart to say about everybody behind their back. I didn't rock like that. If I didn't like you, I wasn't going to pretend that I did. With me, what you see is what you get. No pretense, no folly. I was on the way back to the kitchen when the doorbell rang. We didn't get many visitors.

"Brody?" My heart felt like it was trying to skid out of my chest. *Holy crap! How did he find me?*

"Oh my God, Jordan. It's so good to see you." Brody rushed forward, giving me a big hug.

I pushed him back. "What, what are you doing here?"

His look of confusion could have been comical, if I were in a laughing mood. I felt like my past and present were colliding. It wasn't a pleasant feeling either.

"What a coincidence finding you here. I can't believe it. I asked Max where I could find you and he said he didn't know."

The only person who knew the true circumstance of my being in the home was Mrs. Gates. I wanted to keep it that way. I pushed Brody back on the porch, closing the door behind me. "I've been meaning to call you. Things are a little hectic for me right now." I was shocked to know he'd been asking about me. I was also a little peeved at Max for not mentioning it.

"You just up and disappeared. I came by to pick you up and you were gone."

"I'm sorry about that. When they said I could leave, I left. I was so ready to get away. How did you find me?"

"Actually, I didn't. I'm here for something else."

It was my turn to look confused. What were the odds of his stumbling into me in a state as large as Atlanta? "Oh, really?"

"Yeah. I was at the music festival yesterday and this girl just passed out in front of me. Turns out she lives here. She asked me to get some clothes for her."

"You must mean Lacy. Aren't you acting like Captain Save-A-Ho.?"

"Huh?"

"Never mind, it's a long story. I assume you talked to Keisha. Let me get her. Please don't tell her or anyone else that you know me. I'll call you as soon as I can."

"Oh, okay."

I couldn't stand the crestfallen expression on his face. "I'll call you tomorrow, promise." He had the cutest smile I'd ever seen. It took at least five years off his age, which I guessed to be his early twenties.

"I look forward to it. Maybe we can go to lunch or something."

"We'll see." I wasn't about to make any promises.

"Aren't you going to ask what happened to Lacy?"

"Uh, no. I'm sure she'll tell us when she gets back."

"All righty then. I can almost smell a story out of this."

"Oh no you don't. I'm keeping a low profile." The last thing I needed was to have him blow me up more than he had already had. "I'll go get Keisha." I closed the door leaving Brody grinning on the porch. I considered yelling to Keisha to get the door, but that would have brought the other girls running to see who it was. I walked back upstairs. "There's some dude on the porch, said you were expecting him."

"Right. Tell him I'll be right down."

"Tell him yourself. I'm done." I ran down the stairs and closed the door to my room. Technically, I was supposed to do what I was told. However, given the circumstances, I felt it appropriate to act like an ass. Seeing Brody brought back a rush of emotions I wasn't ready to deal with. In a lot of ways, I owed my life to him. Because of his actions, I was released from the nut house. However grateful I was for his assistance, he reminded me of a time in my life I really wanted to forget. He also had a way of getting information out of me, even when I was reluctant to share.

It was a pity and a shame that Lacy didn't die. Based upon the sentiment of the house, she wouldn't have been missed. It was ironic that she would be the reason why Brody was back in my life. If he was bringing her back, there were some things I needed to do, like getting rid of those cookies and the peanut oil. The last thing I needed was an attempted murder charge. I had a few more things I needed to get done before that happened.

CHAPTER NINETEEN

LACY BATES

Brody pushed open the door to my room after a short knock. "You are looking like a new woman this morning. How do you feel?"

"I'm just grateful to be alive. I've never been so afraid in my entire life." I said smiling.

"I can understand that. You had a near death experience. I heard it can be life changing."

"So what does that mean? Am I going to walk around singing fucking Kumbaya and shit?"

Nonplussed, Brody answered, "it affects people in different ways."

"Are you a frigging doctor or something?"

"No, I'm just someone who was there when you needed help."

I was suddenly feeling angry but I couldn't pinpoint why. One minute I was happy to be alive and the next I was ready to tear shit up. "Did you get my clothes?" It was sort of a dumb question. Why else would he be standing there holding a shopping bag, taking abuse from me?

"Yeah." He walked over and placed the bag on the rollaway table they served meals on.

"Any chance you got any food in that bag? The food in here sucks."

"I actually considered bringing you something to eat, but I wasn't sure what you could eat or what you liked."

I started to tear up for no reason.

"Hey, don't do that. I'm such a sucker for tears. If you want, we can go get something before I take you home."

I wiped the corners of my eyes. "Am I in trouble? I mean at the house and all?"

"I don't think so. They were glad to know you are alright."

"Right. I don't think they care about me at all."

"Well, Keisha was the only person I spoke with."

I was slightly relieved to know Keisha was the person he'd talked to. "Do me a favor and slide that tray over here." He did as I requested and stepped back, as if he were afraid of getting too close.

"Will you relax? I'm not going to bite you."

"I'm good." He looked at his watch. "Did they say when they would be releasing you?"

I felt another flash of irritation. I dumped the bag on the bed, ignoring his last question. "Are you kidding me? What the hell is this?

Brody looked perplexed. "Those are your clothes, right?"

"Of course they're mine but they don't fucking go together. Stripes and polka dots? Where they do that at? People are gonna look at me like I'm some sort of clown."

"No they won't. Besides, you're just going home. You can take them off when you get there."

"What about when we go out to eat? Or did you change your mind about that? I know that bitch did this shit on purpose." I was fit to be tied.

"Oh, yeah. Well, if you keep the hospital identification bracelet on, everyone will know you're just getting released from the hospital."

"They will think I've been in a nut house. I won't fucking do it. I can't. I'll look like a retard."

"I think you are over exaggerating."

"What the fuck do you know anyway? You're not a doctor. You're probably as dumb as a box of rocks."

Brody's face turned red. That was the first sign of emotions I'd seen in him since we'd met. Even when he was saving me, he appeared to be unfazed. That's why I initially assumed he was a doctor.

"You are right. I never professed to be a doctor. And you know what else? I don't have to stay here and take your sh—" He started backing up to the door.

I started crying in earnest. I was ashamed of myself. This man had only shown me kindness and I was attacking him. Unfortunately, this was what I did. My standard mode of operation. I pushed people away before they had a chance to leave. I didn't know any other way to be.

Brody sighed loudly. "Crap. Stop crying. I have an idea. We can go through a drive thru. This way if anyone sees you, it will only be from the waist up." Brody smiled.

I had to give it to the man; he was trying, even though I was making it difficult for him. "What do you do for a living, Brody?"

"I'm a writer."

I snickered. "What are you writing, a fat novel? Are you waiting to be discovered?" My voice was dripping with sarcasm. I couldn't help myself; I was in such a funky mood that made me want to lash out. It was almost as if I wanted him to feel as bad as I did. Thankfully, Brody didn't take my bait.

"Actually, I believe I have a book or two in me. For right now, I'm not that type of writer."

I was still taking verbal jabs at him. "What other kind of writer is there? You probably don't write nothing but your name on your unemployment check." The look on his face was priceless.

"I wish I did have an unemployment check. Money is money. I'm a freelance journalist."

"Don't you dare write about me." I said it jokingly, but I was so serious.

"You do like to flatter yourself, don't you?"

Was that an insult? I wasn't sure. "What have you written? Have you ever had anything published?"

He smiled. It was like milk, it did his body good. "I write a lot of different stuff. Human interest mainly. And all my stuff gets published."

"Sounds like I'm not the only one who likes to flatter themselves."

He popped his collar. "The truth doesn't need flattery. It can stand alone."

I grew weary of our banter. It wasn't important anyway. What was important was what I was going to wear out of the hospital. "You've got to go back and get me something else to wear. I can make you a list so you don't fuck up again." I reached for the pad and pen on the nightstand. In my head, I was already planning my outfit, down to the shoes.

"I think you got me twisted. I don't mind helping out a little but you're trying to play a brother. I suggest you get your narrow ass out that bed, change your clothes and be ready in ten minutes if you expect me to take you home."

I could tell he was dead fucking serious. Since I didn't even have my purse, I couldn't raise bus fare. As much as I hated to, I had no choice but to do as he said. "Fine, but you better not laugh at me." I lowered the bed. Clutching the bottom of my gown as best I could, I stood up. "Turn your back, better yet, wait in the hall," I ordered. I didn't want him trying to sneak a peek at my goodies.

"Girl, if you don't get your butt in that bathroom, I swear to God..." Brody was still mumbling as he stepped out of the room. I said a silent prayer that he'd come back.

CHAPTER TWENTY

BRODY MASON

I was still trying to wrap my head around running into Jordan today. The odds of it happening the way that it did, should have been nil to none. It was pretty amazing given the size of Atlanta. I tried not to view it as some sort of sign. However, it was difficult not to. The woman had literally disappeared from the face of my life. Then boom, there she was. It was a little freaky. Like some sort of cosmic force bought us back together. This time, I was determined not to waste the opportunity to get to know her on a more personal level. But first, I had to deal with the she-devil, Lacy, who was trying to push all of my buttons at once. Had it not been for her, I might not have ever found the woman of my dreams.

Jordan looked good too. Much better than the last time I saw her. She looked to have put on some weight in all the right places. I had to admit, I was completely smitten with Jordan, had been ever since I first laid eyes on her at the hospital. When she left with no forwarding address, it literally tore me apart. Since she didn't wait for me or leave a forwarding address, I assumed she wanted nothing to do with me. Yet, she seemed genuinely happy to see me again. It was puzzling to say the least. If she didn't want to see me, I thought she would've slammed the door in my face.

One of the things that attracted me to Jordan was that she'd tell you exactly what she was thinking. She had no filter. If she thought it, she was going to say it; however inappropriate it may be. She was refreshingly different from the other ladies I had met in Atlanta. There are so many plastic people, with fake nails, hair, eyelashes, boobs, ass, personalities and smiles. It wasn't that I had a problem with women who tried to spruce up what God gave them, I just preferred mine natural.

Stumbling onto Lacy only complicated matters. Based upon the comment Jordan made, which I pretended not to hear, they didn't like each other. Part of me could understand why. Lacy was her boisterous match. Neither one of them gave a damn about what other people thought. At least that was my opinion. But what did I know? I thought Jordan and I were friends. I walked back into Lacy's room.

Lacy edged her way out of the bathroom. She was right, she did look like a clown. I averted my eyes to keep from laughing.

"This is some bullshit right here! I really want to choke the shit out of Keisha right now."

There was no point in my saying anything about the way she looked because I really didn't care. All I really wanted to know was more about Jordan. The trick was getting Lacy to talk about her, without letting on that I knew her? I looked at my watch again. This was taking more time than I wanted to spend.

"You got somewhere to go? You keep looking at your watch and shit like you've got somewhere else to be." She sat back on the bed, folding her arms across her chest.

I struggled to keep the irritation from my voice. "I do have some things I want to get done today. I didn't exactly plan for all this, if you know what I mean. Did the doctor tell you when you would be able to leave?"

"Do you see an IV in my arm? Do you see them coming in pricking me? I was waiting on your ass."

I had had enough of her verbal abuse. "If you're trying to get me to leave your ass in this hospital room, it's working. I think I've gone beyond the call of duty with you. You're the most ungrateful person I've ever met in my life. So if you want my help, I suggest you get your shit together." I was heated. Normally, it took a lot to get my fires going but this little girl had a wicked mouth.

Lacy's face morphed several times before she settled on something akin to outrage. "You're not supposed to cuss at a minor."

"Who says?"

"I, uh …"

"Little girl, you need to know if somebody is trying to help you. You should shut up sometimes and let them. That mouth of yours is gonna get you in big trouble. I really don't have time for that." Our conversation was interrupted when the nurse came in with a wheelchair.

"All ready to go?" she said smiling.

Lacy lowered her head but didn't say a word. "Yeah, she's ready." I looked around the room to see if there was anything I needed to carry. "Do you have everything, Lacy?"

She nodded her head yes, as she got off the bed and took a seat in the chair. She surprised me when she didn't pitch a bitch about getting in the chair. I almost felt bad for chastising her, even though she had it coming. If she acted like this with me, a stranger, I didn't have to wonder how she acted back at the house.

The nurse handed Lacy some forms to sign. She signed them and handed them back, without commenting on them. The nurse tore off one of the copies from each page and handed them to me. I found it odd that the nurse didn't know me from a can of paint, yet she was going to let me leave with this young girl, without requiring so much as a signature from me. If the hospital allowed this, what else would they let me do? I made a mental note to come back one day to test the security measures in place at the hospital. It might even be worthy of another whistle blower story.

***

It was so quiet in the car. I could hear the air circulating. The silence was becoming uncomfortable.

"So tell me about this home you live in?" For a moment, I feared Lacy wasn't going to answer me.

"What's there to tell?"

"Is it like a home for juvenile delinquents or something?"

Her head swung up quickly, her eyes burning brightly. I braced myself for another verbal bashing.

166

"If you must know, it's a home for betweens."

"Betweens? I don't get it."

She exhaled loudly as if frustrated. "We're too old for foster care or adoption but too young to live on our own. Betweens. Get it? I'll be eighteen in a few more months."

"Got it." I was still confused because I knew for a fact Jordan was old enough to live by herself. I decided she must be referring to the other girls living in the house.

"All except one girl, a bitch named Jordan."

I flinched. "How long have you lived there?"

"Almost two years. I came when I was sixteen. I can't wait to get out."

"To do what? Do you have a plan?"

Lacy's brow furrowed. "I'm gonna get me a job."

"Doing what?" She looked like I was trying to back her into the corner. I could almost see the hair standing up on the back of her neck. Much like a cat ready to pounce on its prey.

"I don't know. Something that will make a lot of money. Maybe I'll be a rapper."

I started to laugh, thinking she was joking. I caught myself when I realized she was completely serious. The more I thought about it, the angrier I became. "What about school? Did you finish high school?"

"School is for suckers. Once I'm a rap star, I won't need no high school diploma."

I couldn't believe, in this day and age, I was about to have this kind of conversation with her. I couldn't help but wonder what they were teaching her in the home. "You will always need your education, Lacy. People don't just wake up and decide to become rap stars. Without a diploma, you'll be lucky to get a job at McDonald's."

Lacy shrugged her shoulders. "What's wrong with McDonalds?"

"Nothing, if you intend to live with someone else for the rest of your life. You won't be able to pay rent, buy a car or anything else on those types of wages." This was a problem I was seeing more and more often with children of her generation. No drive or determination to do anything. They were hell bent on fast money.

"Well, I could be a stripper. I got the body for it. I know them bitches get paid."

"Is that really what you see for yourself? What a waste." I was more than a little disgusted. I was also angry that she was wasting my time.

"Why? You don't go to titty bars?" She had the nerve to act indignant. If she were my child, I would've smacked her across the mouth.

"Not that it's any of your business, but no, I don't. I value women too much to see them degrading themselves like that."

"I'm not stupid you know? I was just trying to see where your head was at. Of course I have my diploma. I'm even taking courses on the computer for college, you asshole." Lacy sulked.

I glanced over at her to see if I could tell if she was telling me the truth. "Okay, I'm an asshole. I just assumed —"

"Well you know what they say about people who assume." She folded her arms across her chest and pouted.

"Makes an ass out of me? It wouldn't be the first time." I had been feeling like an ass ever since I'd laid eyes on her.

"And probably not the last."

"Why do you do that? Do you like to fight with everyone and put them on the defensive?" She didn't respond immediately. Which was good. I wasn't trying to be her friend. Jordan's aversion to her made her taboo, as far as I was concerned. Plus, I didn't need that type of toxic energy in my life.

Lacy practically whispered, "I guess I do."

She sounded like she was on the verge of tears again. I hated that shit. Why couldn't women just say what they mean, instead of always resorting to tears? Was it something they learned as children? "Please don't," I said, casting sideway glances at her. This twenty minute car ride seemed like it was taking an eternity. "Do you still want to get something to eat? You might feel better if you put something in your stomach."

"I'm not hungry now."

I breathed a sigh of relief. Once I dropped her off at the house, she would no longer be my responsibility. I pulled up to the front of the house and put the car in park. She didn't make any attempt to open the door. I wasn't sure what I was supposed to do. Did she expect me to walk her to the door, like we had been on some type of fucked up date?

"Thanks," Lacy said looking out the window at the house.

"No problem. Take care of yourself." I was eager to be on my way.

"You too." Once again she made no move to open the door.

"Are you afraid to go in?" I could have kicked myself the moment the words left my lips. Why should I even care?

"A little."

I had to keep reminding myself that although she looked grown up on the outside, she was still a little girl on the inside. "Do you want me to go in with you?"

"Would you?"

Shit. I was such a sucker. "Okay, come on." I took my keys and went around to the passenger side and opened the door. I could see a flutter of movement near one of the windows. Someone was checking us out. Lacy slowly extended her leg from the car, as if she was testing the ground to see if it would open up and swallow her. I wanted to yank her narrow ass from the car.

"It's going to be fine. Don't worry." I tried to give her my arm but she pushed me away. Her eyes glued to the window. Perhaps she saw the movement of the curtains as well.

"Don't. I don't want to give those bitches anything else to talk about."

I froze. "What should I do? Get back in the car?" I whispered.

"No. Just don't touch me. They might get the wrong ideas."

I was fine with that. The shit was getting real now. I was ready for it to be over. We walked up to the porch and stopped. She was looking down at her feet. I stood beside her not knowing what she wanted to do.

"I don't have my key."

Figures. She lost her purse, so it stood to reason her keys were in there. I rang the bell.

"Please don't mention anything about the guy or—"

As the door opened, my heart sank. I was pretty much going to have to follow Lacy's lead and hope that she didn't send us both off a cliff. The woman who opened the door was unfamiliar to me. She looked us both up and down before she held open the door for us to enter. I let Lacy go first. Even though she kept her eyes down on the floor, I noticed her trembling.

"Who are you?" the strange lady asked. She was formidable. She had to be at least six feet tall and thick. She could have easily have passed for a linebacker for the Atlanta Falcons.

"My name is Brody Mason. I'm the one who found Lacy." I pulled her discharge papers from the back pocket of my jeans.

"Found her? Where was she?" The woman's brow creased with apparent distrust. I swallowed a large lump in my throat. I was waiting for Lacy to say something but she was letting me do all the talking.

"In the park. I mean at a concert." This woman was making me nervous and I hadn't done anything.

"Well, which one was it?" She kept looking between Lacy and me, as if she was looking for some sort of correlation between us.

I shook my head to clear it. What the fuck was I scared for? She didn't know me, and after I walked out that door, I didn't have to ever lay eyes on her again. "Actually, it was both. It was at the Sweet Auburn Music Festival in the park. I told all this to Keisha when I came over here to pick up a bag for

Lacy." I attempted to pass on Lacy's release papers but she didn't reach for them. "I'm not sure if you know this, but Lacy has been in the hospital."

"There isn't anything that goes on in this house that I don't know about. I'm Mrs. Gates. I am the head house parent and I run the home. What do you have to say for yourself, Lacy?"

Even I was confused about the question. What could she say, other than she got sick?

"Excuse me?"

Mrs. Gates turned to me again. "What time did you find her?"

I thought quickly. I assumed they had some sort of curfew in the house. "Three or four. Things happened so fast, I don't remember which."

"Um hum. Is that right, Lacy?"

"Yes, I think so." All her bravado was gone. Lacy was literally shaking in her boots.

"So what happened?" Mrs. Gates' voice was still devoid of emotion. Her eyes fierce and unblinking.

"I had an allergic reaction."

"What about your pen?"

"I, uh. Someone stole my purse."

Mrs. Gates looked to me but this part of the story was on Lacy. I could neither confirm nor deny what she was doing before I saw her hit the ground. I was beginning to get a little ticked off. It was obvious to me that Lacy was still a little shaken from her ordeal. It pissed me off that Mrs. Gates had yet to ask her how she was feeling.

"The doctors said she should get plenty of rest. Her body has been through quite a lot." Mrs. Gates ignored me.

"What about your keys? Don't tell me we have to change the locks due to your carelessness." Mrs. Gates turned and started walking down the hallway, leaving us standing in the foyer.

Something inside of me snapped. The sound was so loud to me, I thought everyone heard it. I looked around but Lacy hadn't moved. "Are you friggin' kidding me? This girl damn near died and all you're worried about is her keys? What kind of place is this anyway?" I was furious, but now I understood where Lacy got her tough veneer.

Mrs. Gates spun around and marched back toward me. Her feet pounding the floor like mini earthquakes on the hardwood. "Just who do you think you're talking to? Do you have any idea what it takes to run a facility such as this? Some of the things these girls come up with? You have no idea!"

"Compassion and empathy are free, Mrs. Gates, and neither of those seem present at the moment.

Mrs. Gates directed all of her anger at Lacy. "Can you imagine the scandal if word of this incident got to the press? I never wanted you girls roaming the streets free anyway. I did it against my better judgment, now this. I swear you girls are going to be the death of me."

"Mrs. Gates, it wasn't my fault," Lacy sputtered. Lacy was a bag of bones and quivering cartilage. I was certain the verbal flogging would continue after I left and it made me sad for her.

"Mrs. Gates, I neglected to mention that I'm an independent journalist. Perhaps you've heard about one of my stories? It's been all over the news."

Mrs. Gates' face paled and she appeared to wobble on her feet. I smiled for the first time since entering in the house. Jordan had walked up behind Mrs. Gates and nodded in my direction.

"Hey, Jordan. Small world. Nice to see you again." I held up my thumb and index fingers to my ear and mouthed, 'call me'. Mrs. Gates looked over her shoulder and appeared to swoon. Jordan's timing was impeccable and couldn't have been better staged if it were choreographed. She had to have been the one I saw peeking out the curtains, and eavesdropping on our conversation.

Lacy's mouth was agape. "How do you know her?" She said her, like it was a four letter word.

"Let's just say, Jordan and I did a story together." I winked. I wasn't about to mention the details of the story. I'd leave that to Jordan. I pulled my card out my wallet and handed it to Lacy.

Jordan said, "I'll call you next week, Brody. I might have another story for you."

Mrs. Gates was visibly upset. Her eyes kept switching between Jordan and me. As she seemed to connect the dots, it was like a light came on inside her head. Despite the chilliness of the room, tiny beads of perspiration broke out on her forehead. It was the perfect time for me to leave. "Okay, y'all take care now."

CHAPTER TWENTY-ONE

JORDAN BREE

Things were going exactly as I had planned, with one or two minor exceptions. Both exceptions dealt with Lacy. If she had died outside the home, it would've been safe to assume that whatever happened to her was a direct result of her actions. I needed to find out what, if anything, Lacy knew about her recent confinement. If she were suspicious of foul play, everything I'd done could blow up in my face.

My thoughts were interrupted by a short knock on the door. Disguising my irritation with a smile, I opened the door.

"I need to speak with you for a moment," Mrs. Gates said. This was the first time that she'd come to my room and it surprised me.

"Am I being summoned to your office?"

"No, we can speak here." She seemed uncomfortable but no more so than I was.

"Okay." I stepped back from the door, letting her in. Fortunately, for her, I had just swiped a chair from the dining room. I was waiting for her to realize it and blast me out about it. However, she didn't. I sat on my bed.

"I want to make sure we have an understanding. Things have been a little crazy around here as of late."

I had no idea what she was talking about. "About …"

"This is my home."

"Okay and your point is?" I wasn't sure where she was going with this.

"I opened it up out of the goodness of my heart, to help you girls."

I doubted this was true but I didn't contradict her. I was sure her monetary compensation had something to do with her reasons.

"Now, I realize your circumstances are slightly different than the other girls, I still won't allow my authority to be compromised."

I continued to stare at Mrs. Gates. If she had a point to make, I was hoping she'd get to it soon.

"This is the second time you've introduced someone to me who, in my opinion, has indirectly threatened me."

"Are you serious?" I wanted to laugh. This lady wouldn't know a threat if it hit her in the face.

"I don't know who you think you're fooling, but I'm not the one." The whole time she was talking, her voice remained steady, but I could tell her agitation was growing by the movement of her fingers. She kept rolling the hem of her floral dress.

"I think you need to get your facts straight before you come in my room and start accusing me of anything. I did not bring Brody into this house, Lacy did." I made no attempt to hide the animosity in my voice.

"I knew it. You and Lacy are working together. Well, I'm not going to be bullied in my own house."

She'd gone from stupid to ridiculous. "I don't fuck with Lacy and you know it."

Mrs. Gates got up and walked to the door. She waved her hand up and down in the air, "this isn't working for me. I'm gonna have to think about this some more." Mrs. Gates walked out.

"Now that was funny." I was still perplexed from my conversation with Mrs. Gates when there was another knock on the door. This time, I didn't bother to fake the funk. I yanked open my door. "What?"

Lacy was standing there with her hands clasped in front of her. My first instinct was to shut the door in her face. My curiosity however, got the best of me.

"Can I talk to you for a moment?" She was speaking so low, I had to lean in to hear her. Reluctantly, I agreed.

"May I come in? I don't want everyone in the house to know that I'm here."

I looked around my room. I didn't really want her in my room again. I didn't want to have a confrontation with her all out in the open, just in case things got ugly. Besides, she might have figured out I was the one who tried to kill her. Therefore, speaking in private was probably for the best. I allowed her into my room, taking a seat in the chair, forcing her to stand.

"I know this ain't none of my business, but I saw Mrs. Gates coming out your room."

I didn't say a word. She'd already said it was none of her business and I agreed. Clearly nervous, Lacy shook her head while ringing her hands. "I know what you did."

My heart leaped, but I tried to remain calm. "I beg your pardon," I said feigning ignorance.

She shook her head again. "I mean with the house. How you got Mrs. Gates to change the rules. You helped us. I never got around to saying thanks."

This was not what I was expecting to hear. I slowly exhaled. "I didn't do it for the house. I did it for me."

"Regardless of how it went down, it helped us all. That woman is a bitch."

As much as I hated the word bitch, I understood why she would call Mrs. Gates one. "I know you didn't come in here to tell me this." I was growing impatient.

"Yeah, well I know Mrs. Gates is going to call me down. I wanted to ask you what I should tell her? I don't want her to revoke my privileges and all. You seem to know how to handle her."

I was having a what-the-fuck moment. Two visitors, back to back, left me no time to think. Was Lacy testing me? "I'm sorry to bust your bubble, the only person I know how to handle, is me."

"But you got her to change the rules. How did you do it? She wouldn't even think about doing it before you came here."

"I think it was more of a coincidence that it happened after I came. Nine times out of ten, she made the decision on her own."

"I don't believe that shit. She doesn't give a shit about any of us. I might be young, but I ain't dumb.

All I know is she treats you differently. I was all mad about it, at first, now I don't give a shit. You did us a solid. As far as I'm concerned, my beef with you is squashed."

I thought it was comical that Lacy considered our beef squashed, as if what she said actually mattered. Especially since, I was the one who almost deaded her. That would have squashed our beef most assuredly. I almost laughed out loud. Whatever she felt was irrelevant. I had bigger fish to fry. Lacy was harmless, so I decided to put her out of her misery. "She won't mess with you; it's all good."

"Thanks. I won't bother you any longer but if you ever need my help with something, let me know."

Lacy left, closing the door softly behind her. I might not have any use for her now but she might come in handy later.

CHAPTER TWENTY-TWO

JORDAN BREE

I left the house early before everyone had started moving around. I was hoping to get back before anyone noticed that I'd even been gone. I was going to visit Brody. Fortunately for me, he didn't live far.

Today was another milestone in my life. I was actually going to a man's house. When I phoned him, he invited me over to review his notes. While I was a little nervous about going to his home, I understood why he suggested viewing them in private. He had a valid point. If I wigged out at his house, no one other than him would be the wiser. I was still trying to fly under the radar at the house, keeping the other girls out of my business. As I knocked on the door of his apartment my heart was pounding. He opened it so fast; he must have been standing right beside it.

"Hi." I rushed inside. For some reason, I felt like people were watching me.

"Good morning. I got some coffee brewing; do you want some?"

"No thanks. I'm already nervous enough as it is."

"Why are you nervous?"

Brody seemed genuinely concerned. I marveled again at how attractive he was. For some reason, I felt so safe when I was around him. He was always the gentleman and I enjoyed my time with him. I only wished it were under better circumstances.

"Can we just get to this? I've been up all night thinking about it. Are you going to leave me while I look at it?"

"Sure, if you like. I can go in my bedroom. I really don't think it would be a good idea if you're totally alone. It makes me mad when I watch the tapes, so there's no telling how you will feel once you see them." He walked over to the couch and picked up the remote. "You should probably watch the tapes first before you read my notes."

I sat back on the couch, fighting tears. I guess I didn't really think about the fact that he'd seen the tapes before now. I felt stupid, causing me to lash out. "I'm not crazy. I know I just got out of a mental hospital, but I'm really not crazy. Granted, I do and say inappropriate things but that's not crazy, is it? I mean, that stuff with that lady on the bus, well that was a little crazy, but other than that, I'm okay." I was rambling.

"Jordan, I watched the tapes, so I know you're not crazy. You weren't the only one taunting the lady, you just happened to be the one that got caught."

"You saw that? Someone got it on tape? Did my lawyer see it?" My shame turned to anger. If he was aware of the bigger picture, why wasn't anyone else? Brody didn't say anything for several seconds.

"I don't want to upset you but I think the whole world saw at least one of the videos. I honestly don't know why the other tapes weren't introduced into evidence."

I was only half-way listening to his response. "Are you fucking kidding me? Does that mean I'm a star?"

Brody's mouth fell open. "Technically speaking, I guess you are but not necessarily in a good way."

"I said the wrong thing again, didn't I?"

"It was not something to be proud of. A lot of people got the wrong impression of you. The video that was shown on television didn't show the other people involved. The one they saw was all about you. As if you acted alone."

"Why? That's so unfair," I said as a tear slid down my face. I was tired of crying.

"I agree. That's one of the reasons why I took another look at your case."

"I'm not proud of what I did. I only wanted them to accept me. I wanted to be their friend."

"Is that why things got out of hand on the subway that day? You were trying to be accepted?" Brody asked.

I nodded my head.

"Tell me what happened."

"Every other time I caught the train to school, this one group of kids always called me names. They made fun of the way I dressed, calling me fat and ugly. They were the cool kids at school, real popular. Anyway, this particular day, one of the girls, named Aaryn, started talking to me. At first, I thought it was a joke and didn't pay her any mind. But she kept talking. She introduced me to the rest of her friends.

I figured she wouldn't do that if she was playing a joke. When we got on the train, they invited me to sit with them. I was so happy. I really was. They were the ones that started teasing the old lady. I joined in and you know the rest. I know it was stupid. It was the only time they paid any attention to me." Brody allowed me several minutes to cry. I'd never told anyone what happened the day I'd been arrested.

"It's going to be okay," Brody said, patting my hand while handing me some tissues.

I dried my eyes and wiped the snot dripping from my nose. "Since you've already seen the tape, I don't mind you watching it with me."

"Are you sure? I don't mind stepping out the room."

"It's okay." I took the remote and pressed play. Instantly, I was transported back in time. I saw a little fat girl's desperate cry for attention. I couldn't relate to this little girl. I wasn't that girl anymore.

***

After watching both tapes, I was angry and confused. I was so overwhelmed with emotions, I couldn't even speak. One minute I was sitting on the couch with tears streaming down my face, the next, I'm straddling Brody, riding low on his dick. The move was so smooth, it could have been choreographed. Brody's mouth dropped open as I rocked on his penis. I buried my face in his neck inhaling his scent. I felt his dick rising as I rocked back against it again.

"Jordan, what are you doing?" I heard the alarm in his voice but I ignored it.

"Shush. Don't talk." I grinded down hard on his dick rubbing my clit against his shaft. Brody's look of concern, as he wiped the tears from my face, touched me. I moaned, deep in my throat. He cared about me, I could tell. "Did Max see the tape?" I was still getting my jollies when the question popped into my head. I felt Brody's muscles stiffen under me and not in a good way.

"I couldn't tell you. I know I didn't show it to him." His voice was gruff.

I froze. "You don't like Max do you?"

"I don't care about him one way or the other."

I nuzzled my face against Brody's cheek. Rough stubble tickled my face. "You need a shave."

Brody chuckled, while rubbing his other cheek. "What can I say, I'm very hairy. Sometimes I have to shave twice a day."

I felt like an emotional pendulum. I don't recall ever feeling so unwanted and unloved in my life. I needed to feel something, other than the desolation I had lived with my entire life. I planted a kiss close to Brody's lips. His body trembled as his arms circled my waist. I wiggled closer to his chest. I could feel his heart racing. What started out as a slow burn, turned into a ferocious need. It was like a vortex of sorts. I wanted to fill it with Brody. I grabbed his face and forced his lips to touch mine. I swallowed his essence as we breathed the same air. I pulled him closer as I felt his penis enlarge. My emotional pain was forgotten, replaced by lust. I held his face so tightly, my nails were digging into his flesh. I wanted him like I'd never wanted anything before. Brody pushed me back, a torn look on his face. "Jordan, wait."

My heart felt like it was breaking. He was about to turn me away, much like everyone else in my life had. "What?" I snapped.

"We can't do this." His eyes appeared to be sad.

"You don't want me?" All my feelings of hurt and rejection came back in that moment.

"Of course I do. I've wanted you almost from the first time I saw you."

"You did? Then what is the problem?"

"Timing. You're acting solely on emotions right now. When things calm down, I don't want you to look back on this moment with regrets. You mean too much to me for that to happen."

His mouth was moving but I wasn't trying to hear what he was saying. "If you won't fuck me, I'll find someone else who will." My bluntness shocked me. Normally, I didn't talk that way, but there wasn't anything normal about this day. All I knew was that I was hurting. I needed to feel better. I tried to get up but he held me still.

"You don't mean that." Brody shook his head.

"You have no idea what I mean or don't mean. I know if I call Max —" Brody did not let me finish the sentence. He pulled me in for a deep kiss as he stood up. I wrapped my legs around his waist kissing him deeply. We were breathing so hard. His hands explored my ass. I finally had him where I wanted him. He pushed me against the wall, pinning my body in place while I ravaged his mouth and neck.

"Bedroom," I demanded between breaths.

Brody paused, staring deep into my eyes. His gaze was intense. He pushed back from the wall, stumbled over the leg of the sofa, and for a split second, I thought we were going down. He released one of his hands and stabilized us. "I got you. I will never hurt you." We kissed all the way to the bedroom; his eyes seemed to be burning a hole in my soul. He set me down on the bed breaking the connection between our lips. His eyes that were clouded with lust mere seconds before began to focus.

"Get undressed." I commanded. I was like an army drill instructor barking orders. I took off my shirt and unfastened my bra, tossing them to the floor. He had yet to take off his shirt and I was growing impatient. "What are we waiting for?"

"I think we should talk about this first."

"Are you freaking kidding me?" I was on a slow boil. One minute he was hot, the next he was artic chilly. He sat down on the bed keeping his eyes averted from me and my half naked body.

"If you only knew how hard it is for me to keep away from you right now."

I growled in frustration. Who knew getting a little dick would be so hard. I scrambled to the edge of the bed trying to reach my bra. I didn't like begging and that's exactly what I felt like I was doing. I'd been rejected all my life and this was like the final straw for me.

"What are you doing?"

"Getting my clothes. It's obvious you and I are not on the same page. You have some sort of moral standard. I ain't got no time for that."

"I wouldn't go so far as to say that," he said taking my bra from my hands and tossing it on the chair.

My heart galloped. I flipped on my back and shimmied out of my underwear. Brody looked away again. I was done with this emotional roller coaster. I leaped off the bed and grabbed my clothes, looking around for the bathroom. Brody grabbed my arm and pulled me to him, locking his arms around my waist. I was naked while he was still dressed.

"You're killing me," he whispered against my stomach while feathering me with kisses.

"No, you're killing me. You need to make up your mind what you want to do because I can't do this." My breathing was shallow and labored.

"I just want you to be sure this is what you want. Do you realize how many women make an emotional decision to have sex, and later regret it? Then the first thing they want to do is cry rape. I care too much about you for us to end that way."

"I'm sure, damn it. What more do you want me to do?" I lifted his shirt, running my palms against his skin. A loud moan escaped his lips. His skin felt so good to me. He peeled off his shirt and threw it on the floor. I was breathing so fast. I was getting dizzy. I let him go long enough for him to take off the rest of his clothes. Brody had an amazing body. His cocoa brown skin was stretched, taunt against his long lean frame. His hooded eyes raked my body. I shivered. He gently lowered himself into my outstretched arms.

"Ahh," I murmured as his chest crushed mine. I tried to position my lower body to meet his penis but he artfully evaded me. I groaned again in frustration.

"I need to get a condom," he said between pants and grinds.

While I should have been pleased with his precautionary measures, all of these delays were taking me out of the mood to have sex. He got up from the bed again, giving me an opportunity to fully explore his body with my eyes. His skin was a canvas of art covering the sinewy muscle underneath. "Hurry," I pleaded, impatient for his touch.

He pulled open his nightstand drawer so fast, it fell to the floor. Bending over, his ass pointed toward the ceiling, he searched through the mess he created and found the tiny foiled condoms. "Got it."

I snatched the condom from his hand and ripped it open with my teeth. "Do you want me to do it?" I was feeling confident even though I'd never put on a condom before.

"I got it," A sly smile crossed his face as he shook his head, taking the condom back.

As much as I wanted to control this situation, he was not going to let me. I eased back on my elbows and watched as he swiftly unrolled the condom onto his dick. I was slightly jealous of the rubber sleeve protecting his most sensitive area. I was moist just thinking about it. Brody reminded me of a black panther, as he playfully crawled onto the bed. His head was low as he sniffed the air around my pussy. He kissed my inner thigh. I almost shot off the bed. His hands held me firmly in place as he kissed my other thigh.

"You don't know how long I've wanted to do that." His lips inched higher leaving a warm trail of kisses.

"Really?" I wasn't trying to talk. Why was he trying to make this more than it was? I wasn't expecting him to fall in love or something stupid like that. I bucked against the bed trembling with desire. He captured my legs again, pinning them to the bed.

"Yes," he whispered against my skin.

His breath sent warm tingles through my body, exploding in my head. Exquisite torture. "Show me," I moaned. Foreplay was for losers and fools who believed in love. I was a realist. He slipped in between my thighs, sinking deep inside of me. I wasn't prepared. I gasped. His powerful thrust broke through my hymen causing tears to spill out of my eyes. I held my breath until my body could get use to his girth.

Brody paused in mid-stroke. His eyes seemed to question me. "Are you okay?" An incredulous look was on his face.

"Yes," I panted. I didn't want to discuss my virginity at that moment. I wrapped my legs around his waist to keep him from pulling out.

He remained rigid. "Why didn't you tell me?"

"Would you have touched me if I had?"

He shook his head no. I could still feel his dick pulsating in my pussy. In spite of the pain, I wanted more. I lifted my hips off the mattress thrusting my vagina over his dick.

"Oh, man," he grunted. "This shit feels so good." His body was shaking so badly as if he was in conflict within himself. I could tell he was trying to be gentle; however, I didn't need this from him right now.

"Fuck me," I urged. The pain was gone, leaving a palpitating organ in its place. I sought his face and forced my tongue in his mouth to keep from screaming out in ecstasy. I wrapped my arms around his neck, pulling him closer. I never imagined having sex would feel so good. I could remember listening outside of my mother's door when she was sexing her friends. I thought she was gross. I was sure I'd never make such animalistic sounds. Hearing myself now, I could totally relate to what my mom had to have experienced.

Brody pulled out and I cried. "What are you doing?" I panicked. Was he done? Was it over and I missed it? It felt nice but I just thought it should be more. I felt like I was on a cliff, hanging on with one fingernail.

"No, I want you on top." He flipped on his back. Relieved, I climbed on top positioning myself over his dick. I wasn't sure what I was doing. I allowed my instincts to take over. My hunger forced me on his dick. I couldn't have stopped pounding on that dick if I wanted to. "Aww," I moaned, as I eased him back inside of me. With my eyes closed, head held back, I rode him. He reached up and cupped my breasts, gently fingering my nipples. They were puckered like little raisins.

"I love your boobs. Look at you. You're freaking gorgeous."

My eyes popped open at his compliment. I wasn't used to getting them. His words completely threw me off my stride. His hands guided me back to a gallop. He sat up and started sucking my nipples; the sensation sent my body into a frenzy. "Right there, baby."

"Oh, God, Jordan, I don't think I can hold it." Perspiration the size of dewdrops dotted his face and chest. His fingers dug into my sides as he held on for dear life. He was bucking against me the same way I was thrusting back at him until something inside me imploded. My lips dropped open as a wondrous euphoric wave overtook me, shaking me to my core.

"Oh shit," I said falling forward onto his chest. He wrapped his arms around me, while we both caught our breath. My mind was spinning in a thousand different directions at once. I did not anticipate this rush of emotions. While the physical connection helped get my mind off what I saw on those awful tapes, now that the sex was over, the pain began to seep back in. I pulled back from Brody, wanting to go take a shower or something. I was feeling a little bit embarrassed by my behavior.

"Where are you going?"

"Can I take a shower?"

"Yeah, in a minute. I just want to hold you for a second."

I felt a flash of irritation as he pulled me back in his arms. We laid on our sides, with my back touching his chest. It actually felt good as we spooned. I wasn't under any illusions about Brody's interest in me. He said it himself, he has wanted me from the moment he saw me. Now that he had me, there was no reason for him to stick around. I was okay with that. I was accustomed to being alone.

"So, what do we do now?"

I felt every muscle in my body tense up, including my butt cheeks. "What do you mean, we?" I tried to pull away but he held me tight.

"Jordan, wait. I was just thinking that if you wanted to do some more digging into the past, I'd be willing to help you find the answers you need. And if you want to forget it, I'm fine with that too."

I didn't know what to say. The last thing I wanted was to have him reinvestigating what happened the day I was sent to the hospital. I needed him to let it go. "Honestly, I can't do it anymore. What's done is done. I can't change anything, so I don't see what good it would do to continue looking."

"That's actually quite smart. You shouldn't dwell on the past. When I first saw the tapes, I wondered why you didn't tell the court about the other people involved."

"I tried but my lawyer kept cutting me off. He was trying to get rid of me. He asked the judge to remove me from the courtroom. I don't even know what happened after I left except for ending up in the hospital."

"Excuse my French. That's fucked up." Brody said angrily.

"Tell me about it. And the people at the hospital weren't trying to hear it either. Every time I was cognizant enough to say something about it, someone would come at me with a needle. Lights out for me. Got to a point where it wasn't worth the hassle mentioning it. Max was the only one that seemed to give a shit about me, one way or the other."

Brody appeared to bristle at the mention of Max's name.

"Why do you do that? Why do you get all funny every time I mention his name?"

"He's okay."

I could tell Brody was lying to me and it pissed me off. "You know what; I think I should go home now." I got up to gather my clothes.

"Jordan, wait. Don't leave like this."

I didn't have anything else to say. My mood switched again. I felt trapped and I needed to get some air. I rushed through getting dressed, ignoring Brody's pleas to talk to him.

"I'll call you," I said, as I shut his door behind me. I'd been resting too long. It was time to put some of my plans into motion.

CHAPTER TWENTY-THREE

LACY BATES

I was chillaxing on the front porch when I first noticed Jordan stumbling down the sidewalk. From a distance, she looked stoned and completely oblivious to her surroundings. I don't know what scared me more, her trance like walk, or her getting nailed for coming home high. I rushed down the walk to meet her, while silently praying that she wouldn't fight me.

"Jordan?" I tentatively grabbed her arm and pulled her close to me. I wasn't quite sure what her reaction would be. When she didn't resist, I grew frightened. She was sweating really badly, but that's stopped too. I led her through the gate, pausing to close it behind us. I could feel her body trembling. "What's wrong?" She was so out of it, I wasn't surprised when she didn't respond. I practically dragged her to her room and shut the door behind us. She sat on the bed staring at the floor. I didn't know what to do. If I alerted Mrs. Gates, I knew all hell would break loose. "Honey, you're scaring me. Can I get you something?" Jordan continued to stare at her feet, as if she didn't even know who they belonged to. I took off her shoes, stringing her bag over my shoulder. I pushed her back on the bed. She curled up in a ball, closing her eyes. I thought maybe she needed to sleep, although I kept second guessing myself. I stood there for a few minutes; staring at her while she twitched. When she didn't open her eyes, I backed out of the room and closed the door. I was convinced something had happened to her. I could not imagine what.

I went back to the living room so I could monitor Jordan's room. No one could walk in or out of her room without my knowing it. I was a nervous wreck.

When I saw Jordan sneaking out the house, she appeared to be fine. Six hours later, she's looking like a zombie? It didn't make sense. I looked down and realized I was still holding Jordan's purse. I debated for two or three minutes before I decided to look in her bag to see if I could find some answers as to what was going on with Jordan. I snuck back in her room and sat on the bed beside her. "Jordan, I'm going to go through your bag. If you don't want me too, then you need to say something." I was met with silence.

"Okay, I'm going in." Her purse contained the normal girl shit.: makeup, lipstick, lip gloss, keys, medicine bottle, phone and several business cards.

"Oh shit, where'd you get a phone? You just break all the rules, don't you? What else you got in here?" I might as well have been talking to myself. Jordan was in her own little world. The bottle of Lithobid concerned me. It was half full even though it had only been filled a few days prior. I was no stranger to the drug, so I suspected that she'd taken too much. The question now was what should I do about it? "Fuck." I was pretty sure Jordan wouldn't want to go to the hospital but I didn't know what else to do. If this were an overdose, she was going to need medical attention.

I turned on her phone and looked at her call list. Surprisingly, our friend, Brody was the last person called. I didn't have time to talk myself out of calling him. Rushing to the door, I flipped the lock and dialed his number. He picked up on the first ring.

"Jordan, are you okay? You left so suddenly I've been worried sick about you."

I immediately became suspicious. "Brody, this is Lacy, not Jordan." I waited.

"Uh, oh yeah. Um, I saw the number and assumed…"

"Well, it's not. Jordan came home a little while ago and something is not right. She seems out of it. I don't know what's wrong with her." I was keenly aware he could've been the last person to see Jordan, so his input was crucial.

"What do you mean, out of it?" Brody sounded leery.

I immediately noted the change in his pitch. He was hiding something. I could feel it in my bones. "She's lethargic and not really acting like herself."

"Wait, I didn't realize you two were friends."

I wasn't sure how to take his comment. Was he trying to be her friend or was he hiding something else? "We're cool. We kind of look out for each other. Did you say you saw her recently?"

"Where is she?" He completely ignored my question.

"She's home."

"Can I speak with her?"

"She's not really in a talking kind of mood. If you know what I mean." If he was going to be evasive, so was I.

Brody sighed heavily into the phone. "She wasn't in the best mood when she left my house."

"Why was she at your house?" The hairs on the back of my neck were standing up. I began thinking about all the things that could have happened.

"I don't know how much of this I should tell you."

"You better fucking tell me something, or I'm going to call the police. When I saw her stumbling down the street, my first thought was that she'd been raped." Now that I said the words out loud, I listened with a third ear.

"Police? Now wait a minute. If you are insinuating that I did something to her, you're way off base. She was upset when she left but it's not what you think. Jordan means the world to me. You have to know that."

In my heart, I believed him but I wasn't ready to let him off the hook until he came clean. "Then I suggest you enlighten me right now. Why was she upset? She's shaking and shit." I could feel his hesitation even over the phone.

"Wait, why would she be shaking?" This time there was no denying his obvious concern.

"I'm thinking she might be off her medication."

"Shit. Keep an eye on her for me, I'm going to get in touch with her doctor and call you back."

I was really confused now. "You know her doctor?"

"Just don't leave her alone. I'll call you back." He hung up.

I was left holding the phone, feeling very unsure whether or not I did the right thing by calling Brody. If Jordan truly had a relationship with him, I was scared she'd get mad at me for talking crazy to her man. I put the phone and the medicine back in her bag and waited. Jordan was still curled in a ball, rocking back and forth. She was no longer sweating. Her skin almost felt clammy. I got up from the bed and took a seat at her desk, nervously keeping vigil. If it were a drug overdose, my biggest fear was the possibility of seizures. When I was first diagnosed with bipolar disorder, I was given Lithobid. It didn't work for me, so I was very familiar with its side effects. The buzzing of Jordan's phone caught me completely off guard. I rushed back to the bed and grabbed it, to silence it. Personal phones weren't allowed in the house, so I had to silence the buzzing immediately. As loud as it was, the noise didn't shake Jordan out of her stupor.

"Hello?"

"Lacy, I have Jordan's doctor, Lawrence Maxwell, on the phone with us."

"Okay," I wasn't really comfortable with this third-party conversation. Brody could be lying to me about who this other person was.

"Hello, Lacy. Can you tell me what Jordan is doing?"

"Well, she's curled up in a ball right now, rocking back and forth. Not really doing much of anything else."

"Brody mentioned tremors. Are her pupils dilated?"

"She was shaking when she first got home. That appears to be slacking off. Her eyes seem normal to me. She was also sweating real badly but that's stopped too."

"I still want to check her out. Do you think I could come over there?"

"Not unless you want the whole house to know something is going on."

"Do you think you can get her out of the house for me to examine her?"

"I guess, but I'm coming with you."

"Fine. We'll be there in about twenty minutes," Brody said.

"We don't need everybody to be involved in this," Max objected.

"That's the way it's going to be. I'll pick you up in five, Max." The line went dead in my ear again. I put the phone back in her bag.

"Okay, Jordan, we're going to take a little trip. I've got to put your shoes back on." I pulled her up into a sitting position. She was so pliable, almost like clay, which led me to believe she was aware of everything that was happening. She allowed me to put on her shoes and flatten out her hair, which was a hot-ass mess. "I don't know what happened to you, boo. But I'm going to need you to get your shit together quick, fast and in a hurry."

CHAPTER TWENTY-FOUR

BRODY MASON

I was more than a little nervous as I drove to pick up Max. I was frantically thinking about how much, or how little I needed to tell him about Jordan's visit to my apartment. The fact that Max also had feelings for Jordan complicated things. Where I would normally be forthcoming in a situation like this, I now had to be guarded. My gut told me to withhold the physical aspects of our relationship from him unless it was absolutely necessary. Absolutely necessary to her recovery, that is. Having sex was Jordan's idea but I was afraid Max would think I'd taken advantage of her.

The drive to Max's house was nerve wrecking. For what seemed like the 100th day in a row, it was raining in Atlanta. I was so sick of rain; I didn't know what to do. I just wanted one day of complete sunshine. The rain did provide a distraction from my dilemma. Most of my mind concentrated on the road. A smaller portion was reserved for the mild panic attack I was having. Atlanta was notorious for bad weather drivers. They drive slow as hell every day of the week but the minute the weather takes a turn, they wanted to drive like bats out of hell. Thankfully, I wasn't too far from Max's house. In fact, he was standing on the curb when I turned the corner.

Max was in full nerd/turd mode. I could tell he was amped up by the way he reached for the door before the car came to a complete stop. "What the fuck is going on, Brody? Why didn't they just take Jordan to the emergency room if they were so worried about her? And why the hell did they call you in the first place?"

"Damn, man, chill. You look like you're about to bust a blood vessel."

"Something doesn't feel right about this. Hell, I don't do house calls. I could get in big trouble if this shit goes south."

"You could have said no. I just thought you'd want to help Jordan, especially since you know how she feels about hospitals after all she's been through." I was counting on Max's guilty conscious kicking in. He might not have created the problems with Jordan's care, but he wasn't the one who blew the whistle. I was.

"Oh wow, man. I didn't even think about that aspect of it. I'm just tripping. I'm glad you called." Despite his contrite response, I could still see that Max was worried.

"Exactly. I feel like we are just getting her to talk, so sticking her back into a hospital would be a big mistake."

"What do you mean talk? She talks to you?"

"Uh..."

"You might as well tell me, it might be important." Max began fumbling with his seatbelt. He was yanking the belt like he had a personal vendetta against it.

"Dude, let it go and pull it again. You're about to screw up my ride."

He sighed loudly, as the belt slid back in the holster. This time when he pulled it out, he did it slower.

"So, what did she tell you? What did she say?"

"She said you advised her to remember the past in order to forget it."

"Well yeah, I did. She's been repressing memories for a long time, maybe even before the stint in the hospital. Has she said anything about the hospital or how she came to be in the hospital?"

"She's repressing memories about her family. She doesn't talk much about them at all."

"You seem to have gotten rather close."

There was a hint of sadness in his voice. I almost felt sorry for him. Evidently, he had developed feelings for Jordan, which went beyond the doctor patient relationship. I didn't have the heart to tell him he was wasting his time chasing those emotions. "She wanted my help with filling in the gaps about her past. I shared some of the information I told you about. She was fine when she left my house." If I could have bit off my own damn tongue, I would have. I stole a look at Max to see if he caught my slip of the lips. One look confirmed that he had indeed heard what I said.

"What the hell was she doing at your house?" Max yelled.

"Man, she wanted to see the tapes. What was I supposed to do, take her to the library? Take a risk of her nutting up in a public place again? Seriously?" I honestly never gave the library any thought when she called me. It sounded good to me; I just hoped he brought it.

"You could have figured out some other place, other than your house." Max was pissed, it was written all over his face. I knew it was going to be an issue and that's why I didn't want to tell him.

"Where man? You tell me. Where could I have taken her and still have some privacy? It's on a DVD for crying out loud."

"Did you ever hear of a portable DVD player? I'm betting you had another motive for getting her alone."

I felt a rush of anger and guilt at the same moment, especially in light of how the afternoon ended. However, none of that mattered right at the moment. "I wish you would put that bullshit aside and concentrate on the issue at hand. Jordan and I are friends." I kept the 'with benefits' to myself.

"So, who was the girl on the phone? Don't tell me you know her too."

"Actually, I do. Her name is Lacy. It was through her that I reconnected with Jordan."

"This keeps getting better and better. What did you do? Bribe her to keep track of Jordan?"

"I realize you don't think much of me. I get it. I'm not feeling you either. You can think what you want. It's a free mother-fucking country. What you won't do, is create fictitious stories to massage your ego. If I wasn't so worried about Jordan, I'd kick your ass out my car."

"Oh, there would be some ass kicking alright. All I'm saying is that it seems mighty damn strange this all happened after she left your house."

I couldn't deny that it did sound fishy, especially since, I had all but given up hope on ever seeing Jordan again. However, I resented his insinuating I was to blame. "I couldn't give ten swishes of a ducks tail what you think. It is what it is." I threw the car in park in front of the group home.

"A duck's tail? Really dog?" He opened the door, grabbing his bag.

"Wait, you moron. Let me see if I can get her out the house. If you go in there carrying a medical bag, it's going to throw up all kinds of red flags." I called Jordan's phone. Lacy answered right away. "We're outside," I whispered even though it wasn't necessary.

"We'll be right out."

"Okay, Einstein, where do you propose I examine her? On the floor?"

"Max, you can really be an ass. Are you always this difficult? Or do you save it all for me?" This guy had some serious issues.

"This is unorthodox. I don't understand why we can't do it where she is. What are you trying to hide?"

"I'm not hiding anything you idiot. I just feel like the more people involved, the more likely the home is going to want to send her away. You said it yourself, hospitals are overcrowded and patients can get lost in the system. Make up your damn mind which defense you're going to use for your profession. Not to mention the fact that Jordan was severely traumatized by her last visit to the hospital."

If we weren't in the car, I had no doubt we would have been fighting by now. I was tired of his pompous ass and his attitude.

"Fine, but if she doesn't check out, I'm sending her to the hospital. I'm not trying to lose my license over some bullshit."

Lacy and Jordan came out of the house putting a temporary halt to our feuding. It was immediately apparent why Lacy had called me. Jordan was being led like she couldn't support her own weight, leaning heavily on Lacy.

"What the fuck, dude?" Max cautiously exited the car, opened the back door and slid in. Lacy assisted Jordan into the backseat and closed the door. Lacy climbed into the front seat with me. I was nervous as hell, as I pulled away. I watched Max, as best I could, in the rearview mirror.

Seeing Jordan in this condition made me nervous. "Where should I go?" I was at a complete loss, as to my culpability in all of this.

"Just drive for right now. Let me take her vitals." Max was all business. He had on his game face, concealing all remnants of his prior attitude. There wasn't a trace of the anger or attitude he'd been throwing my way.

While he was busy with Jordan, I asked a few more questions of Lacy. "Did anything happen in the house?"

"No, I told you she was like this when she came home. She was walking down the street like an android. Scared me half to death. I don't know where she came from but she was pretty much gone for most of the day."

I met Max's evil eye in the rearview mirror. I knew then, I was going to have to deal with this fucker sooner, rather than later. This time, he wouldn't be punching me in the face and getting away with it

"Oh, not to worry, Brody knows exactly where she was. Don't you, Brody?"

I ignored Max for the moment. I kept my focus on Lacy. "Did she say anything to you?"

"No, she hasn't said a word. I'm pretty sure that she's aware of what's going on around her. She knows she's safe. This happened to me once before. If it's the same thing, I was aware the entire time; I just didn't want to participate in life."

"Are you bipolar too?" Max questioned.

"Excuse you? I don't know you like that."

I could feel tempers were about to escalate inside the car. "Lacy, this is the doctor I was telling you about, Max. He was the physician treating Jordan when she was confined to the hospital. For what it's worth, Jordan trusts him." She didn't need to know that I didn't.

I continued to drive in circles while Max monitored Jordan. Fortunately, the rain had stopped. I was beginning to relax somewhat.

"Jordan, can you hear me?" Max asked, as he shined a light in Jordan's eyes. Jordan remained silent.

I looked over at Lacy, who was turned half way around in her seat. From the look on her face, she seemed to be legitimately concerned about Jordan's welfare.

I felt the need to reassure Lacy. "You did the right thing calling me. I'm glad she has someone in the house that she can trust."

"She may not know she can trust me. I hope she does because I really do like her."

"Are you for real? What do you mean?"

"When she first got to the house, we butted heads big time. Truth be told, I was a tad bit jealous of her. It was also before I got to know her and shit. What's going to happen to her?"

Max interjected from the peanut gallery. "Lacy, did you tell Brody she was shaking?"

"Yes, her arms and stuff were shaking. When that stopped, it was just her hands."

"Even though she appears stable, I'd like to run her by the hospital to run a few tests."

"No!" Jordan shouted. She began to thrash around in the backseat. For me, it was scary watching her in the rearview mirror. The sudden outburst scared me, so I pulled the car over. Max had his hands full, as Jordan tried to climb over him, to get out of the car. It was like a scene from *Girls Gone Wild*, in the backseat of my car. I got out to help Max control Jordan. I didn't want her to hurt herself trying to get away. "What can I do?"

"Grab her arms."

"Jordan, listen to me. It's Brody; you're safe." I kept my voice conversationally low, in spite of the overwhelming panic I was feeling. Her eyes were wild and haunted. I couldn't help but wonder where she was in her mind, and what was happening to her. Whatever it was, I wanted to save her.

"Brody?" Jordan slumped against my chest, giving up her fight.

Max glared at me with obvious hatred. His eyes demanded answers to unasked questions. To him, this probably looked suspicious. I was caught between a rock and a hard place on what to do.

"Is she going to be okay?" Lacy seemed oblivious to the animosity between Max and me. She was the only person in the car that didn't seem to care that Jordan had collapsed in my arms.

"I guess she didn't need a doctor after all," Max said, as he placed his tools of the trade back in his bag. I didn't have time to nurse his bruised ego.

"Jordan, what happened to you? Did you mix up on your medicines?" I asked, while wiping the hair away from her forehead. Slowly, her eyes began to regain focus.

"I'm fine. I heard everything you all said. I just didn't have the energy to answer." She sat up, pulling away from me and backing up next to Max, who immediately started grinning as if he'd won some type of prize.

"You had us all nervous and afraid," Max patted her hair which had become mushed, while she was tussling. I bristled and climbed out of the backseat. I felt like he was only touching her because he'd seen me do it. I still felt guilty for crossing the line with Jordan. The question now was what we were going to do about it? Jordan's eyes sought mine in the mirror as she pulled away from Max, sitting up straight.

Lacy cleared her throat. "It's getting dark. We should get on home before we miss curfew and we both get in trouble."

I pulled out of the parking lot and headed in the direction of the home.

"I still want to know what happened to you. Do we need to run you past the hospital for a check?" Max intoned.

"I'm fine, Max. I shut down for a minute. I just needed to think, and the best way for me to do it, was to envision myself in a hole. So, I was in a hole and y'all happened to dig me out of it. End of story." She shrugged her shoulders.

I was familiar with her tone. She was getting mad. I'd seen these signs before when I was interviewing her for my article. It wasn't pretty. If she were about to get pissed, I didn't want it to be about me. I had too much to lose if our relationship was exposed.

Max, on the other hand, couldn't let it go. "Have you remembered something? Was something going on when this happened?" Jordan ignored his incessant chatter.

Now that the crisis was over, it seemed like everybody wanted to share their feelings. I felt the sweat before the first drop hit my brow. My eyes locked with Jordan, telepathically begging her to keep her mouth shut. My hands were shaking as I parked the car in front of the home. They got out of the car and Max got back in the front seat. I rolled down the window to say good-bye but the girls were talking.

"Jordan, I'm sorry I called Brody. He was the only person that I knew who knew us both. Girl, I was so nervous. I thought I was going to have a heart attack when I saw you walking down the street."

"Its okay, Lacy. I'm not mad. I should be thanking you." Jordan winked at me as our eyes met.

For a minute, I exhaled. The threat was over. We survived.

Jordan chuckled. "It's not every day a girl loses her virginity. I didn't know it would wipe me out. You know, sensory overload. I'm good now. Bye y'all."

My foot hit the gas and I almost ran my car into a parked vehicle. *Holy shit! What the fuck was she thinking?* I already knew the ride back to Max's house was going to be miserable for me.

Max yelled, "You know what? I should kill you, you smug, son of a bitch. I knew you had something to do with this." Max was going ballistic.

"Max, I know how that sounded but she came on to me." I felt like a dick blaming it all on Jordan especially since she wasn't there to dispute it.

"You perverted fuck. I'll bet you didn't try to stop her either."

"That's where you're wrong. I did. I told her I cared too much about her to rush into anything with her."

"Yeah, right. You couldn't wait to get your hands on her. I could see it in your eyes the first fucking time I met you. She's a child, you sicko."

"She is not a child. She's a grown woman."

"Well, she thinks like a child." Max stared out the window, refusing to meet my eyes.

"You might as well face it Max, her delivery was a little off, but she's made her choice."

"If you didn't do anything wrong, as you claim, why didn't you tell me about it when I first got in the car?"

"Because, it was none of your damn business."

"No, you just gloated like a pompous ass."

"Get real. The only reason why you're upset is because she chose me instead of you."

"Fuck out of here; she's my patient."

"She was your patient."

"Well, I find it mighty funny, that a few months ago, you didn't even know where to find her. Now you're banging her."

"Gee, Max, I sort of like this feisty side of you. Where's all your professionalism now?" I stopped the car in front of Max's house. I didn't bother to turn the car off. As far as I was concerned, me and Max had nothing else to say to each other."

"If you hurt her, you will see just how feisty I can get." Max got out the car slamming the door.

"I'm not going to take too many more of your threats. I get that you're mad or maybe even hurt. But I didn't do it to you. She came on to me, not the other way around." I don't know why it was so important to me that he knew this.

"Whatever. Just remember the next time you call yourself needing my help, go fuck yourself."

"So what are you saying? If something happens to Jordan, you don't want to know about it?"

"Not if it involves you." Max gave me the finger and walked away.

CHAPTER TWENTY-FIVE

JORDAN BREE

For three straight days, I did not come out of my room, except to use the bathroom. I didn't eat. I barely slept. I read every letter, article and post it note in the boxes of material that Brody had gathered. I even attempted to read the files that Max had given me, but they had so much medical jargon in them, I couldn't understand them. During this time, Lacy worried the shit out of me. She was always at my door, checking to make sure I was alright. She bought me food, which I didn't eat and offered me a shoulder when I needed to cry.

I also had numerous telephone calls which I didn't answer. Most of them were from Max. I wasn't ready to face him yet. Letting him know about Brody, the way that I did, was wrong. I now knew I was trying to hurt him like I'd been hurt. Now that my head was clearer, I was deeply ashamed of myself.

As I shifted through the last box, I felt myself getting ill. I couldn't remember the last time I'd eaten. My stomach was riotously acting a fool. The information in the files had given me a bird's eye view of people's candid opinions about me. I didn't like or agree with what they said.

Brody tried to dissuade me from continuing my search but I felt like I needed to know, in order to go forward with my life. I needed to understand how things escalated so far, to have me committed to a mental institution. Now I knew at least three sides to the story. I still hadn't figured out why my family abandoned me.

I threw the last folder against the wall, as tears streamed down my face. "It's lies, all lies," I screamed. Lacy was the only person to come when she heard my screams. No one else had the balls. She picked the lock, her habit of late, and came into my room.

"Girl, you scared the shit out of me," she said, as she rushed to gather me up off the floor. I wasn't sure when we became friends, but we had.

"It's so unfair, it's so unfair." I wailed.

"What's unfair? Talk to me. Look at this mess." She was talking about my room. I had papers everywhere. I could hear the concern in her voice.

"I wasn't the only person, on the bus tormenting the old lady, but I was the only one who caught charges." My legs were trembling when I stood up from the floor. I staggered down the hall to the bathroom, literally blinded by my tears. Lacy was close behind me. "How much more of this shit am I expected to take?" I made it to the toilet before I started retching. The bile burned my throat, causing me to cry even harder. I fell to my knees narrowly missing hitting my head on the brim of the porcelain bowl. I vomited twice more before the pain in my stomach subsided. Lacy helped me to my feet and back to my room. I was madder than I'd ever recalled being.

"Jordan, you can't keep doing this to yourself. You're a mess and you need to eat something."

"I don't need you telling me what to do."

"I wasn't trying to tell you what to do," Lacy patiently responded.

"I don't need your pity either."

"Good, because I didn't bring any with me. Now are you going to clean yourself up so we can eat?"

I wanted to argue with her but she was right. I could smell myself and even if I wasn't hungry, I didn't need to smell like a pig.

"Fine." I went back to the bathroom for a shower. I turned the water on as hot as I could stand it. It actually helped clear my mind. When I returned to my room, I saw that Lacy had begun picking up the papers from the floor and placing them back into boxes. "What do you think you're doing?" I pretended to be mad but I really wasn't. I didn't want to see those offending papers again and I was glad that she took the initiative to put them away.

"Cleaning up this mess, then I'm going to fix us something to eat." Lacy walked out, leaving me to get dressed. When I was finished, I followed my nose to the kitchen. The rest of the girls were gone, so we had the room to ourselves.

Lacy was busy rattling bowls and pans when I walked into the kitchen. I didn't even know she could cook. "What are you making?"

"Bacon, eggs and toast." She fanned the air around the plates as she put them on the table. She also filled two glasses with ice and poured some orange juice.

"How do you know I like eggs?"

"I don't, but it's the only thing I really know how to cook."

"Alrighty then," I laughed. I wasn't sure how they were going to taste, but they smelled good. I sat down in front of my plate and started to eat.

Lacy poured a generous amount of hot sauce over her eggs.

"You should have taken more eggs to go with your hot sauce."

"I don't like eggs so I use the sauce to cover the flavor."

"Then how come you know how to cook them so well?"

Lacy smiled. "Is that you're way of telling me they're good? It's okay for you to compliment my cooking."

"I didn't say I liked it. I'm just saying they looked nice on the plate. Pass me some of that hot sauce." I picked up the bottle and pretended to sprinkle some onto my plate but stopped. "I'm just kidding. They really do taste good." I was impressed. Over the past few weeks, we'd gotten pretty close. She was the first person who seemed to genuinely care about me. Since she did something nice for me, I wanted to do the same for her.

"Let's clean up this kitchen. I wanna do something." Together, we cleaned up the kitchen and got ready to go.

***

The moment Lacy and I walked into DW Salons at Lenox Mall, I wanted to turn around and flee.

There were at least fifteen people in the salon and all of them trained their eyes on us.

Lacy leaned over and whispered in my ear. "Girl, what are we doing here?" She appeared to be anxious.

"This busted look ain't working for me no more. We're about to step it up."

"What do you mean? I can't afford no shop like this."

"Don't worry about it; I got you." Seeing all the beautiful people in the shop, I became overly self-conscious about what we were wearing and the overall unkempt condition of our hair. I hadn't had a perm in years and my natural curls had taken over like weeds in a grassy field.

"Why the fuck are they staring at us?" I grabbed her hand, urging her to be quiet. I didn't like them staring at me either, but we did look like fashion rejects. Judging by the look of the stylists and the patrons, this was the place we needed to be. I swallowed my pride and let them gawk, until someone had the gumption to speak to me.

"Hi, can I help you?" A short, light-skinned lady approached us, while wiping her hands on her apron.

It was hard not to be nervous. I'd never been in a salon before. I fumbled with the ends of my shirt. Lacy was of no help either, she was shaking like a leaf. I wanted to run so badly, or at least put the other people in the shop on the defensive for being so rude, but I didn't. "I, I mean we, need to get something done." We needed so much. I couldn't begin to list it all. Armed with my new debit card, I wasn't the least bit concerned about the price.

"Is this your first time here?" the lady inquired. *Was she making jokes?*

Lacy yanked hard against my hand. I wasn't sure if the lady was playing with us or not. I nodded my head unable to speak. People were still staring at us and it was pissing me off.

"Good. What would you like to have done?" She directed her question to me. I was cool with that.

"Uh, I'm not sure. We'd like to talk to a stylist…in private." I eyed down those nosy people that were all up in my Kool-Aid, trying to guess the flavor. One by one, their eyes turned away, until I felt like I could breathe again.

"Absolutely, but I need to know which stylist you want to consult with. What are you looking to have done?"

"A whole new look, for both of us."

The lady nodded her head. "Natural, chemical, weave, sew-in? Each, of our stylists, specializes in different things."

"Oh, I get it. I need something that is low maintenance. I have no clue on what to do with my hair. What about you Lacy?" I turned and looked at my friend.

"I'm having the same thing you're getting." She looked to be as out of her element as I was.

"Of course, let me get someone to help you." She walked toward the group of people still trying to eavesdrop on our conversation. I hated the scrutiny they were giving us. It almost reminded me of my school days when I was always picked on for the way I looked. It was hard for me to stand there and take it. Although we didn't wait long, it felt like an eternity before we were led to the back of the shop.

"Hi, I'm Mia, the owner." Mia extended her hand and Lacy and I took it while giving her uneasy smiles.

"I'm Jordan and this is my friend Lacy. We need a fashion do-over."

"You ain't kidding a bit. Of course, our services are not cheap but we are the best." She didn't come right out and ask me if I could afford it but I understand where she was going.

"So I'm hearing," I replied.

"Then you've come to the right place. When you leave here, you won't even know each other. If you let me, I'm going to do you myself. Brianna, my assistant, will do your friend. Don't you worry about a thang, I got this."

Mia's station was the farthest away from the other stylists and had a privacy screen. Lacy looked terrified as Mia pulled it closed. I was glad for the privacy screen, as I was tired of being the center of attention. I was ready to fade into the background because being in the spotlight tended to make me antsy.

"So what did you have in mind?" Mia asked after she snapped a cape on me.

"Um ...I'm not sure how I want it. My hair hasn't been cut or styled in years. The only thing I like about my hair is the length."

"Girl, ain't no way I would cut all this hair. I'd have to send you to someone else, if that's what you wanted. I like long hair, the longer the better."

"You do? I thought you hated it the way you were looking at me."

"Oh, hell no. I saw your potential. I wanted to be the one to bring it out in you. Look at you, you have a cute face. All you need is the right hair and clothes. You will be fierce like Tyra Banks!"

"Fierce?"

"Yes, fierce, honey. Mark my words." Mia snapped her hands and spun around like she was modeling. I thought Mia was exaggerating her talents. Mia was a beautiful woman. If she could make me look one-tenth as good, I would be happy. The thought gave me butterflies in my stomach.

"Okay, let's do this."

"Slow down, sister. You still have to tell me what you want. When's the last time you put some perm in this hair?" Mia had spun the chair around so that we both were facing the mirror. She undid my braid that kept my hair from flying all over my head.

"I haven't had a perm in years."

"Is that by choice, or by force?"

I panicked. I wasn't ready to tell anyone where I'd been for the last several years. "I guess you could say force; my mother wouldn't give me the money to take care of it."

"Well, if you're not going to take care of it, then I don't think you should do another perm. I'd hate to see you lose all this hair because you couldn't afford the upkeep."

"Oh, that's not an issue anymore. I—" I stopped myself short. Mia stared at me, waiting for me to finish my sentence but I remained silent.

"You wouldn't be opposed to a perm? What about natural? We could still get it straight without the chemicals, if you want."

I was still uncertain what to do. I knew I wasn't talented when it came to doing my hair. I would, more than likely, wear a ponytail in between visits to the hair salon.

"I don't know. Just do something." I was anxious to get things started.

"Alright, no pressure. Let me show you what I can do without the perm. If you don't like it, we can do the perm the next time. How does that sound to you?"

"Fine. I don't want to talk about it anymore. I just want to do it."

"You need to do something about those eyebrows too. The uni-brow thing, it's got to go."

"I said whatever. Can we get started?"

"Yes we can." Mia led me to the shampoo bowl.

I knew we were in a top notch salon, but I wasn't expecting miracles. Four hours later, Mia was done.

"Well, what do you think?" Mia asked, as she finally turned her chair so I could see my reflection. I was so used to things not turning out well, I was almost afraid to look. I only wanted to look like everyone else; this was my only expectation. I counted to ten and looked up. My breath caught in my throat. I couldn't believe my eyes.

"Shut the front door," I exclaimed, as I jumped up from the chair to get closer to the mirror.

"Say what?" Mia looked confused. Obviously she'd never heard this expression before and didn't know what it meant.

I stole a brief look at Mia. This girl had skills.

"You don't like it?"

"Are you kidding me? I love it. I can't believe it's really me." I rushed toward Mia and gave her a hug.

"Whoa, slow your roll, sugar. Are you trying to give folks the wrong idea? I ain't trying to get your girlfriend all up in my face."

"Huh? Lacy? She's not my girlfriend, like that. She's my friend, who happens to be a girl. Eww, that's disgusting."

"Hey, I didn't know. Y'all came in holding hands. Both of you needed the works, so I just assumed. You feel me?"

"I'm glad you didn't say that in front of Lacy, she might have hit you." I said giggling. I would never be able to communicate to Mia how I was feeling inside. Never in my life, would I have imagined, it possible, for me to look as beautiful as I did right now.

"Do you like it?"

"Are you freaking kidding me? I look like I could be on television."

"Pump your brakes kid. You still have some more work to do before all of that. Those bitches in the shop are going to hate you when you walk in there."

"Work? What kind of work?" I was ready to sit my happy ass back down, for another four hours, if Mia could improve on what I was already seeing.

"Clothes. You've got to do something about that outfit. You do realize that it's one hundred and ten degrees outside and you have on a long sleeved shirt."

"Duh, I know I need some new clothes. Shopping is the next stop on our agenda. Do you have any suggestions on where I should shop?"

"You are in the mall, child, let yourself run free," Mia said laughing. "I had to whack away at your ends, but I left your length. The next time you come, if there is a next time, we'll need to cut some more. I didn't want to traumatize you by doing it all at once."

"Oh, you can bet your ass, I will be back. How much do I owe you for both of us?" I asked, while I flipped my hair from side to side like I'd seen some white people doing on television. I liked the bounce my hair had. I couldn't wait to see what they did to Lacy.

"Three hundred fifty dollars," Mia said.

Mia's prices were steep but definitely worth it. I gave her cash when she showed me the 'credit cards not allowed' sign. Thank God I remembered to bring some money along. I also included an extra hundred for a tip.

"You can make an appointment with the girl at the front desk. I'll see you next time, Jordan."

"Thank you so much, Mia. I really appreciate it." I had an extra bounce in my step when I pulled back the drapes and entered the salon. Once again, all conversation in the room ceased. For such a busy place, it didn't take much to get everyone off their game.

"Damn, Mia, you better work!" shouted one of the stylists.

"Hey, y'all know how I do." Mia patted herself on the back.

I beamed. For the first time in my life, I actually felt pretty and I was enjoying the feeling. When I saw Lacy, I squealed with joy.

"Girl, who knew you, had all this in you?" I shouted.

"Look at you. Damn, girl, Brody is going to shit a brick when he sees you. Those bitches at the house are going to hate big time." I pinched Lacy's arm, pushing her out the salon. She'd almost blown our cover. I made follow-up appointments and joined her outside.

"Don't hurt nobody, Jordan," Mia yelled as I went through the door. I didn't answer, but threw up my hand in acknowledgement. My mind already on the clothes we would get to complete our new looks.

CHAPTER TWENTY-SIX

BRODY MASON

I was a little apprehensive about seeing Jordan again, especially after that stunt she pulled in the car. Despite her theatrics, I missed her. She called me and asked me to meet her in the food court of Lenox Mall. After our last meeting, I had a thousand reasons not to see her again. But when she called, I couldn't think of one.

I couldn't imagine what it was like for her to have lost so many years of her life through no fault of her own. I also couldn't imagine how she'd gotten through it all, without being resentful. If it was me, I'd want revenge of some sort, or payback; starting with the persons I believed to be the root of the problem, her family. Jordan also had reason to hate her so-called friends who betrayed her. I glanced at my watch again for the umpteenth time hoping that it hadn't advanced some more since the last time I looked.

Jordan was over thirty minutes late and I was growing impatient. As much as it bothered me, I had no other choice but to wait, regardless of how long it took. I took a table in the center of the food court, so I could see all the entry points. The last thing I wanted to happen was for us to both be in the same place, and inadvertently miss each other.

"Hi," Jordan said softly, as she slid into the seat across from me.

My mouth dropped open forming a perfect O. "Oh, shit." I was not prepared for Jordan's transformation.

"What's wrong?" Jordan coyly smiled.

"Uh, err…" I coughed. Too much saliva pooled in my mouth. I was practically drooling. Totally, not cool.. I wiped my lips trying to think of something to say other than *wow*.

"Not quite the reaction I was looking for."

"You wanted to shock me? Got me choking, almost kill me." I laughed to mask my embarrassment.

Jordan nodded her head. "Let's just say it was an experiment. You're always so cool. I wanted to see if I could rattle your cage." She seemed very pleased with herself. "Have you been waiting long?" She cocked her head to the side, her long hair framing her face.

I was still trying to catch my breath. I was looking at a total transformation and I suddenly felt out of my league. My reaction felt juvenile. I couldn't even look at her without my heart skipping a beat. "No, I just got here," I lied. I had envisioned our meeting again so many times and none of those images included my making a total fool of myself.

"Stop lying."

I was busted. "Okay, you got me. I've been here about a half an hour. So, what's going on with you?"

Jordan's smile disappeared. "I'm getting by. Trying to pick up the pieces of my life. I'm sorry I outed you in front of Max."

"That was crazy. Max bit my head off during the entire ride back to his house. Have you spoken with him yet?"

"No. I've been trying to let him cool down. Max is a nice enough guy, but he's too old for me."

"I feel you. It's unfortunate for him he developed feelings for you. I can't be mad at him. I completely understand his position."

"Is that your way of saying you like me, Mr. Mason?" she said smiling.

"Backwards, frontwards, anyway you slice it, I think you're amazing." My heart went out to her. On the outside, she looked picture perfect, but on the inside, she was still fragmented.

"Thanks."

"Are you still remembering things?"

She nodded her head as her smile slipped. "It comes and goes. I try not to dwell on them."

"I've been meaning to ask you about the home. What's the deal? Was this your idea?"

"Are you kidding me? Like I would sign up to leave one jail and go to another?"

"That didn't come out right. I'm just trying to understand how that came about."

"Honestly, I think it's something the judge and my attorney cooked up. I can't rightly say. They claim I'm not ready to live alone. I can't tell what, if anything, living in the house is supposed to teach me. It's not like they actually interact with us."

"What's the point?"

"I really don't know. My time there is almost over. But those other girls, I feel sorry for them."

"That doesn't make any sense. Is this a state funded home?"

"I'm thinking Mrs. Gates owns the actual house, but because of some law, the state gives her some compensation for it. Maybe you can do what you do and give me a report."

"Whoa, you want me to do a story on it?"

"No, I just want to know what I'm working with. As surprising as it might sound, I've actually taken a liking to Lacy. I wouldn't be opposed to taking her with me when I leave."

"She seems to genuinely like you. Does she know how you feel?"

"I haven't said anything yet. I wanted to see what you could find out first. Especially, as it relates to her."

"Okay, I'll see what I can do." I didn't want to admit it, but my feelings were a little hurt because we hadn't talked about what happened the last time we were together. I felt stupid bringing it up. Yet, it was something that I felt, shouldn't be ignored.

"I've got so many things to do before I'm officially released from the home. I really want to get my license so I can get a car. Do you think you could help me?" She cocked her head again giving me, what I considered, were her bedroom eyes. Warning bells were dinging in my head. I felt like I was in dangerous waters, not knowing how to proceed.

"Of course, I'll help you. I still can't get over how gorgeous you look. I was sitting here expecting a little school girl and this beautiful woman comes over to me. You totally caught me off my game."

"Game? I don't like games, Brody." She frowned marring her perfect features.

"I didn't mean game like that."

"Well? Are you going to help me or not?" Her tone worried me. She actually sounded like she was mad. My palms felt sweaty and I used my jeans to absorb the moisture.

"How can I say no to you?" I couldn't possibly tell her how much she invaded my thoughts.

"Do you really think I'm pretty?"

"Come on, you probably hear that all the time."

"Actually, I don't. You have to remember my past. The only time anyone paid me any attention, it was to ridicule me. It keeps me on guard all the time."

She seemed genuine. I could not imagine anyone trying to hurt her. "Aren't you glad that chapter of your life is over?"

"It ain't over until I say it's over," Jordan mumbled while looking through her purse.

My eyes were focused on her lips, so I really didn't hear what she said. She was so sensual. "What did you say?"

"If you weren't staring at my lips, you might have heard me." She didn't appear to be mad but I felt ashamed, nevertheless.

"I feel like such a dick right now." I wanted the floor to open up and swallow me whole.

"Dicks can be fun."

It was a good thing I didn't have anything in my mouth or I would have choked to death. Who was this person? Every time I thought I had her figured out, she'd say or do something that would catch me off guard.

"Well, damn. I do believe I'm at a loss for words."

"Seriously? I didn't think I'd ever see that happen, mister master of the pen."

"Me neither. See what you do to me?" I felt totally exposed. I handed her the driver's education booklet I'd snagged earlier that day. I was finding it difficult to look at her so I kept my eyes neutral.

"What's this?" Jordan asked as she reached for the booklet. Our fingers briefly touched.

"You're going to need to study this for your test."

"Did I tell you I needed this? How did you know?" Her look told me she was confused.

"You mentioned it. I was in the area the other day, so I picked one up for you."

"You're so thoughtful. Thanks." Jordan fingered the book for a moment seeming to be lost in thought. She stood and picked up some bags that were at her feet. I had not noticed them until she was standing. Shopping was probably the reason why she was late.

I stood up as well as I admired Jordan's transformation. She looked amazing, like a younger version of Gabrielle Union. I opened my mouth to speak, but nothing came out. I couldn't believe this was happening to me. I could honestly say I'd never met anyone capable of reducing me to a blundering idiot.

"Are we going? These bags are heavy," Jordan said pouting.

"Huh?" I felt like I was in a trance. "Oh damn, I didn't even notice your bags. Here, let me get them for you." Happy that I had something to do, I reached for her bags.

"No thanks. I got them." She turned and started walking away.

I panicked. "Jordan, wait. Where are you going? I'm parked the other way."

"Fine," she continued walking in the same direction. I rushed up behind her confused. She appeared to be mad at me. For the life of me, I couldn't figure out what I'd done.

"Are you mad at me for some reason?" I touched her arm to slow down her angry retreat. I felt an electric jolt, the likes of which I'd never felt before.

"Ouch," she snatched her arm away from my touch.

"You felt that too?" I was surprised. I thought it was just me and was relieved to know that it wasn't.

"Of course I felt it. You shocked me." She started walking again, increasing her stride. My eyes followed up her long, slender legs encased in six-inch heels. When I got to her butt, I thought my eyes were going to pop out of my head.

"Damn, baby got back," I whispered. I knew that it was big, but the booty shorts she wore made it appear larger. I would've stood there staring, if some dude didn't try to step in Jordan's way. I rushed to her side and pulled her closer to me, protectively. Thankfully, she didn't pull away from my grip this time. The guy looked like he was about to say something, but I gave him the 'don't fuck with me look'. The guy kept on walking.

"You can let go of me now," Jordan said between gritted teeth. There was no doubt about it, she was pissed.

"Why are you snapping at me? What the hell did I do?" I didn't mean to cuss, the word slipped out.

She turned on me so fast, we bumped each other. She was so close, her nipples brushed against my chest. My dick bumped her leg, but she didn't move, neither did I. She was so damn sexy, it didn't make sense.

"I did all this shit and you act like you don't even notice." She threw her hands up damn near slapping me with her bag.

"Are you freakin' kidding me? How could I not notice? You got me drooling and shit. What do you expect me to do? We're in a mall damn it." I didn't intend to say all of that. It came out before I could stop it.

Her face softened, "You could have at least said I look nice."

I was confused. I kept telling her she looked nice and she obviously ignored it. I didn't know how many different ways she wanted me to say it. "You look drop dead beautiful; simply amazing. I kid you not. Hell, why you think I was trying to get that other dude off of you?"

"Well, damn. Did I look like a mangy dog before? I don't know whether or not I should feel insulted."

"Oh, please don't be offended. You are the type of pretty that would be beautiful in the dark."

"In the dark?" We were still standing face to face, almost touching. I remembered the feel of her in my arms.

"Yeah," I whispered. Her breath tickled my nose. I had to scratch or I'd sneeze. The movement broke the spell. I stepped back. I had to force myself to do so, especially since we were in the middle of a crowded mall. As I stepped away, I got a whiff of her perfume; it would haunt me at night.

"You smell good too."

"Thanks. Where did you say your car was?" We were good again.

I pointed to another door and reached over, grabbing her bags, which she graciously handed off to me. I placed them in the back of my CRV.

"Wow, when I saw the car the other day, I thought I was dreaming. I would have never pictured you driving something like this."

"What? You thought I'd drive a little sports car?"

"Well ...yeah" she said teasingly.

"I'm freaking six feet tall. What I look like climbing out of a tin can, Shaq? That dude couldn't even move in the car in the commercial. I like to have room when I drive. Especially, if I'm taking a long trip or something. It was a choice between this and a truck. I get better gas mileage with this one. Plus, it can act like a truck when I need it to." I was rambling.

"You almost sound like an infomercial. It's okay, I guess. I was thinking it was more of a family car," she said laughing.

"It could be if I had one, but I don't." My feelings were a little hurt. I felt like she was trying to handle me. She got in the car and put on her seatbelt. I walked around and started the car, still unsure of where we were headed and if I wanted to go with her. Even though I was older than Jordan, she unnerved me to a certain degree.

"I guess I should get home before I get in trouble."

My heart sank a little. I was kind of hoping we could swing by my place for a quickie. Jordan made me second guess myself. I wasn't use to the feeling. Deflated, I drove her back to the home. We didn't talk during the ride even though there were so many things that needed to be said. For some innate reason, I felt compelled to make things right for Jordan. I wanted to fix things but I had no idea how to start. This feeling went beyond the sexual and intellectual attraction I felt for her. It was almost parental in nature, even though I thought I didn't have a parental bone in my body. These feelings baffled me but I knew I couldn't ignore them.

While I was parking the car, I noticed that Jordan had fallen sleep. I sat protectively watching her, wondering what horrors she'd seen in her life. I also wondered about her family. Neither Jordan, nor Max, mentioned them while I was interviewing them. Where were they after all this time? "Wake up sleepy head, we're here." I said softly.

"We got here so fast." She stretched her arms over her head and wiped her eyes. "I'm sorry I zonked out on you, but this medicine usually puts me out, especially after a long day." She started gathering her things from the back seat of the car.

I opened the door and popped the trunk. I gathered her bags and was about to help her get them all inside, when Jordan stopped me.

"Brody, don't. I can get them myself." She jumped from the car and grabbed the bags from my hands, scratching me in the process.

"Ouch," I said, as I stuck my hand in my mouth sucking away the blood. I was confused by her abrupt changes in temperament.

"Oh shit, look what you made me do," she snapped angrily. Her eyes were literally on fire. They could have been heated by some internal fuel source, such as kerosene lanterns. The blaze was that intense, I could almost feel the burn. Instinctively, I wanted to pull her into my arms and tell her everything would be okay. I wanted to let her know, she didn't have to fight anymore because I was there to protect her. Her body language stopped me. I had to keep reminding myself that she wasn't like the rest of the women that I'd been involved with. The same rules didn't apply.

"I'm sorry. I didn't mean to rush you." I wasn't in the habit of apologizing for stuff I didn't do. I didn't know what else to say, so I said nothing.

She snatched the rest of the bags from my hands and walked toward the home. I watched her stomp off, my heart thumping wildly, in tune with the clicking of her heels. I wasn't sure if I'd ever see her again. She opened the door, flipped on the lights and slammed the door. Shaking my head, I stood rooted in place, wondering what the fuck had just happened. I thought if I waited long enough, the answer would come. I only had to be quiet enough to hear it.

"Nothing," I shook my head, quietly laughing at my own foolishness. As much as I wanted to help Jordan, I couldn't do it if, she fights me every step of the way. As I was about to pull away, I heard a door open. I looked up and saw her tiny figure running to catch me.

She whispered, "Max told me these pills I have to take will me better, but sometimes I think they are driving me insane. I can't help it. One minute I'm up and the next, I just don't know. I keep getting this feeling I'm fucking up with you. I am, aren't I?"

"Well, I wouldn't have said it like that." My daddy didn't raise no fool. If I'd have said yeah, our whole conversation would be a wrap and I didn't want it to end, at least not on bad terms.

Jordan stepped back from my car. "You said we were going driving." She said it in a manner that made me feel as if it were my fault that we didn't do it. *Had she forgotten telling me she needed to get home?*

I bit back my gut response before the words could escape my lips. "I know, but since we got such a late start, I didn't want you to miss curfew."

"Okay. I really wanted to make sure you didn't drive away mad."

"I'm not mad at you, Jordan. I don't think there's anything that you could do that would make me mad at you."

"I hope you're right. I can be a handful sometimes. I even drive myself nuts," she said laughing.

"Thanks again, for bringing me home. I'm going to study for my test tonight and maybe, by Friday, you can take me to get my license." She leaned in the car and gave me a slight kiss on the cheek.

"Yeah, sure. Just call me."

"If you get the chance, don't forget to check into the home for me. If I'm gonna be spending a lot of time with you, I can't be worried about no curfew. Bye now."

Just when I was about to give up hope, she left me feeling encouraged. I smiled all the way home.

CHAPTER TWENTY-SEVEN

LAWRENCE MAXWELL

I walked through the empty administrative offices of Northwest Georgia Regional Hospital. Almost all of the staff was let go after the stinging expo by Brody. The hospital was plagued with suicides and unexplained deaths. The medical team allegedly used medication as a chemical retardant. Most of this occurred before my time. I was brought in to clean up the mess. Case in point: Jordan Bree.

Of course, I wasn't told any of this prior to my taking the job with the hospital. I was looking to close my private practice and take a more lucrative position, with seemingly less stress. However, that was not the case. The hospital blamed their woes on understaffing. They neglected to mention the federal push to close all facilities dedicated to mental health. I was duped. Now, I was the last physician standing in the now defunct hospital. Mine was the face of disgrace. I had to evaluate the remaining patients and make the tough decisions on what to do with them, now that the hospital was closed. The problem was I wasn't a facilitator. My passion and dedication was to the patients. I wanted what was best for them, even if it didn't bode well for the hospital.

"Fuck!" I threw a file I'd been reviewing on my desk and sat down. I didn't expect to feel anything for these people so quickly. However, that was not the case. Forty-eight case files littered my desk. All of them had been institutionalized, in my opinion, without proper evaluation or treatment. Drugged for compliance sake, they were forgotten by a social justice system that put them there. It was utterly disgraceful. Jordan was lucky; she had garnered the attention of the world. Eleven patients remained, and I had to figure out what to do with them.

I was not a fan of the immediate push towards group housing for the patients. I'd seen very little proof that these homes offered a better alternative to hospitals. They may have been viable options for those patients living with mild psychiatric problems but the chronic conditions presented a bigger problem. This was why I opted to thoroughly evaluate each of the remaining patients before making my decision. In order to do it, I had to decrease their medications. This presented a challenge, since I was the only doctor left on staff.

Phyllis, one of the attending nurses, knocked on my door. "Dr. Maxwell, you didn't secure the patient in bed five. Should I put her in restraints?"

I felt a surge of anger. "For what? Has she done anything to warrant restraints?"

"I, uh, no. Not really. I was only thinking, as a matter of precaution."

"That won't be necessary, Nurse Phyllis. From now on, restraints will be our last resort, not our first. As long as the patient doesn't exhibit any sign of distress, you should only monitor her."

"What if she gets up and starts wandering the halls? What should I do then?"

"Call me. I'm not going anywhere. I'll be right here going over these records."

"Very well Doctor. If you're sure that's what you want. I might be able to handle two or three of them wandering around, but you're about to wake 'em all up. If you ask me, you are just asking for trouble."

I was seized with doubts. I wasn't absolutely sure I was making the right decisions, but I had to start somewhere. I sighed in frustration. "Nurse, do you know where the rest of the patients' records are kept?"

"The rest, sir?"

"Some of these patients have been here for several years. These files only contain about ten or twenty sheets of paper. Surely there has to be more?"

"I wouldn't know, Doctor."

"How long have you been at this hospital?" I was trying very hard to keep the irritation out of my voice. Ever since I started working at the hospital, I felt like I had to tiptoe around both the patients and the staff. Dealing with the remaining staff was proving to be more difficult than the patients.

"Four, about to be, five years," she answered warily.

"Then you would be the most senior person here, right?"

"I guess." I could tell she was uncomfortable with my questions. In order for me to do my job, I needed her cooperation. "Do you have any idea why you were allowed to stay, while some of your counterparts were dismissed?" I took off my glasses and tossed them on my desk.

"Honestly, I don't know," she snorted.

"I do. I asked them to keep you because I thought you would be the most likely person to work with me, not against me."

"Can I speak truthfully?"

"Yes, of course," I answered, guardedly.

"While I appreciate the opportunity to stay a few more weeks, I'm not trying to risk my life to do it. The only thing you did for me was postpone the inevitable. I need to find another job, so if it's all the same to you, you can let me go now. I can start my unemployment that much sooner."

I didn't expect the rancor I heard in her voice. "Wow, maybe I don't know what I'm doing. I thought I knew people and you impressed me as someone who cared. I wasn't the one who created this mess. When I took this job, I had no idea what I was walking into. I called myself taking a job down south to chill. Ha, I guess the joke is on me."

"The big difference between me and you is you'll be able to move forward without skipping a beat. I'll be on that unemployment line, excuse my analogy, scratching like a dog with fleas."

"Don't you think I want to throw my hands up in the air and walk away too? What makes you think I won't be behind you in that same unemployment line? In case you haven't noticed, people think treating mental health patients is a luxury, not a necessity. Most psychiatrists in private practice aren't thriving in this economy."

There was a knock on the door. "Uh, Dr. Maxwell, there's a Brody Mason here to see you," one of the secretaries said. Nurse Phyllis saw her opportunity to leave and took it.

"Fuck." I was about to send him away, when he barged into my office. It had been a long day and the last thing I wanted to do was get into a sparring match with him. "How dare you barge in my office like a bull in a china shop?" This man had a lot of nerve.

"Because I knew that was the only way you were going to see me." Brody extended his hand in greeting.

I looked at his extended hand with disgust. I'd yet to forgive him for his involvement with Jordan. There was no way I was going to shake his hand like all was forgotten. "I'm a busy man. What do you want?" Brody was way too cocky for my taste. I had already said everything I needed to say to him. Nevertheless, I was curious as to why he was there.

Brody came in, shut the door and took a seat in the chair opposite my desk. "I really need some advice, off the record."

"Why me? Don't you have someone else to torment?" I had pretty much accepted the fact Jordan had chosen him over me. That didn't mean I wanted anything more to do with him.

"Because, regardless of how you feel about me, I know you still care about Jordan."

"What's wrong?" Fear sieged my heart. I hadn't seen or talked to her since the night she broke my heart, a few weeks ago.

"I saw Jordan the other night. Since you accused me of not thinking about the bigger picture, I need your opinion about something she asked me."

"Oh, now you want to ask my opinion? That's rich," Max said, the sarcasm oozing from his voice.

"Come on, man, it's been over three weeks. Van you let this go? I probably shouldn't tell you this, but it only happened once. I hope that makes you feel better."

In a twisted kind of way, it did. I smiled for the first time since he entered my office. "What's going on?" He had my undivided attention.

"Have you spoken with Jordan?"

"Not since that night. She never answers when I call."

"She's making plans to move out of the home. Her six months are almost up. She wants to get her license and I agreed to take her tomorrow."

"So what do you need my opinion on? It seems like you've got things under control."

"That's not the issue I wanted to discuss with you. She already knew how to drive. She only needs me to take her to get the license."

"Indulge me for a minute. I'm still trying to figure out how you got in contact with Jordan anyway. The day she was released from the hospital, you came by here asking where she went. Next thing I know, y'all all chummy." My guard was up. I was lulled into a false sense of comfort by Brody before when he told me he didn't know where Jordan was. I was still pissed, but I tried not to let it show.

"I know you'd like to believe I chased her down, but we really did meet again by accident."

No fucking way. I didn't believe for one moment that he randomly found her. He must think I'm stupid as hell. "Imagine that. What are the odds?"

"I swear that's how it happened. I was at the Sweet Auburn Festival and this girl passed out and stopped breathing. I helped her until the paramedics arrived. Since I was there, I went to the hospital just to make sure she made it. I ended up taking her home the next day. The girl lived in the same home as Jordan."

Brody was grinning his ass off. I just wanted to reach across the desk and punch him in the throat. No doubt about it, he was one lucky son of a bitch. "Wow, that's pretty amazing. So she called you after you dropped the girl off?"

"Yeah, pretty much. When you told her about remembering to forget, she called me."

I didn't like Jordan discussing anything I said with Brody. Not only was he a threat with his pen, I still believed he used her to get what he wanted. "Chances are she's going to remember anyway without any help from you. It would be better for her, in my opinion, if she recalled those events in a controlled environment, on her terms."

He nodded his head as he appeared to digest what I was saying to him. "Well, she went through both our notes, after she saw the DVD. I actually thought she would stop looking but apparently, that's not the case."

"Why is that a problem? She's going to remember eventually. If you have some information she needs to know, by all means, show it to her."

Brody seemed pensive. "I'm not worried about my notes, they are pretty straight forward. She keeps on harping on the DVD's. That's what has me worried. She might need to talk to someone about it. In the event she does, I wanted to know if you would be there for her."

"I haven't seen the DVD's. If I had, maybe I would see the significance of all your concern."

"Dude, the video went viral. Jordan taunted this old lady on the bus and the lady snapped on her. She was wrong but she didn't act alone. If you want to see it, all you have to do is Google it."

"The tape I saw showed only Jordan."

"Oh, maybe you didn't see the second one. Now that I think about it, it may have been removed."

"What's on the tape?" Now he made me curious. I wanted to see the damn tape too but wasn't about to ask him for it.

"This fucking bitch kicked Jordan when she was down. I mean, kicked the shit out of her several times. Pisses me off every time I see it."

"What girl? I didn't see no girl. I just saw the woman and the bus driver trying to control Jordan."

Brody got up and started pacing before my desk. It was like he was working up to a dramatic overture. I wanted him to tell me the story without the theatrics.

"I haven't spoken to Jordan about this, so I can only assume this person was a friend. I don't know who took the video but Jordan was standing off to the side talking to this girl. The girl said something to Jordan. The next thing I see is Jordan going off on the lady. The lady brandishes a cane and proceeds to whip the crap out of Jordan."

"I saw all that." Brody was pissing me off.

"Wait, let me finish. When Jordan fell, the girl she was speaking to ran up behind Jordan and started stomping her. If you could see the girl's face, it was personal. This chick was all up in the mix but she didn't testify in court."

"I'm confused."

"The other girl, her name is Aaryn Chattem, she was also teasing the lady but she was edited out of the viral video. In this second video, it was a group of kids, just fucking with folks on the bus."

"Are you kidding me? Why wasn't this brought up at Jordan's trial."

"That was the basis of my article against the state. Jordan wasn't given adequate counsel, and given her mental state, she didn't dispute the charges. The way I see it, all of them should have been charged with disorderly conduct. Jordan took the blame for everything."

"How did you find out about the tape?"

"A random search on chaos on buses. I looked at hundreds until I found it."

"You must have had a lot of time on your hands."

"I believe in being thorough. I figured if there was one tape, there might be more. Hell, even the onboard video from the bus showed the other students involved but they weren't shown in court either. Jordan really got railroaded."

"She carries around a lot of guilt from that day. This would in no way excuse her behavior, but it does explain it. Probably, peer pressure."

"I was thinking the exact same thing."

I shook my head. "If she wants to talk to me about it, I'll make myself available to her."

Brody smiled. "I was hoping you would say that. If she doesn't feel comfortable talking to me, I am going to make sure she speaks to you. I really do believe she needs to talk to someone about it."

"Need I remind you that I'm the professional here?" I couldn't stand this man.

"Pump the brakes, Max. If I didn't respect your opinion, I wouldn't be here."

I stood up. "Yeah, well thanks for coming by." I walked over to the door and held it open for him.

"Oh, okay. Thanks for your time."

He didn't look too happy when he left but I could care less. I felt confident Jordan would seek me out, and when she did, I'd be ready to make my move.

CHAPTER TWENTY-EIGHT

BRODY MASON

I was smiling from ear to ear. "Well?"

"Well, what?" Jordan asked as she got into my car and put on her seatbelt.

"How does it feel to have your license? You made up your mind what you wanted to do and you did it." She was so nonchalant; I couldn't get a read on her.

"I guess it still feels the same. It ain't no big deal."

"The hell it ain't a big deal! When I first got my license, you couldn't tell me shit. I thought I was the man," I said laughing.

"Well, maybe I would feel differently, if I was driving. With me in the passenger seat and you driving, it feels the same."

"You can drive if you want to. This is your day."

She seemed to think about it for a few seconds. A slow smile spread across her face. It was moments like this that I cherished. I started to undo my belt.

"I don't want to drive your car. I want to drive my own."

"Wow, for real. You ready to make that step?"

She nodded her head vigorously, her expression hopeful. Seeing her like this made me realize how much I'd grown to love her. I'd do anything to make sure she had something to smile about. "What kind of car do you want?" I already knew she didn't want a CRV. She'd made it perfectly clear.

"I always wanted to have an Audi convertible, preferably, white."

"You ain't playing are you? Do you want to go look at one now?"

"Can we?" She clapped her hands excitedly, looking like a little kid at Christmas.

"Sure, we can. If that's what you want to do." I pulled out my iPhone and asked Siri to locate the nearest dealer. Once I had the directions, we took off. I was a little nervous about guiding her in taking such a big step. I had to keep reminding myself she was a grown woman. "Are you thinking about a new or used car?" I asked to pass the time.

"Definitely new. I don't want to inherit someone else's problems."

"Do you have any idea how much those babies cost?" I was sure she'd get a reality check as soon as we got booted off the lot. Then, we could go right down the street to the Toyota dealer for a more sensible purchase.

"Not really. I have always wanted one ever since I saw NeNe, from The Real Housewives of Atlanta, driving one."

I wasn't going to be the one to bust her bubble. Some of those housewives had long paper. "Why a convertible? You wanna feel the wind rushing through your hair?" I was trying to keep the conversation light-hearted, to displace some of the misgivings I was having.

"No," she said pouting.

"Did I say something wrong?" I was concerned.

"I think you're making fun of me."

"No I'm not. I've heard a lot of people who have bought convertibles say that. Two months later, they almost never put the tops down."

"So you think I'll get bored with it? Is that what you're saying?"

"It shouldn't be the reason why you want a particular car. When you buy a car, there are a lot of things to consider. Such as mileage, value retention, road safety, dependability and insurance rates. What a car looks like, should be the least of your concerns. I'm not saying you should get a 'family car', but you need to keep those things in mind when shopping for a vehicle."

"I never thought about it that way. I appreciate your 'schooling me'. Which kind of car would you recommend for me that fit those criteria?"

If she wanted me to tell her, I had no problem sharing my knowledge. However, I wanted it to be her choice. Last thing I needed was for her to come back at me later and blame me for ruining her dream. She seemed to be truly interested, so I gave her my views. "In my opinion, Toyota's retain their value. They have been ranked among the highest in safety and their repairs won't break the bank. Honda's are also good cars."

"What if you had millions of dollars? Would you still pick the same cars?"

"Honestly, I probably would. But, I'd also have a play car, like an Aston Martin, to kick it in."

"Maybe I will get a Toyota. Do they have convertibles?"

"Nonsense, we're here now. I wasn't trying to get you to change your mind. If this is the car you see yourself in, then you should get it. At least now, you can make an informed decision."

"Brody, I respect your opinion."

"Well, some people say, opinions are like assholes,everyone has one. I want you to follow your heart. As long as you are not getting the car to impress people. That would be asinine because if you have to impress someone in order for them to like you, they will most likely be the very people trying to use you. The one thing you have to remember, since you have money, someone is going to try to use you. It's just a matter of time and a matter of who it's going to be. If you're careful, you'll be fine. One other thing before we go in, don't let this salesman try to sell you the first car you see. And no matter what happens, don't accept his first offer."

"Wow, this is so confusing. Will you help me?"

"Of course I will. I'm going to pretty much let you handle it, but if I say walk away, follow my lead. I'm not about to let anyone punk you."

***

"So are you happy now, Miss Big Time Car Owner? I haven't heard a peep out of you, since you signed your name on the dotted line. How does this feel?"

"Oh, it's nice. I love it. I still can't believe I actually got it."

"Truth be told, I can't believe you got it either. When that guy said sixty-eight thousand dollars, I almost choked. I knew these cars were expensive but I didn't know it would be that much. These days, you can almost get a house for that amount. While I was spitting and gagging at the price, you didn't even bat an eye. It was classic. You really impressed me with the way you haggled down the price since you were paying cash. You really didn't need my help after all. "

"If you hadn't warned me before we went in, I probably would have paid full price. I might be new to money but it ain't new to me. Thanks for your help."

"So what do you want to do now?" I knew what I wanted to do but I certainly wasn't going to suggest it.

"You want to go for a ride?"

It wasn't exactly what I had in mind, but I'd take it. I was happy to be spending time with her. "Why not? I like new car smells too. But first, I need to drop off my car. Will you follow me to my house?"

"Sure, I'll probably beat you there."

"Be careful, you haven't gotten insurance yet. You don't want to get a ticket the first day you get your license."

"Spoil sport. I'll be careful." She playfully answered.

As I drove to my house, I couldn't help but to wonder what Max would think about this. Would he accuse me of influencing her in this decision as well? It was obvious Jordan got a lot of money from her settlement with the state. The fact that she didn't even blink when the salesman quoted her the price, hipped me to that. I wasn't mad. She deserved nice things. I also had to admit, she did look good in that car.

I got in her car and buckled up. I thought I was going to feel cramped in her two-seater but it was surprisingly roomy for a sports car. "You gonna pop the top?"

"And mess up my hair? I don't think so," she said laughing. "Where would you like to go?" Her excitement was contagious.

"Doesn't really matter, I just want to fill my lungs with the smell of plastic and leather."

"You're too funny."

"Since this is your day, you pick the place."

"How much time do you have?"

"I'm at your disposal. I don't have a job, remember?" I chuckled. Jordan pursed her lips and I worried that she didn't get my humor.

"Have you ever been to Helen, Georgia? I went there on a field trip with my school. I always said I wanted to go back during this time of year to see the leaves change color."

"It's a short trip. I think we can do it. I wouldn't have figured you to be a nature buff."

"Why you trying to figure me out?" She stopped the car in the middle of the street, as her whole demeanor changed.

"Awe, man. Don't trip on me, girl. It was just a figure of speech." Her personality disorder was exactly what I was afraid of when she mentioned getting a car. If she were going to nut up, I'd prefer she not do it while we were in the car.

"Ain't nobody tripping. I was just asking a question." She resumed driving.

"Asking a question is one thing, but you can't be stopping in the middle of the street like that. You could cause an accident. You know folks don't be paying attention all that well. Some of them texting and talking on the phone. All it takes is for one of them not to have their mind on the road—"

"Okay Brody, I get it. It won't happen again."

She turned the satellite radio on, keeping time with the music. I breathed a sigh of relief. Potential crisis avoided. I inhaled deeply, as if my very life depended on it. As she merged her car onto the freeway, she was smiling.

"I was always fascinated by the change of seasons. We didn't have many trees where I grew up." Her voice sounded wistful.

"If that's the case, then I'm glad I'm here to share it with you. I'm not much of a nature buff. In fact, to me, the only good leaf is one still stuck on a tree. Obviously, you've never had to spend the entire weekend raking up leaves only to have them fall back down again."

"Well, no. I can't say I have. However, it still doesn't take away from the beauty of it all."

"You're right. I just never looked at it that way."

"Tell me about yourself, Brody. I don't know anything about you."

"What do you want to know?"

"When did you start writing?"

"In college, mostly. I mean, I did some short stories when I was a kid but they never really amounted to anything. I always told myself I'd write a book. Although I haven't gotten around to it yet, it's still a dream of mine."

"What are you waiting for?"

"I have a short attention span. I've got to find something that keeps my attention for more than a week or two."

"I hope you're not writing a book about me?" She turned and gave me a searching look.

"No, why would you think that?"

She shrugged her shoulders. "Maybe because I've kept your attention for longer than two weeks."

This was it…my shit or get off the pot moment where I tell her exactly how I feel about her. The question was, would I be a man and put it all on the line, or would I punk out and say something stupid. The seconds ticked while I contemplated how I was going to play it. "Jordan, you are not book material."

"What do you mean by that? I'm not exciting?"

I couldn't tell if she was relieved or disappointed. Tiny butterflies fluttered in my stomach. It was a trick question and I knew it. I could be screwed, either way it went.

"If I were to write about you, trust me, it would be a fantastic story." I felt like I dodged a bullet.

"Oh yeah? How so?"

"Aw, man, do I have to?" I could feel the sweat popping on my brow. She must have sensed my trepidation.

"Do you have any sisters or brothers, Brody?"

This was seemly a safe topic, which I didn't hesitate to answer. "Yeah, I have two brothers and a sister."

"Did y'all get along?" She was doing about seventy miles an hour.

"My sister was a pain in the ass, but we got along."

I felt a surge in speed as Jordan's foot pressed against the gas pedal and her fingers tightened around the steering wheel. "Why would you call your sister a pain in the ass? That's rude."

Luckily, the mid-day traffic was light. "'Cause she was. She tried to be the boss of me just because she was older. She never let me get away with anything."

"But she loved you right?" Jordan inquired, as her fingers gripped the steering wheel even tighter.

My eyes kept darting from her, to the road, as I attempted to remain calm. "Yeah, she loved me. She'd do anything for me." I said, smiling. I hadn't seen my sister in a couple of years and talking about her reminded me that it was my turn to make the call.

"What about your sister? Are you close?"

"No. Not really." Jordan flexed her fingers on the steering wheel, staring straight ahead. Her lips were pressed together, as if she were thinking about something deeply intellectual. The air inside the car was charged.

"Then you were lucky. My sister trashed my cigarettes and threw away all my porno magazines."

Jordan laughed, her foot easing off the gas. "You know you shouldn't have been smoking anyway."

"I had a mother. I didn't need two." I feigned anger with my sister. I liked to complain about her but I appreciated my sister's efforts.

Jordan's hands clinched again. I could tell she was being affected by our talk about family. It wasn't fair. I knew she didn't have any fond memories to make her smile. All she had inside was pain and rejection.

"What about a dad? Did you have one of those too?"

I wasn't oblivious to Jordan's growing agitation. I didn't talk much about myself and while I enjoyed our thought provoking conversation, it was taking a toll on Jordan.

"Are you sure you want to talk about this? We could talk about something else or just listen to the music."

"I want to listen, Brody. I never get to listen."

I sighed. "My father was a hot mess. You would have liked him."

"Would have? Did he leave you too?"

"He died." I turned my head and looked out the window. We were getting up in the mountains and the trees were really beautiful.

Jordan gasped, "I'm sorry. I didn't know."

"Don't worry about it. You couldn't have known. He's in a better place, so I'm cool." This was a patent response that I gave, anytime someone spoke of my father's passing. It wasn't something that I actually believed but it appeared to make others feel better about mentioning him.

"Do you really believe that or are you just saying it?" Jordan's insight was uncanny. Either she was very perceptive, or I was a horrible liar.

"Does it make a difference?" I wasn't trying to be flippant, despite how it may have sounded.

"I heard that. Don't mind me, I'm just trying to make conversation."

"Hey, did your ears just pop?" I asked, as I wiggled my earlobes.

"Yeah, I thought it was just me. That shit hurts a little bit."

"Keep your mouth open. It should help relieve the pressure."

"Keep my mouth open? For how long?" She took her eyes off the road for a second and stared at me.

"I don't know; until it stops I guess."

"You're making this up. How is keeping my mouth open going to help my ears?"

"Have your ears popped again? Your mouth has been open the entire time, so you tell me if it worked." She stole another look at me and smiled. I could tell by her smile it had stopped. "Is that a smile I'm seeing?"

"What?" Jordan cheesed harder.

"There, on your face. I do believe I see a genuine smile."

"I doubt that. I don't smile much."

"Well, you should because it takes my breath away when you do."

"Yeah, right," Jordan sarcastically said.

"I'm serious, Jordan; you have a beautiful smile. Why do you hide it?"

"Because I don't have a whole lot to smile about." Her smile turned into a frown.

"Nonsense. You woke up this morning, right? Everybody can't say that."

"Those that can't are dead. So what are you saying?"

"You know good and well what I mean. Don't try to play like you don't understand me."

"So, I should smile all day because I woke up from last night?"

She kept looking from me to the road, which was scary because the roads should have been commanding all of her attention. She was still a new driver and these steep hills were a bit intimidating, even to me. I tried not to let her see how nervous I was.

"No, not exactly but it's a start. I wake up smiling, period. Then I look for other things to keep it going. Like my first cup of coffee, a warm sticky bun and a beautiful lady."

"I can get with the coffee, maybe even a sticky bun but ladies don't do anything for me," Jordan said laughingly.

"What about a sexy man?" I pumped my arms like a body builder, hoping to impress her.

Jordan giggled. It was refreshing, since I never recalled her doing it before. The sound not only surprised me, but I think it surprised her too. "See there. You found your happy. Hey, wait. Pull over. Don't you want to check out the view?" We'd reached the lookout point for vehicles to pull safely off the road to see the mountain trees. She smoothly pulled her car off the road and cut the engine.

I opened my door and came around and opened the door for her. Her hands were shaking a little bit when I grabbed them. We walked to the railing, arm in arm. Together, we gazed at the mountains and the sea of colors before us.

"Breathtaking, isn't it?" Jordan asked.

"Yes. When I was a little boy my father used to take me and my brother camping in woods much like this." At the time, we hated it. Now that I'm older, I can appreciate what he was trying to show us."

"What was he trying to show you?"

"That he didn't know a damn thing about camping but he wasn't afraid to try. He damn near set those woods on fire. He took us out there with kerosene instead of lighter fluid. Scared them white folks camping in the woods half to death. They were yelling, 'them niggas trying to burn up the forest.'"

I could almost feel Jordan's mood shift. She pulled her hand from mines. "You ready to go?" Jordan turned to go back to her car.

"Wait, what's wrong?"

"Nothing. We came to see the leaves. We saw them. Now we can go."

I was not about to let this opportunity pass. "Something happened to turn that smile upside down. Tell me." I folded my arms across my chest, with my back resting against the railing. Although Jordan was looking right at me, I could tell she wasn't seeing me.

"There's nothing to tell. Besides, I'd hate to think about what you would say about me in another one of your stories."

Icy slithers of dread crept up my spine. Something happened to our beautiful sunny day and it felt like a dreary cloud was looming overhead. "Jordan, you can't be serious. I already told you, I wouldn't write a story about you. Do you honestly think I'm spending time with you because I want to write another story?"

Jordan yanked her hand back from the car and marched back over to me. I could tell she was fuming but I didn't understand why. "What do you want from me?"

Her eyes held me captive. Her lips had me enslaved. I wanted nothing more than to take her in my arms and suckle her plump lips. I chose my words carefully. "I want to see you smile." Her look of confusion tore at my heart strings. I knew she was young and inexperienced, but her eyes were old and tortured. My common sense told me to get as far away from her as I could get, but my heart wanted to protect her from the cruelties of the world. She folded like a marionette, whose strings were cut. I caught her limp body before she could hit the ground. I carried her back to the car, placing her in the passenger seat. Her reaction scared me. She offered no objection to my driving her car. She sat with a rigid torso, as her head lulled to the side.

"Jordan, I hope you are listening to what I'm about to say to you. You've spent most of your life hiding from people whose sole intent was to hurt you. That was your past. It is not your future. You need to make a list of all those people, write them down, so you won't forget and mentally tell all those fuckers to catch fire. Then I want you to lock that list away, and never dwell on it again. Just as I told you there are going to be people in your life that will try to use and abuse you, I am also telling you I am not one of them. Do you hear what I'm saying to you?"

Jordan remained in the same position she was in when I first placed her in the car. I couldn't tell if she heard me or not. Uncertain what I should do next, I drove her home with me. Consulting Max was out of the question. This was a fragile moment and I didn't want to risk her breaking down at the home. I'd rather she do it with me. I could only pray I made the right decision.

CHAPTER TWENTY-NINE

JORDAN BREE

As difficult as it was to process, I heard everything Brody was saying to me. After he bought me home, it took me two full days to get up the courage to start working on my list. Sitting at my makeshift desk, sipping lukewarm coffee, I carefully crafted a list of people who could, in Brody's words, 'catch fire'. As much as I wanted to forget everything that had happened to me prior to my release from the hospital, I couldn't. Now that the list was finished, I had to find a way to let it go. All the yelling, crying and stomping I did while making the list, didn't take away the pain or anger.

I grabbed the list off my desk and drove over to Brody's house, without calling. I pounded on his door until he answered. He stood at the door, naked from the waist up. A brown towel was wrapped low on his hip. Water glistened off his muscles. I swallowed hard.

"Writing this list has to be the dumbest shit I've ever done in my life. How is making this ridiculous list going to make me feel any better? What I really want to do is punch the shit out of somebody." I pushed past his beautiful body and walked inside.

"Good morning to you too."

Even though I wasn't looking at Brody's face, I could tell he was smiling. He was always smiling. Perhaps that was why I had a hard time taking him seriously. "I'm glad one of us finds this situation funny, 'cause it sure ain't me."

"Who said I thought anything was funny?"

"Aren't you smiling?" I demanded.

"Well, yeah, I guess I am," Brody admitted.

"Then obviously you find something humorous."

"Jordan, I can smile without laughing. That's not the only reason to smile. Don't you ever just smile because you feel good? Haven't you ever heard it takes more muscles to frown than it does to smile?"

"Well, I'm exercising them, because I'm pissed the fuck off. You said this stupid list was going to make me feel better. You lied to me. I should have known better than to listen to your stupid ass."

Brody laughed long and hard. "Why I got to be a stupid ass? I never said making the list would make you feel better. What I said was, once you make the list, the people on it could never hurt you because you will know who they are. But, it only works if you're willing to let them go.

"What's going to stop them from coming after me again?"

"They can't come for you unless you send for them, Jordan. You're not a child anymore and you're certainly not defenseless. Everything that happens to you, from now on, should be of your own making. You don't have to rely on anyone to do anything for you because you can do those things for yourself. Don't you see the power in that? If you don't like the way things are going, you have the ability to change it and do something different."

I didn't know how I felt about what Brody was saying. On the one hand, he was making a lot of sense. On the other, I felt like he gave me way too much credit. I was afraid I didn't have the strength he thought I had. On the outside, I might look like an adult, but on the inside, where it mattered, I was still very much a child.

"Why do I have to put the list away? Why can't I hang it up on the wall as a reminder?"

"No, you have to put the list away. Burn it if it makes you feel better. Whatever you do, don't put it up on the wall, like a badge or banner. Then, it can still have the power to hurt you. By burning the list, you relinquish its power over you."

Brody made a good argument but it still sounded stupid to me. I tucked the list back in my purse. "Okay, I'll try it your way. I'm sorry I can't stay. I've got some things I need to take care of. Did you have any luck finding out anything about the home? I want to talk to Lacy today to see if she wants to blow the joint with me." I was doing my best not to look in Brody's direction. He was still dripping, making it difficult for me to concentrate.

"Yeah, I did. It doesn't look like there are any court related documents or orders requiring Lacy to reside in the home. You were right about Mrs. Gates owning the house. Therefore, it should be a matter of giving notice and leaving. Since you only have a few weeks left, I don't suspect you will have any problems."

"Good. I want to start looking for an apartment today. I'm going to stop back by the home and get Lacy. I'll catch you later." I got on my tippy toes and gave Brody a kiss.

"Um, I wish you could stay awhile," he said as he wrapped his arms around my waist, drawing me into him. I felt his nature rising. He was such a sexy man, I was tempted.

"Not today. Soon." I kissed him again and gently pulled away. Unexpectedly, I felt happy, and it worried me. I liked having Brody in my life. I liked the way he took the time to explain things to me without being condescending. I also liked the way he flipped my ass and made it sing.

***

I parked my car around the corner from the home and locked the doors. I was still getting used to having a car, and the novelty hadn't worn off yet. So far, I'd managed to keep it a secret but I planned on telling Lacy today, when I dropped the news on her about moving out.

When I was in my funk, she consistently came to my room to check on me. It was a lot more than I could say about the other women in the house. Even the RA's had kept their distance, which suited me just fine. I jogged back to the house, taking the stairs two at a time, till I got to Lacy's room. It was the first time I'd ever knocked on her door.

"What do you want?" She said when she snatched open the door. I could tell by the surprised expression on her face, I was the last person she expected to see. "Jordan, what's wrong? I came down to check on you after breakfast but you'd already left."

"Ain't nothing wrong. What are you doing?"

"Nothing. Ain't nothing to do in this bitch."

"Put some clothes on and go with me?"

"Where are we going?" Lacy asked smiling.

"Don't worry about it. Just get cute. I'm about to change too."

"Alright then. Give me about fifteen minutes. I already had my shower."

"Cool, I'll meet you downstairs." I quickly went to my room to change. We'd bought some really nice outfits when we went shopping a few weeks ago and some of them still had price tags on them. I was dressed in less than ten minutes and was waiting for Lacy at the door.

"Where you think you going all dressed up and stuff?" Keisha asked.

I was not about to let her nosy ass ruin my good mood. "Lacy and I are going to catch a movie and hang out at the mall."

"Humph, for two people who claim they don't like each other, you sure are spending a lot of time together."

"We're in a different space." I wasn't about to explain my relationship with Lacy to Keisha. Especially, when I didn't understand it myself. At one point, I actually hated Lacy.

"I'm really glad to hear it. You two are a lot alike. I always felt like it was such a shame that because of the fighting, you couldn't see it."

"Gee, thanks." Keisha surprised me. I expected her to hate on us like the rest of the ladies. She actually was being pretty nice. Lacy was all smiles as she came rushing down the stairs. She stopped mid-way when she noticed Keisha standing by the door.

"You ready?" I walked past Keisha and opened the door.

"Yeah. See you later Keisha."

"Y'all look nice. Have fun."

Lacy waited until we closed the gate and were down the sidewalk before she turned to me. "What the fuck was that?" she asked astonished.

"Girl, you got me. She was really being sweet; it was weird." We rounded the corner and stopped at my car. I opened the door and got in while trying to hide my smile.

"What the fuck are you doing? Are you out your mind?" Lacy was looking all wild-eyed, frantically motioning for me to get out of the car.

"Keep your voice down before someone calls the cops."

"Look, you're my girl and all, and I like to fuck with you but I'm not about to go to jail on no bullshit robbery job. I don't have no problems catching the bus." She folded her arms in front of her chest.

"Will you get your ass in the car?"

"No. I just got some freedom and you're trying to mess that all up. You must have forgotten your meds this morning. Now get your ass out this car before I have to drag you out."

"It's my car you idiot. Check the glove compartment if you don't believe me." I was holding up the keys, dangling them in her air.

"Shut the fuck up! When the hell did you get a car?"

"Do you like it? I got it a couple of days ago. I didn't want the rest of the girls to know. Put your seatbelt on."

Lacy did as I said, but she still hadn't shut her mouth. I felt like she really did want to check the glove compartment and was afraid to do it. "Girl, relax. I promise you it's all mine."

"Who are you? First you surprise me and take us to this swanky hair salon. Then, you splurge on a shopping spree and now this. If you're fucking a drug dude, can you hook me up with one of his workers?"

"I am not dating a drug dude. I came into some money and I wanted to share some of it with you." I wasn't ready to tell Lacy all of the gritty details as to how I'd come upon the money. It was still difficult to talk about.

"I knew you were a bad bitch the first time I laid eyes on you."

"If you want to remain friends, do not call me a bitch again. I hate that word. My mom used to call me that all the time."

"My mom used to call me a bitch too, especially when one of her men was trying to get in my pants. I don't even know why I still say it."

"It took me a while to stop saying it too. I still might slip up when someone pisses me off, but in general, there are so many other things I could call someone other than a bitch."

"So, where are we going?"

I stole a quick look at Lacy. She was finally looking more relaxed. "Apartment hunting?" I counted for two seconds before I stole another look at her. She was looking out the window. "Aren't you going to say something?"

"I don't know what you want me to say? I mean, I'm happy for you and shit."

"I hope you are happy for me. It would be pretty fucked up if you weren't."

"Forgive me for not doing fucking cartwheels." Lacy's lower lip was quivering.

"Are you about to cry? What the hell are you crying for?" I pulled the car into a McDonald's parking lot and shut off the engine.

"Because I'm going to miss your stank ass."

"You are not going to miss me."

"How the fuck you know how I'll be feeling?" She used the back of her hand to wipe her nose.

"Eww!" I got out of the car and ran into the restaurant and grabbed some napkins. "Don't you get that stuff on my leather seats."

"I could give a fuck about your seats right now. I think I'm going to get out here. I don't want to spoil your good day with my selfish behavior." Lacy reached for the handle and I could not continue with the pretense any longer.

"Will you please chill out? I asked you to come along with me because I want you to move in with me." She didn't respond right away and I was almost afraid she was going to tell me no.

"I don't think that's funny."

"Do I look like I'm laughing?"

"Are you serious?" A hint of a smile was beginning to blossom.

"I'm dead serious. If you want to, the offer is on the table."

"Wait, I almost got caught up in the hype. I ain't rolling like you seem to be. I can pay the rent at home, but unless I get a job, that's it."

This time, I was the one to get mad. "Did I ask you to pay any rent? Unless you have some secret reason for sticking it out in that hell hole, then I suggest you get with the program."

"And you're really, really serious?"

"I'm really, really serious. Now can we go?"

"Hell yeah! I can't wait to tell Mrs. Gates! She's gonna bust a blood vessel."

"Do me a favor. I have the list of apartments I want to check out in my purse. I need you to put the address in the navigation system."

"Damn, you got one of those two. This car is the shit." Lacy grabbed my purse off the backseat and began looking through it. She pulled out a weathered sheet of paper and unfolded it. "I don't see any addresses on this, wait, what is this?"

My heart nearly missed a beat. She was holding my bloody list. How could I have forgotten to put it away? Now I understood why Brody told me to burn it. Lacy didn't even know what it represented and it still hurt me that she found it. "It's nothing. That's not it. The addresses have to be in there somewhere. Dump the whole bag out if you have to."

"You are lying like a rug. If it were nothing, it wouldn't have what looks like tears stains on it and you wouldn't be fucking shaking right now."

"I really don't want to talk about it. Could you just put it away and find what I asked you to find?" At this point, I didn't feel like apartment hunting. The only thing I wanted to do was go back to the home and curl up in my bed.

"You don't have to get all huffy with me. I'll put the damn thing back." She shoved the paper back in my purse, zipped it and threw it in the back seat.

"Bitch, are you out your damn mind?" I pulled the car over again for an entirely different reason.

"Bitch? Oh, you mad now? Well I'm mad too. I told you, I fucks with you. That means I'm with you like pancakes with syrup. One don't go without the other. If you and I are going to be friends, that also means we got each other's backs. I can't have your back when you're keeping secrets. It ain't finna be that way. Not with me it ain't." She was breathing all fast. I thought she was about to bust her own blood vessel.

"Can we talk about this later?" I needed a chance to get myself together, and so did she.

"Alright then. We can do it later but I mean what I say."

CHAPTER THIRTY

LACY BATES

After the fight with Jordan, I didn't think either one of us really wanted to apartment shop. We had some issues to work through if this arrangement was going to work. The number one issue was trust. Unlike Jordan, I wasn't holding onto luggage from the past. My problems were pretty much clear cut. I sensed Jordan's water ran deeper. We were both diagnosed with the same illness, yet mine appeared to be under control, while she continued to have episodes.

Realistically, our friendship was doomed to fail if she didn't get a handle on what was causing her to zap out.

"Where do you want to have our talk?" We'd been riding around in circles for what felt like hours.

"I got to show you something first." I used my Bluetooth to access my phone. "Call Brody," she said.

"Oh shit, this car can do everything."

Jordan raised her fingers to her lips, signaling me to be quiet. After a few rings, Brody answered the phone.

"Hey, Jordan. What's up?"

"I have Lacy in the car. I wanted to ask you if we could come over. I want to show her the tape and I couldn't think of anywhere else to show it to her."

"That's not a problem. I got to run out for a while but I'll leave the key under the mat."

"Thanks, Brody. We're on our way. We should be there in about fifteen minutes."

"You got that man whipped." I said.

"Brody is not whipped. It's not like that. Brody and I are friends," she stated.

"With benefits, right? I heard you tell that guy, Max, that you'd lost your virginity to him. I almost felt sorry for Max."

"It's complicated."

I was impressed. I had yet to find one man, let alone two, who expressed an interest in me, other than, my mother's boyfriends. Truth be told, I wasn't ready for the headache. Maybe once I got settled, I'd change my mind. For the moment, I was content. We didn't talk for the remainder of the ride to Brody's house. You could feel the tension in the air.

When we got to his apartment, Jordan found the key and let us in. She immediately went to his mini bar and poured herself a drink. This was when I realized that whatever it was she was going to tell me, was serious.

"Wait, don't I get a drink to?"

"Brody might get upset; he doesn't like for me to drink either. If you fix one, make it quick since I don't know when he is coming back."

I wasn't about to pass up an opportunity to have a drink. Now that I knew it was a possibility that we were moving, I wasn't as worried about getting kicked out the house. "You know you have me nervous, don't you? Whatever it is you have to tell me, it can't be that bad."

"For you maybe. It's hard for me to talk about this. You know there's a whole lot about you that I don't know either."

"I don't have a problem telling you about me. What do you want to know?"

"We can do that later. I need to show you this DVD. Since we don't have access to a television that we can privately watch, I brought you here. I'm nervous, therefore, the drink. It's not easy for me to open up and share. Jordan curled up on the couch with her feet under her. With her drink in her hand, she pressed play on the remote.

I asked, "What are we looking at?" She was being very mysterious.

"I'll explain it as we go."

"Jordan, turn around so we can see your face."

"Wait, is that you over there?" I jumped up from my seat on the floor and pointed at one of the people on the video. She was a fat little girl but I heard someone call her Jordan.

"Yeah, that's me."

"You were a little butterball weren't you?"

"Watch it, Lacy." I could hear the warning in her voice.

"My bad. I wish I had videos of me when I was a little girl. You wouldn't be able to recognize me either. That doesn't even look like you. What are y'all doing?"

"It's the last day of school and we're waiting for the train." Jordan's emotionless voice was a little alarming.

"At least you have a lot of friends. I didn't have any friends when I was going to school." I went back to sitting on the floor.

"Those weren't my friends. This was the one and only time that they ever paid me any attention. I was so young and dumb; I didn't even recognize what they were doing."

On the video, when the train came, Jordan was huddled in a group of teens who appeared to be whispering.

"Uh oh, y'all look like you're up to no good." The camera followed them onto the train.

"They were. I didn't even know someone recorded this."

"What you mean? You were looking right at the camera, boo. Look right there, it looks like you're striking a pose."

"I wasn't posing for this camera. My 'friends' said we were going to make a video on the train. We were going to put on a show. You know how they got them cameras installed on all the trains now."

"Yeah, but why?"

"I wish I knew what I was thinking that day…"

Jordan began chanting, a stupid ditty in this little old black lady's face. The lady looked to be in her late sixties or early seventies. She had short, gray hair, which peeked out of a ratty knitted hat. The other teens repeated Jordan's words. "Put your shirt in your mouth and sit on your head," Jordan chanted in her sing-song voice. She used her hands to keep time with her words.

The woman appeared to be trying to ignore Jordan and the other children. *"Go on and get away from me child,"* the woman turned around in her chair, putting her head down. The small crowd of students laughed, and encouraged Jordan to continue taunting the lady. "Go big or go home!" Someone else yelled. For a moment, Jordan paused.

I wasn't sure what I was looking at. "What does that mean? You look confused."

Jordan slurped her drink. "I was. Don't you see me trying to sit down?"

"Yeah, fuck you playing for?" Another boy shouted. The other students laughed. Jordan was off camera for a brief moment. Suddenly, Jordan jumped right in front of the camera. Sticking her face very close to the older woman, Jordan yelled. "Sit on your head, shirt in mouth and piss in your eyes ..."

The woman appeared to be frazzled. "What are you saying? Why don't you sit down somewhere and leave me alone?" The woman looked around at the other

passengers on the train. They appeared
not to notice or care what was going on.
Maybe they didn't want to get involved.
Jordan was clowning, looking right at the
camera. With her head mere inches from
the woman's face, Jordan shouted, "Balls
to the walls, bitch." Everyone laughed,
including Jordan.

To me, Jordan actually appeared to be proud of
herself. "Hold up. Can you pause this for a minute
because I am so lost?"

Jordan stopped the video and got up to fix herself
another drink. "Before you ask me a gazillion
questions, I have no idea what the fuck I was talking
about. All I knew was we were supposed to tease the
lady. I didn't even know what to say. I said anything
that came to my mind. At the time, I didn't think we
were doing anything wrong."

"That was some wack-ass shit. Y'all were bugging
out, big time. You're lucky you didn't get in any
trouble."

"You ain't seen the rest of the tape." Something
about the way she said this scared me. Jordan went
back to the sofa and pressed play. I could only watch
the rest with my mouth hanging down. Something
about the video seemed vaguely familiar.

The lady must have decided she'd had
enough. She grabbed her cane, which was
under her seat, and began beating Jordan
over the head. Jordan seemed surprised by
the attack. She tried to get out of the way
of the swinging stick but she had nowhere
to run. Those very same passengers, who

had previously ignored the situation, woke the fuck up and were blocking her escape. This ugly mob was cheering the old lady on but she didn't need or want their help.

"Didn't your momma ever tell you to respect your elders?" The woman emphasized each word with a wicked blow to Jordan's arms and legs.

Jordan looked frantic as she looked around. I assumed she was looking for her friends. I was not ready for what I saw next. Her friends had switched sides and were cheering the lady on. Jordan was crying as she fell to the floor. Her arms were wrapped protectively over her head while her friends kicked and stomped at her.

The train appeared to come to a sudden stop, pitching the belligerent woman in the air. Jordan got to her feet and rushed to the now opened doors. She didn't get far. Metro police was waiting for her. As she was being led away, one of her friends yelled, "See you on YouTube, bitch." They were laughing as they led her away.

Jordan cried softly on the sofa. For several moments, I continued to sit on the floor, stunned. I didn't know what I was expecting when she first started the tape but it wasn't this. Slowly, I rose from the floor and went to where Jordan was sitting. "Don't cry, boo. Don't cry." I was angry. I didn't like seeing my friends in handcuffs.

Between sniffs, Jordan told me the rest of the story. "Of course, I was arrested. They charged me with disorderly conduct."

"What happened to the rest of the people? I didn't see them in handcuffs."

"Nothing happened to them. The tape you saw wasn't even shown in court. Brody found this one. The tape they played in court only showed me acting an ass. My court appointed attorney tried to say I was crazy, so the judge sent me to a hospital for evaluation. That was almost five years ago."

I pushed Jordan away so I could see her face. "Are you fucking kidding me? That ain't right. How could they do that to you? Those other people were just as responsible as you were."

"They set me up. I didn't have no beef with that lady. I'd seen her a hundred times or more; never said a word to her, except for that day. Those kids knew I was desperate to fit in. I let them punk me into doing something stupid."

"Wow. I bet you beat the brakes off of them bitches when you got out."

"No I didn't. When I got out, I moved into the home."

"Fuck you mean? You said that was almost five years ago. They locked you up in jail for four years, for that?" I could not believe what I was hearing. This was some bullshit.

"Not jail. They left me in that mental institution the entire time. I was lost until Brody wrote a story about people just like me. That's where my money came from. I sued the state for wrongful imprisonment."

"What about your family? What did they say? What the fuck?"

"They ain't say shit. I didn't even talk to them until I got out. They didn't even show up in court."

"That's fucked up."

"You keep saying that, but it's true. I couldn't make this shit up if I tried. You see how I did free-styling," She attempted to laugh but it fell short.

"Yeah, you sucked big, black, donkey balls. I still can't believe this shit. I don't mean no harm but it seems like I have seen parts of this video before."

"You probably did. Brody said it went viral and was on all the television stations. That's how he found me, the video."

"Shut up. This is crazy. No wonder you two are so close. He really is a nice man." At that moment, I liked Brody even more than when I first met him.

"He is really trying to help me. The list you saw in my purse that was his idea. He told me to write down all the people in my life who had done me wrong. He said I should burn it when I was finished but I didn't."

"Oh. Now it's starting to make sense." My heart went out to Jordan. She'd been through some terrible shit in her life. Nothing compared to what I'd been through. If all of these things started as the result of something as innocent as a prank gone bad, how did it escalate into her losing five years of her life? The more I thought about it, the madder I got. Granted, Jordan was financially compensated but how did it compare to what she had lost?

"Well, now you know the gritty details. Are you going to hate me too?" Her voice was so low, I almost didn't hear her.

"I should punch you in your face right now. I told you how I get down. That there was some bullshit. Let's get out of here before Brody gets back and finds out we have been drinking. Maybe tomorrow we can go looking for that apartment."

Jordan took our glasses to the kitchen and washed them. "I'm going to brush my teeth, I'll be right back."

Watching the tape gave me some of the answers to the questions I had regarding who Jordan really was. I felt honored that she was comfortable enough with me to share it. It said a lot, especially when I recalled how bad our relationship was in the beginning. She hated me. I hated her.

CHAPTER THIRTY ONE

JORDAN BREE

"I am not believing this shit." I pounded my hand on the steering wheel.

"What?" Lacy looked around. "Did we leave something?"

"No. I think I just saw number three on my list, Aaryn Chattem."

"No shit? Where?"

"If it was her, she was just getting into a car behind me."

"Girl, turn this car around and make sure. Aren't you curious what the bitch is into?"

"I could care less. That chick can kiss my ass."

"Well, I want to see this bitch for myself. Can you please turn around? Let's at least see where she's going."

The woman was riding in a busted up blue, Ford Focus. Since she was right behind me, I had to think fast. Although it might not have been in my best interest, I took the next left, went around the block and came up behind her car.

"Is that her?"

"Yeah, I think so."

"Don't you want to be sure? You could be hating on a bitch that's already dead."

Her choice of words almost left me speechless. As weird as it sounded, I did want to know for my own sanity if this really was the witch that changed my life. "What should I do?"

"Follow her. If you let her get away, you might not ever know. Worst thing that happens we follow the wrong bitch." Lacy was perched on the edge of the seat, eagerly watching the car's tail lights.

"I hope I don't live to regret this."

"What is the harm in seeing if this is really her? I'm telling you, if you don't put this to rest, it's going to haunt you in your sleep."

I understood Lacy's train of thought. Over the years, I had blocked out the memories of that tragic day. Watching those tapes brought those painful moments back with such clarity, it was frightening. I was also beginning to believe my thoughts had somehow caused me to conjure up Aaryn. "We don't have enough time to be chasing this chick all over Atlanta."

"With that raggedy car, trust me, that bitch ain't going far. If we were thinking, we could have looked up everyone on your list on Instagram and Facebook. All we needed was internet connection."

"I don't even know what you're talking about." I was concentrating on keeping a safe distance from Aaryn's car.

"Instagram and Facebook are social networking programs. Almost everyone in our age bracket use one or the other. Remind me to show it to you the next time we're on a computer."

"I'm buying a computer the first chance I get. We definitely need one for our apartment."

"No doubt. Hey see, the trick looks like she's stopping at that laundry mat. Pull up next to her car so you can get a good look."

"I don't know about this."

"Just pull the car up. If you don't want to get a good look at her, then I do."

I did as Lacy asked. Part of me wanted it to be someone else because I wasn't ready to deal with how I would feel if it actually was her. I pulled up my car alongside her parked car. Aaryn had already gotten out. She was taking clothes from the backseat.

"It's most definitely her." My heart was hammering against my chest.

"Hey! Hey, bitch. I'm talking to you." Lacy had her window down and was half-way out the car yelling at Aaryn. She turned around with a mean expression on her face.

"I know you ain't talking to me," Aaryn yelled back.

My hands were sweating and I felt like I was unable to move. This could not be happening.

"I don't see no other bitches scratching around." Lacy took something from her purse and drew a line on Aaryn's car.

"What the fuck did you do to my car?" Aaryn dropped her laundry basket and ran around to see what had been done.

"I put your name on it, bitch. How you like it?"

"What the fuck? You keyed my car! I'm calling the police."

I was about to pull off when Lacy opened the door and stepped out next to Aaryn. I saw her arm lash out and then she was back in the car.

"Go," Lacy yelled as she patted her hand on the dashboard.

I didn't even think about it, my foot hit the accelerator. My only thought was getting away before anyone could copy my temporary tags. When I looked in the rearview mirror, Aaryn was no longer standing in the street. She was lying on the ground. My foot slipped off the gas. "Oh my God, Lacy! What did you do?" I was a nervous wreck.

"Slice her femoral artery and scratched one name off your list. Let's get out of here. I may have gotten some blood on my shirt and I'd hate to get it in your car. Better yet, let's find a car wash. Since you got this white ass car, blood will stand out on it like dirt. We can go through the self-serve line and take care of two problems with one stone."

I could not believe how collected Lacy was compared to my scary ass. "What if someone finds her? She can identify us. She'll tell them about this car for sure." I keep looking in the mirror just to make sure we weren't being followed.

"Trust me; she was probably dead before she hit the asphalt. I got her good. It doesn't take long to bleed out when you cut the right one."

"Damn. Should I be scared of you? Where did you learn some shit like that?"

"Biology 101. I never thought I would use anything I learned in class. I'm glad I paid attention."

"I am too. You were so smooth. I thought you only punched her."

"I did punch her, with my knife. I never leave home without it."

"I'm making a note to myself—never get on your bad side."

"You were on my bad side, remember? I fucking hated you in the beginning."

"That seems like an eternity ago. I'm glad we're friends now."

One of the good things about all of the rain we'd been having was no one was washing their cars. We pulled into the carwash and had the place to ourselves. Lacy opened the door. "I got this. Ain't no need for both of us to get wet."

I marveled at Lacy's nonchalant attitude about what she'd done. You would think she'd just picked up our order of takeout, instead of taking out another human being. What she did for me was huge. I wasn't even aware that I wanted Aaryn dead until I saw her lying in the street. The only remorse I had was that I didn't get to do it myself.

"Lacy, I don't know how I'm ever going to repay you for what you did. I mean how did you even know I was thinking it?"

"You might not have thought about it. For me, it was simple. I feel like the stars were aligned for it to happen. I mean, why else would she have magically appeared right when we were talking about it? When I let the window down and thought back to the way she kicked you when you were on the ground, it's like a light went off in my head. I didn't do what I did for you. I did it for me. I couldn't have stopped myself if I wanted to."

"So, I'm not this terrible person because I don't feel bad about it?"

"If I don't feel bad, why should you? Did she feel bad while your ass was rotting away in the mental hospital? Did she come to visit you or send you a letter saying she was sorry?"

"No, she didn't."

"Then fuck her. I'm hungry. I wonder if we have any leftovers at the house."

"I sure hope so. Let's go home. I could eat something too."

***

"I think there's enough spaghetti for both of us. Is that alright with you?"

"That will work," I said. Now that we were home, the paranoia was beginning to creep in. Even though I didn't commit the actual murder, I didn't report it. The mere fact that I drove away from the scene, made me an accomplice. It wasn't that I gave a good two shits about Aaryn; I just didn't want to end up in jail for the rest of my natural life for her sorry ass. As far as I was concerned, payback was a motherfucker and she got what she deserved.

Lacy seemed to read my mind. "Jordan, don't worry about that chick. Ain't nobody going to be the wiser. Did you notice where we were? We were in the straight up hood and she's just another dead nigger in the street. Nine times out of ten, somebody has already rolled up on her body and frisked it for money. There's no way they could trace that shit back to us."

"How can you be so sure?"

"I wouldn't have done it if I didn't think I could get away with it. There were no cameras and no witnesses. If anybody should be worried, it should be me. And I'm not worried. Believe that! Now could you please pass me the red pepper? They never make this spaghetti hot enough for me."

CHAPTER THIRTY-TWO

JORDAN BREE

"That's it. I got the last box from the car. Now all I have to do is start putting things away. Thanks for helping me get settled."

"Getting a furnished apartment was probably the best move too. This way, you won't have to sit on the floor." Lacy moved a box off the sofa and sat down. She was sulking and neither of us was ready to talk about the elephant in the room.

"Girl, sitting on the floor was never my plans. If I had to, I would have delayed the move until we had some decent furniture in this piece."

"I hear you." Lacy had tears in her eyes.

"Look, I know you're upset that you aren't here with me now. But, it's only temporary. You can come over here anytime you want. Then, at the end of the month, you can move too. When it's time, I'll come over and help you too."

"I hope you're not just saying that. It's going to be terrible for me without you there."

"I couldn't stay. After my fight I had with Mrs. Gates, there was no way I could do it. I would have killed that bitch in her sleep."

Lacy nodded her head indicating she heard me. "I still can't believe you did it. I thought for sure Mrs. Gates was going to try to do something to keep you there."

"I knew she wasn't going to try to stop me. I was a pain in her ass and she had no problem telling me as much. When she showed her ass, she only made me move up my timeline."

"Yeah, she had no right to tell the other girls that you'd been in a mental hospital. I wanted to slice the bitch myself for that."

"Then we would have played right into her hands. Mrs. Gates is no dummy. If you or I had clowned up, she could have called the police and made trouble for us. If the police came, who do you think they would have believed?"

"Mrs. Gates. That bitch better sleep with one eye open."

"Lacy, you can't retaliate against her. You would be the first one they brought in to question."

"I know, but it still sucks."

"Mrs. Gates thought she controlled me with a roof over my head. You always wanted to know how I kept her in check. Well, it was Brody. He was my secret weapon. Mrs. Gates knew about the article that Brody wrote. It caused a statewide investigation, which resulted in over half the mental hospitals in the state, to close their doors."

"Brody is a bad dude."

"All I had to do was mention his name and I was getting things done. What she didn't know, was how much money I have. Up until recently, I kept it a secret. When she threatened to kick me out, I called her bluff."

"We would have both gotten away, if only my birthday would have been twenty-five days sooner. I could have called her bluff too."

"It's a risk we didn't need to take. At first, I thought she was going to ask you to leave too. She only bought up your age because she knew we planned on living together. She's a spiteful old lady and she wanted to hurt me."

"Well, she hurt us both. That bitch could fuck up a wet dream."

"It's going to be okay. I'll have this place all fixed up by the time you move in. And, if shit gets bad over there, you can just come over here and chill. Or, better yet, call Brody. I'm sure he won't mind helping you out too. "

"You won't forget about me?"

"You should kill yourself right now after what we've been through? You're like my family. Or, at least what I think family should be." It was my turn to get all teary eyed. My family was still a sore spot with me.

"You're like my family too." Lacy said, with the hint of a smile on her face.

"You know who surprised me the most as I was leaving?"

"Who?"

"Keisha! I never expected her to cry. I mean, she was cool sometimes, but we weren't that close."

Lacy played with the corners of one of the boxes. "We had some conversations. Mainly they were about you."

"Me? Why would y'all be talking about me?" I didn't like the sound of that. The less people talked about me, the better I felt.

"It was before, you know, when we weren't friends. She knew I admired you. Things like that. It was nothing too bad."

"That was kind of creepy. You know that, right? You were such a pain in the ass," I said laughing.

"I know. Don't remind me of what a jerk I was. I liked you because you stood up for yourself. I respected that. Those other girls at the home are cool sometimes, but they don't count. Once you and I started hanging out together, they wanted to throw shade on you."

"Whatever. I won't be missing them girls at all. I do have something I want to talk to you about. Let's open up some champagne. I got some in the frig."

"Ooh, champagne. What are we celebrating?"

"We have a new place, silly. I'll get the glasses, if you open the bottle. I'm such a wuss. Those corks scare me."

I waited for Lacy to return with the open bottle before I started talking.

"Cheers." We brought our glasses together.

"So, this is what I wanted to talk to you about. I knew it was going to fuck you up when I moved before you did. I don't want you to have any worries about that. When I asked you to move in, I meant it. That's why I insisted that your name go on the lease with me." I placed the lease on the table for her to see it.

"Seriously?"

"I just need your signature on it."

Lacy was smiling sincerely as she signed her name on the spaces indicated. "I say cheers to that."

"This apartment will give both of us rental history. If we ever decide to live alone, we can use this place as a reference."

"I don't know how to thank you. You seem to think about everything."

"Trust me. There are a whole lot of things I haven't thought about. Problem is, I don't know what they are," I said laughing.

"I got to tell you, since we both suffer from personality disorders, I was worried that you might wake up one day and tell me to get the fuck out."

"Exactly. This lease will prevent me from doing that. Although, I could still tell you to get the fuck out, legally, I wouldn't be able to get away with it."

"Well, I hope it never comes down to that. You know I don't have a lot of money. I don't know what I would do if I had to stay at the home for any longer than I have to. Or worse, crawl back there if this doesn't work out and have to beg for a room."

I got up and went to get my purse. "Money was another thing I wanted to talk to you about. You are going to have to have your own. You can't come running to me every time you want to do something."

"Damn, I said I'd get a job. I'll start looking in the morning. Until then, I get a little something each month. I've made it work before and I'll do it again." Lacy placed her half empty glass on the table, folding her arms across her chest.

"I wasn't finished." Lacy had her panties in a knot.

"Well excuse me."

"I asked my lawyer to write you a check, Negro." I took the check from my bag and put it on the table next to the lease and her glass. Lacy leaned forward, her eyes wide as saucers.

"Are you fucking kidding me? Wait, look at all those zeros! Stop lying. That's a million dollars! Why would you give me a million dollars? Are you crazy?"

"I may have ninety-nine thousand problems but money isn't one of them. My lawyers settled my case and I'm set. My motives with you are very simple. You're going to need a lot of stuff to settle in. I'm about to redo my resume and create a new persona that doesn't include a brief interlude at the home. That part of my life is over. You're gonna need to do that as well. After you move in, I don't even want to talk about that place again."

Lacy shook her head no. "I can't take this. It's too much."

"You can and you will. You're going to have bills to pay. You ain't gonna stay here with me and not pay your share. You're going to need a car, insurance, a phone, a computer. You've got a little over twenty days to get it done."

"With all this money, I can get all that stuff and still have change left over. Tell me the real reason why you are doing this? If this is about what happened a couple weeks ago, it isn't necessary for you to do all this."

"Even before you did that, I had decided I was going to ask you if you wanted to move in with me. I even asked Brody to check it out, to see if it were possible, especially since you haven't turned eighteen yet. He told me it could go either way. In any event, I was going to give you some money. I really want this friendship to work. I honestly don't want to live alone. If you have to come to me for everything, it would be only a matter of time before you'd grow to resent me. This way, we both have a chance at making things work."

"I don't know what to say."

"Oh, and you're going to have to pay your own taxes on the money too. My lawyer can help you. I'll take you down to meet him this week. He can also help you to invest some of the money. This way, you can make the money work for you, instead of the other way around.

"I could kiss you right now."

"You do and I'll punch you right in the throat." We both laughed and I had to admit, it felt good. I wasn't at the point where I did it every day but I was working on it.

"I think I'm gonna need another bottle of this champagne. I'm about to get drunk."

"Oh no you're not. You can't go back to the home drunk. You can't get in any trouble there. We don't want to give Mrs. Gates any reason to get in your ass."

"Damn. That sucks donkey dicks."

"You have the most colorful way of saying things I've ever heard."

"What can I say?" We laughed again.

"If we leave now, we can get to the bank and put some money in your pocket."

"Fuck, that's going to present a problem for me, I don't have any identification. Remember that night I got sick? This bastard stole my purse and I haven't gotten around to replacing it.

"If you have your birth certificate and know your social security number, we can take care of that today."

"I, uh. I'm sure I got it there somewhere. We can do that once I move."

"Come on then, let me turn in this lease and get you a key. Don't forget your check."

"Hell yeah, I'm gonna get that."

CHAPTER THIRTY-THREE

JORDAN BREE

I had one other loose end to tie before Lacy moved in. Although I trusted her completely, this was something I had to deal with myself. I had to talk to my mother.

No matter how I looked at it, I was still baffled by the way she treated me when I needed her the most. Growing up, she might not have been the best mother, but she was all I had. The last time I went to the house, my sister made it clear that I was not welcome. I wanted to know why. Talking to my mother, in my sister's presence, wasn't going to work. So I needed to meet her somewhere other than her apartment. Fortunately, I pretty sure where I could find her. All I had to do was be patient.

Lanetta Bree stumbled out of the crack house on the corner of Memorial Drive and 2nd Avenue. If I had bet money on it, I would have won. She only came out when her money or her credit ran out. By the looks of her, I was guessing it was a combination of both. She looked terrible, much worse than I'd ever seen her. As a child, I remember sitting with her during her 'bad' days. Those days when she couldn't get up enough money for her next hit. Those memories came rushing back like a strong gust of wind. I shuddered.

"This is some bullshit. Why am I even here, Lord?" I asked myself aloud. I knew the answer before I even asked the question. I needed closure. I started the car and followed behind my mother. She didn't look left or right. She shuffled like her feet weighed a ton. I could only imagine what she smelled like. Her long hair, which I used to brush at night, was gone. She had cut it short and bleached it blonde. Perhaps she thought it made her look younger. She was wrong. I followed her for half a block before I got up the nerve to call out to her.

"Lanetta!" I yelled. The child in me screamed. I had never addressed my mother by her first name before. To me, it was the ultimate sign of disrespect. My sister used to call her that all the time. I hated it.

"What?" My mom turned around so fast, she almost fell over. Her beady eyes focused on me in the car. Somehow, I'd forgotten how menacing her eyes could be. "What the fuck you want?"

"I just want to talk to you."

"Talking ain't free and I don't lick no pussy."

I was appalled. She didn't know who I was. She must have thought I was trying to pick her ass up or something. My good common sense told me to drive the fuck away. The bad part said, get what you came for and be done with it.

"I could get you something to eat." Lord knows she looked like she needed it.

"Fuck I want to eat for? I needs me some money." She stepped closer to the car. "You got some money for me, honey?" She smiled. Her teeth, what was left of them, were brown and rotted. Her breath reeked, as if she'd been swirling garbage in her mouth. Her claw like fingers gripped the door on the passenger side. Her nails, once long and polished, were short and bitten to the quick and dirty.

I swallowed hard to keep from gagging. There was no way I was going to be able to let her get in my car unless I put down the top. Even with that, I'd still have to get the car detailed to get rid of the stench. "Yeah, I got some money for you. But I don't have it with me."

"Get the fuck out of here wasting my time. What you want me to do, wait for you to go get it?"

I had to know. "Do you know who I am?" She laughed so long and loud, it reminded me of a cackle. All she needed was a green face and a pointed hat and she would look just like the wicked witch from The Wizard of Oz. The sound sent shivers down my spine.

"You might have gotten your hair did, lost some of that fat, put on some fancy clothes and stole a car but you're still the same old bitch to me."

Her words were like chalk on a board to me. Cutting away what little self-esteem, I'd managed to keep after my ordeals. My gut told me to get as far away from this woman as I could but I came to get some answers and I'd be damn if I was going to let her leave without them.

"Your sister told me she saw you. I thought the bitch was fucking high but I guess she wasn't. What do you want from us? Why you keep sniffing around here?" She showered me with a spray of spittle, which I tried to dodge like projectiles.

"I'll tell you but not here. You need a bath, bad. You can get one at my house. Then we'll talk." I put the top down.

"Talk hell, what about the money?"

"You'll get your money too, but first, the bath. I might even wash your nasty clothes." If she wanted to be a bitch to me, I could certainly give it back to her. Mother or not, there was only so much I was going to take from her.

"This better not be some sort of trick. I've got things to do. I might be little but I can still whip your ass," she said, as she opened the door and got in. The smell was even worse close up. I turned on the air.

"It's a good thing I don't live far from here. You are burning up the hair in my nose."

"I didn't ask your ass for nothing," she huffed.

She must have forgotten asking me about money a few minutes ago. It didn't matter, I'd give her a couple of hundred and send her on her way. After today, I never wanted to see her again.

"Theresa told me you had another kid."

"And…what else did she tell you?"

I had to think. She'd said so much in our short conversation. "Not much else, other than there wasn't any room for me there."

"Damn right. They cut the water off. Ain't had no electricity in a week."

This was a little more information than I wanted to hear. I could care less about their hardships. We'd lived through similar circumstances before. Somebody always came through. Usually, it was from one of my mother's men. Judging from the looks of her now, I doubted if she could get anyone to do anything for her. It really served them right. "Thank God, I don't need to move back in there. I got me a place of my own."

"So I heard. You think you're the shit now don't you? Driving this fancy car and all. Don't forget, the bigger they are, the harder they fall."

I wasn't sure what the fuck that was supposed to mean to me. I had already fallen down to the lowest common denominator. For me, things were on the way up. "I don't think I will ever forget where I came from." If she didn't like them apples, she could catch fire. How she could twist her lips to say these awful things to me was mind boggling.

"Good. Your sister got the case of the fancy pants after you left. But her ass is right back at the house, worse off than me."

I liked the way she referred to me as leaving as if I had done so voluntarily, as if I had some sort of choice. I had half a mind to open her door and push her ass out my car. "You still didn't tell me about the baby."

"Ain't nothing to tell. DFCS got her."

I was delighted for the child. Maybe she would grow up normal, without the issues that plagued me. I tried to keep my joy out of my voice. "I'm sorry to hear that." I actually wasn't. The way I saw it, there would be one less fucked up child in the world because of it.

"Yeah, whatever. She was just another mouth to feed. I don't miss all that crying either. That baby was worse than you. All the time needing something."

It was almost as if my mother was going out of her way to hurt me. I pulled up in front of my apartment right as I was about to change my mind about letting her inside.

"Bringing you here was a mistake." I wanted to cry so badly but I wasn't about to give her the satisfaction of seeing me do it.

"Damn, this your place?" I almost thought I heard some pride in her voice.

"I'm renting it."

"Figures. Niggas don't know how to buy nothing these days."

She had a lot of damn nerve. She never owned a damn thing in her life but a stinky ass attitude. Before I could totally change my mind, I rushed to open the door. I had neighbors to think of and having them see me with her, wasn't good for my image or my sanity.

"You are going to need that bath first, before you sit down on any of my furniture."

"Uppity bitch. Who you think you are telling me I need a bath?" She wiped her nose with her sleeve.

"You want money from me? That's the deal. Take it or leave. It's up to you." Now that I had her where I wanted her, I could afford to be more brazen.

"I should slap the shit out of you."

"I wouldn't suggest you try it. I'm not that kid anymore." I was over being afraid. As a matter of fact, I didn't really need answers from her anymore. I'd done what I wanted to do. I showed her that in spite of the way she'd treated me, I did good.

"Fine. I'll take a shitty bath but then I'm gonna need that money, and I'm outta here."

I wanted to laugh. She talked like she was doing me a favor by taking a bath. I even changed my mind about washing her clothes. She wasn't about to fuck up my washing machine.

"I put some clean towels in the guest bathroom. I might even be able to find you something to wear too. That shit you wearing can go in this trash bag." I handed her the bag I had snatched from the kitchen, as I pointed to the bathroom. She could act up if she wanted to. I was ready to put her out if I had to.

"Fine. But don't you try no funny shit. I will still whip your ass." She walked away grumbling under her breath.

I wasn't about to give her any of my new clothes. I did have some bum jeans that I used to wear around the home that I was meaning to get rid of. She was on her own with shoes, unless she wanted to wear a pair of my flip-flops. While she was in the bath, I took the time to light some candles and spray the air. I didn't know it was possible for one person to smell so badly. Even on my worse day, I never stunk the way she did. I took one more look around the living room before I went into the kitchen to fix a late breakfast. Everything was exactly where it was supposed to be.

Lanetta stayed in the bathroom for a very long time. I was sure washing off all that filth had to take a while. Part of me expected to see a different person come out than the one that went in there. Those hopes were dashed the second she opened her mouth.

"These fucking jeans are too big." She stood there clutching the front of them, as if they would fall if she weren't holding them up.

"They're not that big."

"The hell you say; can't nobody see my ass." She turned around to show me. If she weren't so sincere, it might have been funny.

"What ass? I think you lost your ass a long time ago."

"Well everybody can't be a fat—" She stopped talking midsentence. I couldn't help but smile.

"You can't call me fat anymore." It was my turn to let her see my body.

"Bout time you lost that extra weight. You were the fattest one of my kids. Ain't nary one of them could eat as much as you. You acted like you were going to eat me out of house and home."

"Don't you have anything nice you could say out your nasty mouth? Why do you have to be so vicious?" I was done. I had given this bitch every opportunity to make things right and she hadn't taken any of them.

"There you go again. Always needing something. What difference does it make what I say to you? I can't change you. I can't wave my hand and make things better. Shit is what it is. Bout time you accepted it."

"Did I ask you to change anything? Did I ask you for a motherfucking thing? You hate me. I get it. I only wanted to know why. But you know what, none of that shit matters to me anymore. You can walk out that door and continue with what's left of your miserable life. The way I see it, at the end of the day, I'm winning. I don't have to crawl home to some fucked up apartment, living with a pack of animals you call children. And most of all, I don't have to deal with you. You're an old, disgusting piece of low class trash and a fucking addict. I hate you for what you did to me. I despise what you've become. Why don't you just do us all a favor and kill yourself? Does that sound familiar? You used to say that shit to me every night before I went to bed. I'm going to do you one better, bitch. I'm gonna live." I had forgotten she used to say that to me until that moment.

Lanetta opened and closed her mouth repeatedly. The queen of quick retorts was speechless. The moment was priceless. I never thought I'd see the day. She stood there, water dripping from her still wet hair, looking pathetic. When she finally found her voice, it didn't matter to me what she said. "You can't speak to me that way. I'm still your mother."

"In your fucking dreams. All you were was a fucking oven. You kept me warm for nine fucking months and I've been freezing ever since." During the entire exchange, I didn't raise my voice once.

"What about the money? You said you were going to give me some money." Her lower lip quivered.

She had the nerve to put her hands where her hips used to be. I could no longer contain my laughter. "I've already given you more than you deserve. I got a belt, and some shoes in the back bedroom. I suggest you take them and get the hell out my house."

"What? You're not even going to take me back home?"

She was really shaking now. I knew her addiction was kicking in. "What did you ever give me, except a hard way to go? You lucky I gave you some clothes and a bath. Take this ten dollars and get out." I pulled the money out my bra and threw it on the floor.

Lanetta stared at the money before using one of her hands to reach down and pick it up. "I'm gonna get your sister to come over here and fuck you up. She won't let you get away with this." She pointed her finger at me menacingly.

"If either one of you step foot in this neighborhood, so help me God, I'll call the cops on you so fast it will make your head spin. You don't know who you are messing with. I can make it rain shit on all of you. Now I suggest you get the belt, and get the fuck out, before I change my mind about that too. Had you been just a little bit nicer, I might have written you a fat check."

"Fuck I need a check for? I ain't got no bank account. You said you were going to give me some money. My time ain't free."

"You are really pressing your luck with me. The little girl who used to love you, don't live here no more."

"Bitch, you really are fucking crazy. All the money in the world ain't gonna change that shit."

Even though I thought I was past caring about what she thought, her words continued to hurt me. "Maybe I am crazy. Crazy enough to think I should do anything to help you. You called me bitch so much growing up, I thought it was my real name. I'm so done with you and your family. Now, I'm not going to say this again. Go before I slap the piss out of you." I was so angry, I was hyperventilating. I walked over to the coffee table and picked up my phone.

"You gonna call the police on me? And tell them what? You brought me here. It ain't my fault you changed your mind."

Ugh, I hated to admit it, she had a point. If I called the cops, I'd end up looking like a fool. "Fine, get the belt and I'll drop you off."

"What about—"

"You better hurry up before I change my mind." I went into the kitchen to throw away the eggs and bacon I'd made for us while she was taking a shower. I could hear Lanetta knocking things over in the bedroom. I didn't even care. There was nothing in there that couldn't be replaced. "I'm leaving," I shouted.

Lanetta shuffled out to the car. Her flip-flops flapping noisily as she tried to keep up with my angry stride. I wanted to get her as far away from my house as I could. We didn't talk during the entire trip, which suited me just fine. I had said all that I was going to say to her.

When I pulled up to the corner that I'd picked her up at, Lanetta got out of the car, slamming the door. "So that's it? You ain't got nothing else to say to me?"

"Does fuck off count?"

"You stank bitch. I should've killed you my damn self."

"Funny, I was thinking the same thing about you." I pulled away from the curb, anxious to get away. I drove straight to the car wash and had my car detailed. As I waited for my car to get finished, I went into the bathroom and I cried. I cried until it seemed as if I didn't have any more tears left. And then, I cried some more.

I called Lacy when I got back to our apartment.

"Is it done?"

"Yes," I was really tired and I wanted to crawl into bed.

"How did it go? Are you alright?"

"It went about as well as can be expected."

"You sound like you've been crying. Do you need me to come over there?" I could hear the genuine concern in Lacy's voice.

"I'm fine. I'm just tired. I'm glad you weren't here to see it. It got ugly."

"I'll bet. If I was there, we'd be cleaning up blood right about now."

"I know that's right. Then we'd have to move before you even got a chance to move in."

"Then I'm glad it worked out the way you wanted it to. Did you get the closure that you needed?"

"Yes and no. Seeing her brought back so many memories that I'd forgotten about. It's no wonder I was fucked up in the head."

"You are not fucked up in the head. I don't even want to hear you say that again."

"I know. My mother felt the need to say that to me before she left. She also said I should pretty much do the world a favor and kill myself. Hearing it again, after so long, I realized that she used to say this to me every night before I went to bed."

"Wow, that's fucked up. Are you sure you don't want me to come over there?"

"I'll be alright. What about you? Are you doing okay?" I didn't want to think about me right now.

"I'm good. No one around here speaks to me but it's cool. I am just counting down the days until I can leave too."

"You'll let me know if it gets bad won't you? I'll send Brody over there so fast, they won't know what hit them."

"I can take care of myself. If Mrs. Gates was going to do something, she would have done it already."

"You've got a point. Besides, Gates ain't crazy. She knows there is nothing that she can do to keep you there. We just have to wait a few more days. I'm about to go to bed. Call me in the morning."

"Okay, have a good night."

I was feeling better by the time I hung up the phone. I finally had the courage to do something that I'd been dreading since I came home. I walked the short corridor to the bedroom. I was almost afraid to see what damage Lanetta had done in the bedroom. Just like having the car detailed, I needed to detail my mother out my apartment.

For a moment, my heart sank. The little ceramic pots on the dresser did not look disturbed. Everything else that had been on the dresser was on the floor. My heart was beating very fast as I opened the first dish. It was empty. The second dish was also empty. I was so excited, I threw the lid up in the air, not caring whether it broke or not. I rushed back into the living room to call Lacy.

"Girl, she took the bait."

"You are shitting me. How could you ever be so sure that she would?"

"Because, I know this bitch like the back of my hand. Once she found out I wasn't going to give her any money. I knew she was going to be looking around for something to steal."

"What if she takes the drugs and sells them? Wouldn't that just fry your ass if you inadvertently gave her the money she asked for?"

"My mother is an addict. There is no way she's going to let those drugs out of her hands. Especially, since she was already feigning. It's only a matter of time. At the very least, she'll get careless and show them to someone who bashes her in the head. But if I really know her, and I believe I do, she's somewhere right now getting high. And she won't stop until they kill her."

"Girl, you don't know how much I just want to go by your old neighborhood and wait for the meat wagon to come pick her up."

"If I thought she was home, I'd tell you where to go. She told me they didn't have any electricity in her house. She also said they didn't have any water."

"Girl, if she's getting high, all she needs is a lighter and a spoon."

"I didn't think about that. She just might go home."

"Doesn't the not knowing bother you? It's working my nerves and it don't have anything to do with me."

"I guess that's where we differ. I don't have to see her dead. I really don't want to. As much as I hate her, I don't want that image in my head. It's enough for me to know I had a hand in her demise."

"What about your sister? How are you going to deal with her?"

"I think she's going to get hers too. Part of me believes she will find the dope after my mother overdoses and use the same shit. I truly believe she is stupid enough to think she would have different results."

"Good Lord, girl, how did you manage to stay sane in a household like that?"

"If you let my mom tell it, I didn't. I can't even repeat some of the things she said to me."

"I'm sorry, boo. I hate that you had to go through that. What are you going to do with your list now?"

"I haven't really thought about it. Brody wants me to burn it."

"Is Brody a doctor now?"

For some reason, I felt like I had to defend Brody to her. "He isn't a doctor but it was his idea to create the list. Naturally, he had suggestions on what to do with it once it's finished."

"Oh shit, did you show him the list?"

"No. I wasn't going to show it to anyone. If you hadn't seen it in my purse, I probably wouldn't have shown it to you."

"Good. I didn't think about it before. But the list does tie your dead friend back to us. Maybe you should get rid of it."

"It would make sense, yet—"

"You don't have to say it."

I nodded my head even though I knew she couldn't see me. I could lie and pretend that I did get rid of it but what good would that do? Now that I had a taste of vengeance, I'd be lying if I said I didn't want more. However, I wasn't about to risk my freedom again. "Am I wrong for feeling this way? Do you think less of me as a person?"

"If I thought it was wrong, I wouldn't have done what I did. Does that answer your questions?"

"Have you ever done anything like that before? I mean, I'm not trying to get all up in your business. I'm just asking."

"Not like that. I thought I was going to feel bad, maybe even have bad dreams, but I've been sleeping like a baby."

"To be honest, so have I. I guess I am still in shock. I keep waiting to see something about it on the television. It's just like you said, no one cares."

"Right. It would have been different if she'd done something with her life."

"But we didn't know what she was doing."

"That one was given to us by God. If we were to do it again, we'd have to be more careful. You know, check them out first, before we strike."

"Next time? I thought we said it couldn't be a next time."

"I'm following your lead. If you want to let sleeping dogs lie, I'm good with that. But if you want to mix things up a bit, I'm down and ready for that as well."

"Are you for real? You'd do that for me? Why?"

"That's what friends are for. I would hope if situations were reverse, you'd do the same thing for me."

"I would. I've never had anyone in my life that has shown me the kindness you've shown me." I meant it from the bottom of my heart. Lacy had proven herself to really be a friend and another gift from God. He protected her from me. Had I been successful and killed her, I'm so sure I would have blocked my blessing. This was another reason why I gave her as much money as I did.

"Hypothetically, if you were to keep working on your list, which number would you scratch off next?"

"Hypothetically speaking?"

"Absolutely."

"Let me think about it," I said laughing. "I feel like we never talk about you. I'm not that selfish that I don't notice."

"I have never, for one moment, thought you were selfish. Right now, we're doing what's in front of us. When I get there, maybe we'll start on my own list."

"Sounds like a plan to me."

"What are you going to do about Brody? I haven't heard you mention anything about him."

"Honestly, I haven't decided. He's a good guy, for sure. But, I'm not sure I'm ready for a relationship. I've got too many issues."

"I can tell he really likes you."

"I like him too. I just don't want to rush into anything that I might regret."

"Makes sense to me. It's getting late, so I'm going to let you go."

"Okay, goodnight. We can pick this up tomorrow."

ABOUT THE AUTHOR

Tina Brooks McKinney began her writing career as a dare. As an avid reader, writing was the next step for her. Armed with a very active imagination and a story to tell, Tina penned her first novel All That Drama. Readers fell in love with Tina's no-nonsense characters and her comedic style of weaving a story. Since then, Tina has written eight novels and two novellas. Her titles include, All That Drama, Lawd, Mo' Drama, Fool, Stop Trippin', Dubious, Deep Deception, Snapped, Got Me Twisted, Deep Deception 2, Snapped 2: The Redemption, Betta Not Tell and Catch Fire.

Catch Fire 2 is anticipated for a December release.

A wife and mother of two, Tina uses real life situations to both entertain and inspire her readers. You can find out more information about her by visiting her website, www.tinamckinney.com or drop her email at tybrooks2@yahoo.com. She would love to hear from you.

www.ingramcontent.com/pod-product-compliance
Lightning Source LLC
Chambersburg PA
CBHW021458240626
47154CB00002B/418